PUBLISHING

WEDDING
IN
THE PINES

A perfect feel-good romance

CASSIDY CARTER

ACKNOWLEDGEMENTS

Welcome back to Cabins in the Pines! I'm so thrilled to revisit old friends from *Love on Location* and introduce you to a few new ones.

One of the things I love about writing is bringing my own experience into my books. In *Love on Location*, much of the setting was taken from my childhood in rural Tennessee and time spent in my recent years in breathtaking Northern Arizona. In *Wedding in the Pines*, I was able to draw on stories from the Jewish side of my family; in particular, a cousin who eschewed a traditional work life for the pursuit of music and became a prominent and successful cellist.

I also love the idea of second chances, and *Wedding in the Pines* highlights so many—but my *favorite* second-chance possibility lies in the journey of our heroine, Hope. I think the struggle between fulfilling family obligations and finding what truly makes her happy is universally relatable, and so many of us might have had to find that same balance, no matter our career or outside passion.

This book would not have been possible if not for a list of people to whom I owe much gratitude.

Thank you to Stacey Donovan for taking (another) chance on my little lakeside world. Your positivity and expert guidance are always amazing and appreciated. Thank you to Gwyn Jordan for thoughtful and on-point story notes, which were invaluable. And thanks go to the entire Hallmark Publishing team for making every book we make together exceed in reality what I start out with in my head.

All my appreciation to and for my remarkable husband and girls. Through many drafts and other daftness, you're my people, and my dreams are possible because of your love and support. God gave me everything when he gave me all of you.

To Dad, Aunt Susan, and Aunt Patricia, thank you for sharing so many wonderful family stories. I love knowing you all and cherish our time together. I look forward to making future memories.

And last but never least, a huge thank-you to my readers. You're the reason I'm here, and I'm blessed by your kind and continued support. I can't wait for our next adventure together.

I'm delighted to return with you to the Cabins in the Pines. I hope you enjoy taking the trip as much as I enjoyed planning it.

DEDICATION

To my daughters—it takes courage to grow
up and become who you really are. May
you always follow your dreams.

CHAPTER 1

S*UMMER'S COMING,* H*OPE* T*HOUGHT,* L*OOKING* down at the cement plaza below her. It was so early that only a few office workers had made appearances, and the window of her sixth-floor office framed them as they shuffled across the courtyard on their way to another monotonous day. The plaza was a perfectly landscaped square, a patch of carefully controlled "nature" that was meant to provide a respite from the generic space between her building and other surrounding structures.

The rays of the rising sun peeked up, reflecting off the glass-and-chrome towers of the downtown business district. It wouldn't be long before the same sun began baking the pavement. That warmth never reached her office, though. It was always a little too chilly on the sixth floor for Hope. But she never complained. The chill kept her hustling.

Speaking of which...

Hope turned back to her desk.

The morning light was starting to take some of the harsh, fluorescent glow out of her office. The single-cup coffeemaker she kept on a side table burbled merrily when she fired it up and the smell of coffee filled her office. Hope enjoyed being in the office before anyone else, taking the time to putter, get organized, and pop into her father's empty office to drop off a bag from Kahn's Bakery. It wasn't the same bag that he used to carry in with him from home every morning, but he did still eat his breakfast at his desk—a habit he'd formed long before Hope had come to work here.

Some things never change.

Hope sighed, twisting her long, blond hair up and securing it with the pins she'd briefly forgotten she was holding. It was time to get to another unshakable institution of her days: that to-do list.

"What are you daydreaming about?"

Hope turned and smiled as Annie Goodman, wearing a smart skirt suit, entered the room.

As much as Hope loved her right-hand woman, she wasn't in the mood to wax nostalgic this morning. No, there was just too much to get done, and the clock was ticking. "Oh, nothing. I was thinking about what the weather will be like during the conference."

Annie smiled back, hoisting her bulging briefcase. As Hope came forward to help with the heavy bag, Annie shoved her slipping glasses up her nose with her free hand and swatted Hope's fingers away from her bag good-naturedly.

"Well, I don't care what the weather is like. I'm just ready to get all of the arrangements done. Do you know that I spent an hour on the phone yesterday for custom napkins?"

Hope put a hand to her lips, her breath catching on a laugh. "Oh, Annie, I'm so sorry. You couldn't order online?"

Annie deposited her bag, slid into Hope's desk chair, and groaned as she spun in it once. Her perfectly blown-out, strawberry-blond bob cut bounced back into place again.

"Mr. Bergman insisted on this place in town that has *no* website. But he says they did the napkins for his cousin's wedding a couple years ago." Annie put a hand to her forehead.

Hope's office phone rang, and Annie picked up. "Beacon Financial Planning and Wealth Management. Hope Bergman's office."

Hope heard voices in the hallway, laughter, the sound of someone rolling a package cart down the hallway. Beacon Financial Planning was waking up. Hope needed to do the same. She bustled over to the side table and busied herself with starting a second cup of coffee.

"Sweet fancy molasses," Annie offered, hanging up the receiver.

"Trouble?" Hope asked, sipping from her mug as she handed a steaming coffee cup over to Annie.

"They misprinted the napkins for the conference. Instead of the acronym for *Beacon Optimum Retirement Planning*, they substituted a U for the other vowel."

Hope's smile returned as she pictured the new acronym in place of the correct one. "And why did Mr. Bergman want to use this place?"

"He said he remembers he really liked the owner."

Hope's grin stretched wider. "When he likes you, he likes you. Luckily, he likes us."

"He *has* to like you. You're his daughter. Me? I make a misstep, and I'll be job searching on the same internet where BURP seminars will have probably gone viral."

Hope and Annie shared a laugh, which faded after

3

a moment. Hope looked back out the window for a moment, watching a bird soar on the other side of the glass, before admitting, "He's actually tougher on me than anyone else around here. I'm the crown princess of this investment and retirement planning kingdom." She waved a hand in the air and tried to keep her voice light, but a hint of bitterness crept in. Hope could hear it in her own words.

"Don't most princesses find adventure outside the castle?"

"They *do*," Hope said, smiling wanly. "I have my share of adventures."

"True. We always have open mic Monday nights at Latte Da."

"Is singing at a coffee house an adventure?"

Annie nodded emphatically. "Absolutely! Especially when your voice catches the ear of that *prince* of a barista who always checks you out."

Hope stifled another laugh, rolling her eyes. "*This* princess has sworn off love. Let's get to work." She picked up Annie's coffee cup and nodded toward the settee at the far side of her office, where she had already laid out the materials they needed to start on their day. Annie rummaged in her bag and pulled out several files, a tablet, and her phone.

"What else needs done? What about the venue?" Hope asked.

Annie consulted her tablet. "Booked, actually."

"Oh? Wow. That was fast."

A mischievous smile played on Annie's lips. "I mean, I might have been swayed by the fact that there's also a full spa there. All work and no play—"

"Is exactly what my father would suggest," Hope finished. She and Annie both shared another laugh. Hope cradled her coffee, feeling her spirits lift.

At the sound of someone nearby clearing their throat, both Annie and Hope jumped. Hope's father, Dan Bergman, stood in the doorway of her office, frowning heavily. She felt her cheeks get hot. She checked her watch and sat up a little straighter.

"Dad, hi. You're in early today. How was the freeway?"

Her father settled in the wing chair across from them. "Traffic was a bother, but I set out earlier than normal." Wasting no time on any further pleasantries, he pointed to the various gadgets and papers in front of them. "What's all this, then?"

"Seminar planning," Hope explained. "We're going to try a new venue this time."

His frown returned. Hope wondered how long it had been since she'd seen him smile. In fact, she could not remember for the life of her how long it had been since his last good mood. Just yesterday, she'd passed his closed office door and overheard him in a heated discussion with someone on the phone. Though there could be complications with clients in their line of work, she'd never heard him argue so loudly before.

Hope would normally ask what had happened, but she knew she'd only be met with stony silence. Since her mother's passing, there'd been so much distance between Hope and her father.

He said, "The summer seminar is responsible for twenty percent of our new business every year. I'm counting on you to maintain—no, *improve*—on that number."

"Yes, I know," Hope said, hoping that her tone didn't bely her sudden mild annoyance.

After a moment, he cleared his throat again and stood,

nodding stiffly. "Looks like you've got it all handled. That business degree didn't go to waste." He smiled, but it was thin, and it held none of the warmth Hope longed to see again. "I'll expect an update at day's end." Straightening the front placket of his suit jacket, he left Hope's office.

Hope swallowed down a lump of apprehension that rose in her throat.

Annie gave her a look of concern. "I thought he was going to start quizzing you on vested percentages and risk appraisal."

Hope smirked. "I'll have you know that I would have come through with flying colors. I *have* been an investment professional since a very young age. All my Barbies had solid 401(k) diversification, and they're all sitting pretty with paid-off dream houses and money in the bank, thanks to yours truly."

Hope's joking seemed to lighten the tension in the room, but she still felt the weight of her father's words. It was time to put her head down. If she buried herself in work, she would forget the pressure as the days between now and the seminar ticked away.

Hunched over in her office chair, staring at a monitor full of numbers that were beginning to blur, Hope had gotten to the point in her day where she'd kicked off her heels and let down her hair. Scrunching her toes into the carpet underneath her desk, she called over to Annie.

"I'll be here *at least* a couple more hours."

Annie was glowering at her tablet. "At this rate, I might as well just sleep here. And *you've* been talking to your computer."

Hope needed a break. She grabbed the remote to the

small stereo that sat on a side table nearby. "I'm going to put on some music. Do you mind?"

Annie shook her head. Hope turned on the local easy listening station. Soft, almost plaintive vocals drifted out of the speakers. She knew this song. It had been a while, but the slow, bittersweet lyrics brought to mind some-thing—*someone*—that Hope would rather forget.

Hope's finger hovered over the remote, but then she put it down and let the song play. As she tried to decipher the lines of numbers on her screen, she found herself singing along. It made her feel better, singing, and filled her with a renewed sense of energy.

"You should do this song at the next open mic," Annie suggested.

Hope nodded as the end notes of the music faded out and a commercial took the air. "Maybe," she said non-committally. She wasn't sure she wanted to taint the fun of open mic night with all the sour memories attached to that particular song.

Hope didn't see the throw pillow that Annie launched at her.

"Oof! What was that for?" Hope felt herself laughing, at least. That had to mean that the memory of he-who-was-attached-to-the-music didn't quite hit her as hard anymore, right? *Right.*

"What are you not telling me?"

"I'm just tired." *And reminiscing way too much.* Annie studied Hope closely, but didn't press her.

Hope needed a change of focus, so she clicked around for the seminar file, sorting through digital brochures un-til one made her stop. Lush, green pine trees surrounded a rustic-yet-upscale-looking building that somehow managed to both blend in with the idyllic surroundings and stand out impressively against them.

"Cabins in the Pines Executive Retreat? Not a typical corporate setting."

Annie looked up. "I think it's the very thing we need. People will feel comfortable, and with comfort comes trust, hopefully."

"You think a zip line and nature walks will make new clients trust us with their futures?" In a promotional photo, a smiling couple embraced by a picturesque lake. There was a roaring campfire on the lakeshore, and a guitar was propped up on a log bench, fireside.

Oy. Now all Hope could think about was a tall, broad-shouldered man with slightly shaggy hair that would fall into his warm, hazel eyes as he strummed a guitar...

Annie came over to look at the image. "The camp vibe is cute. I could do with a romantic campfire evening."

Hope lifted a hand and traced the couple in the photo. She hooked her thumb over her bare ring finger and rubbed absentmindedly. "I wonder if it's really this nice?"

"If you want to find somewhere else..."

"No, no! I trust your judgment completely, Annie. I'm sure it'll work out perfectly."

Hope brought her spreadsheet back onscreen and pushed firmly against the memories that had been sparked by the song. Despite the fact that her start at Beacon had not been completely her choice, Hope still felt proud of what she'd done in her years here, and she had a duty to show her dad that she could handle a big responsibility like the seminar. So what if it wasn't as exciting a career, a life, as she'd dreamed of when she was younger? Hope still wanted to succeed.

Time was ticking. Soon, they would be headed to the

Cabins in the Pines. It would be nice to bond with her father over *something*. Maybe the success of the seminar could be a starting point, a way for them to start growing close again. If it failed, Hope worried that the chasm between them would only grow wider.

"Well, isn't this gorgeous?" Hope twisted her head to look back as Annie drove their rental car up the gentle slope toward the entrance to the Cabins in the Pines Executive Resort. Hope checked her watch—it was around two, so the timing was perfect. She had the window down, and the smell of pine trees mixed with the fresh, damp smell of earth filled the car as the wind whipped her hair. They were going too fast for Hope to make out anything in the tree line, but she pictured delicate deer edging out of the trees every morning, ears pricked up in the light mist as the same breeze that wound around them now blew in to clear the dew.

"It sure is," Annie agreed, looking out the opposite window. "This looks like paradise."

Hope's father sat silently in the back seat, saying nothing about their surroundings.

Hope was so glad to be arriving at their destination. After an early flight that had been too long to be comfortable even in business class, the drive here had been mercifully quick. Hope had been confused by the circuitous route they'd had to take to get here off of the main highway, though. Luckily, the GPS knew exactly where they were going.

They crested the incline and took a slight turn that put them at the front of the main building. Annie and Hope both gasped.

The resort was sprawling, and Hope could see the many pods of balconied rooms stretching out into the distance, built in such a way that they blended in with their surroundings. The resort was fronted by a rustic lodge-style main hall. Their car slowed to a stop at the end of a small stone bridge that led over a pond and to the front doors.

"We have to walk?" Hope's father groused. "You can't pull up right to the front?"

Hope leaned into the back from the passenger's seat and patted her father's sleeve. "Dad, it's right there. And, look, there's a bellhop." As they popped open their car doors, an efficient young man in a starched blue uniform came their way, rolling a shiny, gold luggage cart. They met him at the edge of the bridge.

"Welcome to the Cabins in the Pines Executive Resort."

"Thank you. We're Beacon Financial Planning and Wealth Management," Hope said, looking past the man to the calm waters of the pond beneath the stone bridge. A family of ducks swam there, three little ducklings diving and splashing and being honked at by their mother, who soon crowded them together and aimed them toward the under-bridge arches. *How cute.*

The bellhop pulled out a small tablet. "Ah, yes. You're Annie Goodman?"

"Hope Bergman."

The bellhop looked perplexed. "I have an Annie Goodman down as representative."

Annie stepped forward and held out her hand. "What do you need me to..."

"Nothing at all. I've marked you as arrived, so if you'll hand me the keys, the valet can park your car. Then just go over the bridge and through the double doors. You'll see the front desk. Deanna will be there, ready to give you your room assignments and explain how the scheduling will work with your events. We'll be sure to get your luggage to your rooms."

Annie handed him the keys. As soon as the three of them were out of earshot of the bellhop, Hope's father said gruffly, "I thought you picked this place. You left this up to your assistant?"

Hope was determined not to let his mood ruin the lovely surroundings. "A good boss knows how to delegate. I have total faith in Annie. And look around you." She gestured broadly. "Faith rewarded."

He snorted, but let it drop. Annie smiled gratefully at Hope.

They had reached the front doors, and the peaked portico rising above them shaded them from the early afternoon sun. Up close, Hope admired the beautiful detail in the stonework that wrapped the lodge, and as she passed through the wide front doors, nodding her thanks to the doorman who held one open, she could see that the same attention to detail had been taken on the interior.

They walked together across polished hardwood floors toward a massive check-in desk that looked as though it had been hewn out of the largest tree around. The varnished rings and swirls of the woodgrain were like abstract art.

Beyond the check-in desk was a lounge area with a see-through fireplace as tall as Hope was, and she imagined how cozy it would be when a fire was lit in it. Overstuffed chairs, chaises, and a loveseat surrounded the fireplace. Thick, polished cuts of tree stump that looked to have been taken from the same tree as the front desk stood as occasional tables, their varnished surfaces reflecting the light from the crystal chandeliers above. The overall effect was one of both natural simplicity and absolute luxury. Hope thought she could have spent the whole trip in the lobby and been perfectly content.

"Welcome!" the woman behind the huge front desk said. "I can get you checked in."

Annie and Hope's father walked toward her. She was maybe twenty, fresh-faced and smiling, her button-up, logo-emblazoned shirt crisp and professional. Hope trailed after, still in awe of the place.

"Beacon Financial Planning and Wealth Management," her father said. His tone was a little more pleasant than it had been outside.

The woman, whose name tag read *Amelia*, tapped efficiently at her keyboard, bringing up their reservations. "I have you right here. Can you tell me the names for the rooms?" Her father supplied them, and she was equally as efficient with arranging their keycards and getting them each a packet of information about the resort.

Hope's father waved his keycard. "Now that we're checked in, let's get to our rooms and get ready for the mixer this evening. We'll need to be at our best, and I'm a little road-weary."

Annie nodded, but she leaned back and waved the brochure at Hope, mouthing, "Spa?"

Hope, trying to keep a straight face, nodded, mouthing back, "Absolutely!"

"Before you go, Mr. Bergman," the woman behind the desk said, "let me just print your seminar itinerary with the events marked on our property map. We'll be giving these out to all of your attendees."

A few more taps, and then she froze, with a fleeting expression of panic.

Oh no, Hope thought. *What's wrong?*

Her father echoed her unspoken question. "Something wrong, miss?"

The woman tapped a few more keys, bit her lower lip, and then plastered on a smile that Hope didn't fully believe. "We have new software, and it's a bit of a learning curve." Behind the clerk, a large office printer spit out several sheets of paper, and the woman made three neat packets from them, stapled them, and handed them to Annie, Hope, and her father.

"Here you are. Everything is mapped with your room number as the origin point. Is there anything else I can help you with?" Her smile was still on, and Hope was still worried.

"That'll be all," her father said, turning and motioning for Hope and Annie to follow. He studied his map, then charged ahead to lead the way. Hope followed, preoccupied with what might have thrown off the clerk.

Nothing could go wrong with this seminar. This was Hope's chance to reconnect with her father, and if she couldn't find the way back to their previously warm relationship through giving him time and space and making small gestures to let him know she was there, well, she would grab his attention with how perfectly she could manage his business—and then they would restore the closeness they once had.

They crossed the lobby to the elevator and her father pressed the up button. Hope looked over her shoulder at the front desk clerk, who was now speaking with another employee—her manager? Both of them were sneaking glances at her, her dad, and Annie as they waited for the doors to open. Hope turned away as the elevator doors dinged and slid open. With a silent prayer to whatever patron saint watched over investment managers, she followed her father and Annie onto the elevator.

CHAPTER 2

A SUMMER BREEZE BLEW THROUGH THE branches of the towering trees that surrounded the Cabins in the Pines, creating a light susurrus that should have calmed Slater Evans as he leaned against his company truck, squinting in the noonday sunlight. It *should* have calmed him. But it didn't. Slater had too much to do.

"Rach, come on," he called over his shoulder at the open office door. "We've got to get the rest of this lumber across the lake,"

While he waited for his boss's teenage daughter, he studied the building for anything wrong—an old habit from his years as head maintenance at the campground. But the heavy timbers that made up the structure were smooth, varnished, and pristine. The new red tin roof was cheery and perfect at every seam. The building fit into the lush, verdant landscape as though it had simply sprung up out of the ground—even more so now, after the recent renovations. No, there was nothing to do here.

Slater fidgeted, practically feeling the minutes of the day ticking away. Aside from his new job duties across the lake, there were wedding projects to attend to. This was the second wedding that they'd held for a member of his close circle of friends here at the Cabins, but he was unusually antsy about this one. He didn't want to think about why, even though he had a good idea.

Several more minutes passed. Just as Slater was about to go in, Rachel came barreling out of the office, her long, wheat-colored hair escaping from her own baseball cap and flying behind her. She was holding her hand up triumphantly. "I found them! I found them!"

Slater grinned at her when the kid—nope, now she was a *teenager,* almost taller than her mother—skidded to a stop in front of him and held out a handful of photos. "They were in a box way up high in the storage closet in Mom's office. I'm going to put them right in the center. Do you think Mom and Wyatt will be embarrassed?" Her giggle was pure mischief.

Slater took the photos from Rachel's outstretched hand and looked them over. He had to admit, he'd never seen his two bosses quite like this. One of the photos showed a teenaged Wyatt, now the owner of the Cabins in the Pines, posing outside with long, surfer-style hair, wearing a T-shirt that was so neon it was blinding. In the other picture, boys and girls danced by Lake Fairwood at what looked like an old end-of-camp dance. Neither Wyatt nor Rachel's mom, Delaney, could have been over thirteen in the second photo—younger than Rachel was now. They were as far apart in the photo as their stiff arms could keep them. Wyatt looked sheepish and uncomfortable. Delaney was beaming at him.

Slater grinned. Wyatt was anything but sheepish around Delaney now. In fact, most of the time, he beamed at his wife-to-be the same way she was looking at him in the photo. It was great that the two of them had gotten a second chance at love after Delaney's divorce.

"I think these are sweet, actually," Slater said, handing them back. "Well, maybe not that T-shirt. Probably want to put that picture off to the side so as not to blind anyone." Slater gestured toward the truck behind him. "Ready to go? If we don't get there soon, Wyatt—"

"You mean *Groomzilla*," Rachel corrected cheekily.

Slater clicked his tongue, feeling like he had to stick up for his friend. "Now, now, the man is just stressed. But he's still my boss, and he's going to be blowing up my phone."

Rachel went around the truck and climbed in. Slater slid into the driver's side, settling behind the steering wheel and buckling his seat belt. Once Rachel did the same, he fired up the vehicle. Shiny and new, with the spiffed-up Cabins in the Pines logo emblazoned across each side, the truck was better transportation than the old golf cart they'd driven years ago—though Slater missed cruising the camp with the wind blowing through the open frame of the old buggy.

Time had flown, months stacking up incredibly fast, and not only had the Cabins continued to expand—thanks to their appearance on a reality TV show and the subsequent deal they'd struck with its star-investor host—but Slater's role and responsibilities had also grown enormously. With Alexandra Brent-Collingsworth's help, the original campground had gone from the small site that Wyatt had inherited from his parents to a property that offered both family- and business-centered facilities.

That was another thing that had changed over the past two years. Alex had traded most of her jet-setting time for time in the trees, and she'd even handed *The ABCs of Business* over to a new host last season. It was good that she was here. Every time the original episode re-aired, they were inundated with bookings.

Business was booming, and Slater never quite managed to catch his breath. He bet this was exactly how Wyatt and Delany had felt when the Cabins had been at the edge of ruin, only then they were trying to keep things from falling apart, and not trying to make sure all the cogs in a very successful machine ran smoothly on a daily basis.

True to his own prediction, Slater's phone suddenly dinged twice. The console screen of the truck showed that there were texts from Wyatt.

"Are you gonna read those?" Rachel asked, excitement in her voice.

"Nope," Slater said. "I will when I'm not driving."

Rachel sighed. "How am I supposed to keep up with the wedding drama?"

He laughed. "I suppose you'll have to go straight to the source."

Rachel wrinkled her nose. "No fun. I bet you wouldn't even be a Groomzilla yourself."

I was nearly there, once, he almost said. An image of long, soft blond hair and sky-blue eyes flashed into his brain for the first time in forever, and carried with it the ghost of a song that he couldn't quite remember. Despite the time, though, he could still picture her as clearly as if she were standing right in front of him. He could feel the guitar strings under his fingers and hear her singing. He could see the velvet box and her happy tears when she'd said yes.

Slater had a strong feeling that the time of year—just

when his own wedding-that-never-was had been supposed to happen—was amplifying all the nostalgia he
was feeling surrounding his friends' nuptials. He had to
constantly push thoughts of his past from his mind to
focus on work.

Even as he drove with Rachel to the resort, a short
jaunt across Lake Fairwood from the original camp, he
was cataloging all the things he had to do when they
arrived. The warm breeze whipped into their open windows, and on either side, the tall pines flew past. The
same sun that had dappled down on Slater moments ago
now rushed full-force across the surface of the lake, so
that if he turned his head to look out across it, he would
be greeted by a million sparkling points of brilliance. But
he didn't turn his head.

*Finish the framing on the guest wall. Call and check on
how many folding chairs we have in storage. Remember
to ask Ursula the count for extra staff she has scheduled
on the day of the ceremony. Did I tell Maisie about the
acting class thing that needs to host their luncheon at the
Bean Pot?* There was so much to do. Moving up from
maintenance to management had certainly cranked up
the pressure. He was constantly worried about messing
something up or forgetting something.

"Slater?" Rachel's voice broke into his thoughts.

"Hmm?"

"You missed our turn."

Yikes. Slater shot an apologetic look at Rachel and
used the next pull-off to flip around and direct them back
toward their destination.

"Sorry, kiddo. I'm just in my head a bit. Lots to do."

Rachel nodded in sympathy. "Did you know that Wyatt was pacing around the living room this morning *way*

too early, muttering about tulle versus organza for the reception table centerpieces? My mom was calmly making pancakes, and he was walking crazy laps around the couch, frantically Googling."

Slater turned up the winding driveway to the executive resort. The sunlight half disappeared, and the cooler, shadier atmosphere calmed him—slightly. "There's a difference?"

"Apparently." Rachel sounded both amused and skeptical.

The main entrance to the resort was a mammoth sprawl of natural rock, timber, and tin, crowned with a grand portico that swept skyward to a point, supported by massive stone columns that perfectly framed the barn-style lantern lights that would, come evening, light the way to the entrance. As they eased past the main building, Rachel continued.

"I keep telling Wyatt that he should relax and not freak over the details."

"Easier said than done," Slater said, taking the final turn that put them at a wide stretch of grass where a group was gathered. As they slowed to a stop and parked, Slater pointed out the front windshield toward where Wyatt Andrews—owner of the Cabins in the Pines and recently monikered Groomzilla—stood, looking concerned. He was running a hand through sandy-colored hair, talking animatedly—and pacing.

Beside him stood Delaney, Wyatt's soon-to-be-wife and general manager of the Cabins. She didn't wear the same look of worry. But Slater was surprised that she hadn't pulled out every strand of her own dark-brown locks, dealing with Wyatt and the wedding planning.

Behind them were Alexandra Brent-Collingsworth of

ABCs of Business fame, sitting in an Adirondack chair and being light-tested by *ABCs* director, Norman Gilmore, who was dressed in his normal all-black slacks and t-shirt, wielding a camera and clicking off photographs of Alex as she posed on an antique pale-peach settee that had been carried out just an hour prior to become the centerpiece of the wedding guest photo-op spot. They seemed to be goofing off, which would have been—in the past—very out of character for the pair. Alex's normally perfectly coiffed blond hair was pulled up in a simple bun, and she'd seemed to pull away more and more from her makeup-heavy, on-camera look; the same they'd all seen when she had first come to town with her TV show. Now, she wore softer, more natural makeup, and Slater found her out on a hiking trail as often as he did in her office at the resort.

Rachel squinted at Wyatt and Delaney. "What do you think the issue is now? Is the problem tulle or organza?" she quipped.

Slater shook his head. "I don't know. I'm a tool guy, not a tulle guy."

"Well," Rachel said with a sigh, "let's go, Mr. Deputy Assistant Manager. It looks like my mom might need some assistance managing."

They both unbuckled and popped the doors on their respective sides, climbing out and making their way over the pillow-soft carpet of freshly-shorn grass between them and their destination. At the sight of Rachel and Slater, Wyatt's expression softened a bit. Rachel tucked the photos she'd retrieved into her back pocket as she approached her mom. Slater raised a hand at Alex and Norman as the pair caught sight of the new arrivals.

"Hey, guys!" Wyatt said, jogging lightly to meet them.

He accepted a squeeze from Rachel, and then, clapping Slater on the back, Wyatt gushed, "My best man. Glad you're back. I need to ask your opinion on something."

Slater hesitated. "Okay..." He drew out the last sound a little, unsure of what he was about to get himself into. Wyatt turned Slater toward the lake, gesturing out over the water.

"If we have the guest wall face this way, the guests will have the lake as a backdrop. But if we have the wall face this way"—Wyatt spun Slater 180 degrees, backs to the lake—"we'll have light for longer, so any late arrivals will see the wall lit by the pathway lights."

Slater nodded, still not sure of the real importance of the question. He made eye contact with Delaney, who shrugged and made a helpless face.

"Well, man, in my opinion..."

Slater looked over at Rachel and Delaney again. Alex and Norman had joined them, and everyone—excluding Delaney, who continued to look a tad paralyzed—was flashing fingers at him. *Option one. No, two. No, now two of them say one. Or is that two for two?*

"Yes?" Wyatt looked as though Slater's answer would make or break the whole event. Not even the pressures of his new job could top this.

"Facing away from the lake. You really want that lasting light."

Wyatt's face flooded with relief. And Slater noticed that relief was reflected on all four of the faces behind Wyatt. The four took the opportunity to turn and flee.

Seriously? he thought as he watched them scurry away. Now he was out here in best-man bedlam, *alone*.

"Yeah," Wyatt agreed, nodding. "That's perfect. You're right."

"You just want everything to be perfect. I get it." Slater returned the clap on the back that Wyatt had given him earlier. "Look, it's about lunchtime, right? Why don't you take Rachel and Delaney down to the Bean Pot? Maisie said she was planning to make buttermilk pies for today, and I bet the girls would enjoy a break. It's so stressful for them, all this wedding chaos."

Wyatt nodded at the suggestion. Slater hoped that Maisie—manager of the on-site restaurant and A+ people-whisperer—would help soothe Wyatt's nerves. "That's a great idea. Maybe Del wants to talk over lunch about how we'll split the chairs at the ceremony. I mean, there's the traditional, which is bride-side-groom-side, but—"

Slater held up a hand, halting his friend mid-speech. "How about no wedding talk during lunch?"

Slater watched as realization dawned on the other man's face. "You think I'm stressing everyone out. With the wedding stuff. And the stressing."

It was Slater's turn to nod. "Did you have a sort of fabric dilemma this morning?"

"It was…I mean…there's a difference in the stretch—"

"Wyatt."

Wyatt's mouth snapped shut.

"You're a week away from marrying the perfect woman. You have an amazing stepdaughter, a thriving business, and a group of friends who have your back. Including me."

Wyatt turned, and Slater followed his gaze to where Delaney and Rachel were now hamming it up at the photo setup. Alex was laughing as Norman made exaggerated hand motions and called out to them like they were all at a fashion shoot.

"You're right, Slater. Thanks, man."

23

Wyatt turned back, and Slater was already there with a strong hug. Wyatt, Rachel, and Delaney headed off toward Wyatt's truck, which was parked a few yards away, and Norman and Alex came to meet Slater.

Alex brushed a quick kiss over both of Slater's cheeks before fussing with the collar of his polo shirt. "Darling, you handled that beautifully. You're so good at managing difficult situations. I was telling Delaney again this morning what a brilliant move it was promoting you."

"Leave the man alone, Alex. Can't you see he has work to do? And you do, too."

"Oh, hush," Alex shushed Norman as he came forward to shake hands with Slater. "Norman doesn't want me to spend all day involved in wedding activities. We have a very high-profile group coming in today."

Slater frowned slightly, trying to mentally scroll through the schedule he'd looked at that morning. Things were different with the new software they'd upgraded to—gosh, they'd outgrown three scheduling systems in the last two years—and he kept picturing the last schedule's layout, with all the particulars scrambled in his mind's eye.

"The actor's thing?" It was the only group he could immediately recall. "Are we still keeping that a surprise for Rachel?"

"Yes, we're surprising her. And no, no, dear, I mean the wealth management company. They do their new-client seminar yearly, and they're expanding their seat offerings this year. We can accommodate the extra twenty percent attendance they were looking for, and, even better, every spot is filled."

"Right! They're here for the whole week."

"Yes. If they like us, I have a strong feeling that they'll

be a return booking." Alex practically vibrated with excitement. "And with the wedding happening, well, it absolutely couldn't be a more wonderful week." She ended her speech with a flurry of claps and a few bounces on the balls of her high-heeled feet.

"Guess this place is perfect for bringing together almost anybody," Slater agreed.

Alex pursed her lips. "Speaking of, I never see you bringing anyone home to the family. How are we going to host your wedding in the pines if you don't ever bring us someone to approve of?"

"Well, I..." The question was like a bolt of lightning to Slater's chest. Despite how often the upcoming wedding made him flash back to his past, none of his recent thoughts had made it so sharply clear that he'd been flying pretty much solo for the past several years. He allowed himself to entertain, briefly, the idea of asking someone to be his wedding date. Maybe it was because he'd been remembering too much lately—spoiling himself with images of a heart-shaped face and a laugh that made his heart expand—but he couldn't think of anyone he knew now who he wanted to spend that kind of time with.

Alex snapped her fingers sharply to get Slater's attention. "Evans, come back to us. If you can't stomach the idea of a full-blown relationship, tell me you're at least bringing a date to the wedding."

Slater took the out, giving Alex a pat on the shoulder. "I'll try my best, Alex."

"Good. It would be dreadful if the best man were there *alone.*"

Slater and his love life were forgotten as Alex flipped the camera and powered on the review screen, starting to thumb through the photos they'd all taken. "I'll just go see how these test shots turned out. Ta!" Norman trailed after Alex with a wave at Slater.

Slater unloaded the lumber from the truck. For the next hour, he worked to build the freestanding wall that would greet attendees as they walked up from the large side parking lot. From there, they would be ushered to a fun photo and then the welcome party at the resort.

The wall took shape quickly, and Slater recruited a couple of extra staff members to set it into place in the heavy base stand. Slater hoped it held all week. If it fell, they would have to deal with Groomzilla. For now, it held firm.

High-fives were given all around, and Slater sent the two other men back to their regular duties. He stood back from the wall to examine it, proud of his creation. He imagined the items that would cover it by week's end—not only Rachel's photos, but messages from wedding guests and mementos that would be pinned on to create a collaborative telling of Wyatt and Delaney's story. It would be great. His friends deserved to see others celebrate their love.

Alex's question came, unbidden, back into Slater's mind. *How are we going to host your wedding in the pines if you don't ever bring us someone?*

Slater took in a breath of the warm, forest-scented air. He closed his eyes and listened to the rustling of leaves as a slight breeze wafted through, and smiled a little sadly when he opened his eyes to the chittering argument between a pair of chipmunks that skittered up a nearby tree.

He wasn't even thinking of romance right now. He was happy here, happier than he'd been in a very long time, and he knew from unfortunate experience that love could be a gamble.

Luckily for his two best friends, the gamble had paid off. But Slater had been there, done that, and it wasn't a path he wanted to tread again any time soon.

"It looks good."

Slater turned from surveying his work to find Maisie behind him. Her large, green eyes were smiling. The scarf tied around her sleek, pixie-cut hair was the same color as the retro dress she wore. A pair of cat-eye sunglasses, and Maisie wouldn't be out of place at a sock hop.

"Are you escaping the wedding hullaballoo, too?"

"Goodness, yes. It's like everyone's in a jack-in-the-box that's wound too tight. I remember how anxious I was the week before Charles and I got married. It's supposed to be the most joyous occasion of your life, but I was as nervous as a long-tailed cat in a room full of rocking chairs."

"Love conquered all," Slater observed.

Maisie sighed dreamily. "It did, indeed." Again, Slater's heart panged just a touch. He rubbed at his chest. Maisie surveyed the guest wall and the array of paintbrushes, gold- and silver-ink markers, and small jars of paint. "What a fantastic wedding gift!"

Slater froze at the mention. *Wedding gift?* "This isn't their..."

Maisie looked sideways at him, waiting for him to finish.

"What did you guys get them?" he finished lamely.

Maisie pursed her lips. "Well, don't tell, but Charles built a little arbor out back of the Bean Pot, and yesterday I went and picked up a half-dozen blueberry bushes to grow around it. To make pancakes out of every summer. Rachel helped him, actually. It was sweet. He's really good with kids."

Slater nudged Maisie with his shoulder. "He'll make a good dad someday."

Her grin stretched wide. "How about you? Alex says you got *a date* for the wedding?"

The groan slipped out before Slater could stop it. "No. Alex *wants* me to bring a date. She thinks it's a *faux pas* for the best man to be without one. I have no one in mind." He looked over at Maisie pleadingly. "Do you maybe have a sister?"

"Well, someone as close as a sister, but she's marrying Wyatt this week, so she's busy."

Slater sighed. "No wedding gift. No wedding date. What else could go wrong this week?"

Maisie's eyes widened as she looped her arm around his and put her finger to her lips. "Shush! You don't want to jinx anything! And don't worry, things have a way of working out around here." She jostled him until he felt his furrowed brow relax.

Behind them, Slater suddenly heard a voice calling. They turned as a pair to see Charles—Maisie's bespectacled, adoring husband—approaching on the path.

Slater had just taken a single step with Maisie when his cell phone rang at his hip. The screen showed the number of the front desk on the resort side. *A manager's work is never done*, he thought.

"Mais, go head. I'll catch up. Gotta get this." Giving his arm a squeeze, she left him to his call and skipped giddily toward Charles. Slater swiped to answer, musing about how it actually felt normal now, when cell service at the campground had historically been dismal before the reality show had stepped in.

"Evans, what can I do for you?"

"Slater, it's Ursula."

Wyatt's aunt did not sound happy. He knew she was up at the resort today, handling staff scheduling, and it was a stressful, time-consuming task. He pictured her standing at the front desk, swathed in one of the gauzy flower-child dresses that she favored, with her wild, curly red hair flying everywhere.

"We have a problem, but you have to *promise* you won't say anything to Wyatt or Delaney until we have a solution."

Slater's heart jumped. *Well, shoot.* "What's going on?"

"We double-booked the ballroom. On the day we need it for the reception."

Slater's anxiety actually dropped a few notches. "Okay, just move the other party to the east conference hall and comp the inconvenienced group a day at the spa."

"I can't do that. It's the Beacon Financial Awards Ceremony. And that's not the only conflict between the wedding itinerary and the Beacon events."

Slater blew out a breath. "Okay. Tell the front desk at exec to sit tight. I'm on my way."

As soon as she agreed, Slater hung up, his heart racing a little. One more crisis to avert.

CHAPTER 3

S LATER RUBBED THE BRIDGE OF his nose as he walked into the lobby of the executive resort. He found Alex waiting for him, leaned over the computer at the front desk, frowning.

"Alex, what's the scoop?" Slater rounded the corner to stand behind the desk and lean over Alex's shoulder. He squinted at the computer screen, which displayed the weekly bookings.

"I've sent Amelia to fetch a representative from the seminar, but look here." Alex pointed with one manicured finger. "Wyatt and Delaney's reception was never on this schedule."

Slater sighed. "But they put it on the books six months ago!"

"And it was probably there until the recent software change. It looks like when they imported all of the pre-scheduled events from the old software into the new software, the new software just blanked out the reservation for the reception, along with a couple of other wedding events."

"Leaving those schedule spots open, so when Beacon called to schedule—"

"—it appeared to be available," Alex finished.

They both stared at one another for a moment, thoughtful. Slater leaned in to make a few mouse clicks, tallying up the conflicts he could see off the top of his head.

Alex's voice drew Slater from his focus on the schedule. "Ah, here's Amelia with the young lady now. We'll get all this sorted."

Slater stood, raising his eyes to see the front-desk clerk coming from the direction of the central lounge, escorting an elegantly dressed blonde whose head was bent slightly as they conversed. The soft, golden overhead lights made her carefully coiffed hair seem to glow. She was dressed in a flowing, one-shoulder dress, the material a powder blue that reminded him of the color of summer skies. A slight buzz started behind his eyes, and he knew it wasn't from the small, nagging headache he'd been nursing.

She never looked up the whole walk down the plush-carpeted hall. Slater watched, intrigued. He could hear her talking to Amelia, but couldn't make out what they were saying. That voice, though. It sounded *so* familiar.

And then she laughed.

Slater didn't need her to look up. He knew, in detail, what she looked like—every beautiful feature. Everything about her was etched into his memory permanently, and there wasn't an expression, angle, or gesture that he didn't recall with painful clarity. His heart seemed to twist savagely in his chest.

Oh, no. She's going to look up, and I'll be—

"Slater?"

Time froze when her eyes finally met his. The clear, sparkling blue that he'd lost himself in years ago did the same thing to him now that it had when they'd been younger—knocked him flat. And beneath the blue was an unexpected sadness that put the steamroller in reverse and backed over his prone heart. He knew he was standing there woodenly, awkwardly, but he couldn't force words out of his mouth. The sight of her was at once so unexpected, so painful, and yet so *welcome*, that he didn't know how to react.

He wanted to wrap his arms around her. He wanted to ban her from the property. He wanted to pull a bumbling Buster Keaton leap-and-scramble over the front desk, run into the woods, and hide there until her company left at the end of the week.

Except...the wedding.

Wyatt and Delaney's wedding—not the wedding that he'd longed for, but that had never happened, between him and the woman standing in front of him.

"You two know each other?" Alex asked, crossing her arms and looking between Hope and Slater, eyes narrowed. Amelia, the clerk, looked alternately confused and intrigued.

Hope, at least, had the wherewithal to not freeze like a deer in the headlights. She'd always been more composed than he had, anyway.

"We, uh, actually went to college together. It's great to see you, Slater." Her pinched smile still wasn't the best cover-up.

"You look good," he managed to say softly.

"Thanks. You too."

There was a moment of silence before Hope changed the subject to the problem at hand and distracted Alex—

who Slater knew would only grill him later. Hope's cheeks were tinged pink, and her words stuttered slightly. "I hear there's an issue with scheduling?"

"Umm, yes. There seems to be." Alex gestured for Hope to come around behind the front desk.

Slater decided that it was way too warm in here.

"Excuse me," he said, sliding past Alex and heading to the front doors. He felt Alex's curious gaze on him the whole walk. He needed out. He needed air. He needed a deep, internal shake to clear the impact of seeing the woman who'd broken his heart. It was as if his reminiscing this past week had conjured her out of thin air. *How?*

"Slater, stay close. I have a few things to talk to you about when we're done here," Alex called as he neared the exit. He threw up a hand and waved in response. He pushed outside and grabbed the first chair he saw, a plush patio recliner that was one of many circled around the front fire pit. He took a few deep, steadying breaths.

And here Slater had thought this would be one of the happiest weeks of his life. His two best friends were getting married. His Pines family would all be here. But now, there was an unwelcome guest, a ghost from the past—one who filled Slater with the deepest of dread *and* the slightest shimmer of a longing he knew he'd never really let go of.

Hope couldn't concentrate on what Alex was showing her. She stared at the printed page with the new seminar schedule, but all she could see was Slater Evans. Everything in her was transported back to the first moment they'd met, freshman year, and then fast-forwarded through days in cramped dorm rooms and at campus parties, spending late nights at coffee-shop open mics. And woven into every happy memory was the man who'd been standing in front of her.

And his proposal. The ring box sitting on her stool onstage where they'd performed together. The small crowd, all in on it, waiting for her to notice. Her heart had soared when she'd opened the box and he had slipped to one knee.

How was it possible that he was here? True, she'd never kept track of him after their breakup, but what were the chances that they'd both be in the same place ever again? And how absolutely unfair was it that, all these years later, he was even more handsome than he'd been...

When you left him?

It stung to remember, but it was the truth. Hope had broken the heart inside that tall, rugged man with the million-watt-smile. It was his smile that she remembered the most, or maybe his laugh, or possibly the beautiful hazel eyes that crinkled at the corners when he was happy, or just the way he used to look at her when he'd lazily strummed a series of chords to warm up right before they went out on stage.

A few faint lines of song came floating into Hope's mind. She pressed her lips together against them.

"—and so that should set everything straight, but I need to make sure that you're okay with having your awards ceremony out in the open-air amphitheater rather than the ballroom."

Hope blinked as she realized what Alex was asking. "Outdoors?" Reminded of the task at hand, Hope thought immediately of her father and his expectations. There was no way that he would go for an outdoor event to cap off the week. "No, no, we couldn't possibly. It's a black-tie event."

Hope watched the worry flit across Alex's face. "We had a wedding reception there previously." Then Alex's face brightened a bit. "I have an idea. Let me run it by the bride and groom, and I'll let you know. Does everything else look okay to you?"

Hope scanned the paper again. "Yes, thank you. You'll let me know about the ballroom?"

Alex nodded.

"And your...umm...Mr. Evans?"

Alex's eyes took on a sparkle that Hope didn't miss. "He's the deputy assistant manager of the property. Did you need to speak with him?" Alex gestured out toward the front doors. "I expect he's out front somewhere. And can you ask him to come in once you're finished?"

Hope nodded, squared her shoulders, and marched toward the same doors that her very first love had walked out of moments before.

Slater was, as Alex had predicted, sitting outside. When Hope neared, he stood and wiped his palms on the front of his slacks.

He's nervous too.

He had no reason to be. Well, maybe he was nervous about what she might say. They hadn't parted on the best of terms, or with the kindest of words. But she had been the one to break it off. And look where life had taken her—she was established in her career, and successful, and as far as anyone else knew, happy. She started speaking before he could. He started a split second after.

"I know this is a little awkward, but I'm only here a week, and—"

"It's not a problem that you're here. I hope you don't thi—"

They both broke off, laughing. Hope felt a flush of heat in her cheeks as the crinkles appeared at the corners of his eyes.

"I was surprised to see you. I mean, I saw Beacon Financial on the registration, but that isn't your father's business, is it?"

"It is. It used to be Bergman Financial. Around the time you and I...umm, when my mom passed, my father renamed the company. Her maiden name was Deacon, so Bergman and Deacon..."

Thankfully, he let her almost-mention of their break-up slide without comment. His eyes softened when she mentioned her mother, but he didn't press her to talk about it.

"Ahhh, Beacon. I gct it."

"She was always his light," Hope added. She knew she must be staring, but she couldn't help letting her eyes pass over his sharp-jawed face again and again. The years had been way too kind to him—and it was hard to look away. "And your dad? How's he doing?"

"Good, good," Slater assured. "He runs a fishing company up in Alaska now. After all those years of working for someone else, he went out on his own."

Hope felt a spark of joy at the mention of the senior Evans's success. "That's amazing!"

"Yeah, it's something. I keep meaning to call him and set the date for my next trip up there to visit, but I've been so busy with wedding plans."

"Wedding? You're getting married?" Hope's stomach lurched a little.

He studied her face for a beat before answering, and

the barest ghost of a smile formed on his lips. "No, my two best friends are. Wyatt and Delaney. Wyatt owns the place. Delaney helps run it. Your group is actually double booked into the ballroom where they were going to have their wedding reception."

"Oh. Oh, well, that's unfortunate. But your...friend? Alex? She wants you to come back inside when you're able."

Slater's smile became a grin. "Alex is an investor here. She helped us expand, made all of this"—he swept a hand outward toward the broad area of the resort—"possible. Are you trying to ask if I'm still single?"

Hope's face heated even further. "No! I mean, not at all. That's none of my business. Alex told me she would figure out the ballroom dilemma. But we simply can't give it up. My father's—*our* clients expect a certain level of chic."

Slater hummed noncommittally, shoving his hands into his pockets. "How's work treating you?"

She felt her spine stiffen. They were on sensitive ground now. "It's great."

"Putting that business degree to use?"

"Every day." She waited for the old speech about passions versus obligation, but it didn't come. Instead, Slater stepped closer to her, reached up, and tucked a stray strand of hair behind her ear. She had to will herself not to react.

He cleared his throat and looked at some spot past her as he spoke, seeming to avoid her eyes. "Look, I have a lot of work to do this week for the wedding. You've got this Beacon Financial thing. I think we can both agree to pretend the other isn't here this week. It's been a long time. No need to open up old wounds, okay?"

She couldn't keep the ice out of her voice. What had she expected—that he would still be pining for her? "Agreed. This is just an unfortunate coincidental meeting."

His answering smile was a little sad. "I don't think it's so unfortunate. It was nice to see you." And then he nodded, once, before stepping past her to reenter the resort lobby.

Hope's mind was far from the warm and inviting room in front of her. Annie had selected the perfect professional party decorators to set things up for the mixer. The room was just right.

Soft, thick dark-burgundy carpeting gave underfoot. The lighting was dimmable, and she had it set to half brightness. Tall, linen-swathed tables dotted the room, each with a cluster of lit tea lights on them. Long side tables were laden with chafing dishes that held a bevy of appetizers—again, planned perfectly by Annie. And in front of the room sat a dark-wood podium, draped with a banner bearing their company logo, where her father would be giving the welcome speech to open the annual seminar.

Every seat had booked up, which made Hope, well, hopeful that they would see the client gains that her father had been so adamant about from this event. Hope smoothed her hands down over the front of her dress. She had to push her run-in with Slater from her mind and focus on the seminar. *Stick to the plan. Not the past.*

She refocused on the clipboard in front of her. Slowly, she rescanned the attendees list that she'd had the front desk print, verifying each name as one having a seat in all of the events through the week, as well as making sure that everyone had arrived and checked in. She made it rapidly through the names but stalled when she hit one marked as not arrived. Ralph Murphy—one of her father's oldest friends—had come to all of their conferences for the past ten years. But he hadn't made it in yet. Hope felt a stab of worry—had he decided not to attend? Maybe he'd just been delayed for some reason.

Annie sidled up and tapped Hope's clipboard. "No Ralph yet? That's strange..."

Before they could discuss Ralph, the sharp, metallic sound of the double doors opening behind them rang out. Hope didn't recognize the voice that projected into the room as they turned.

"Well, aren't you both visions!"

Hope and Annie both swiveled to see her father walking in, accompanied by a strikingly handsome man that Hope had never seen before—obviously the man who'd called out the compliment. Well, on second glance, he did look familiar, but she couldn't quite place him.

The pair stopped just short of where Annie and Hope stood, and her father gestured to his companion. "Ladies, this is Jack Allen. Jack, this is my daughter, Hope, and her assistant, Annie."

Jack Allen shook Annie's hand, but when his fingers slid into Hope's, he held on a tiny bit longer, giving her a charming, roguish grin. That smile...

Hope had the nagging feeling of having seen Jack Allen before. Of course, she would have thought that a man who looked like him would stand out in her mind. Tall, trim, and clothed in what was obviously a designer suit, Jack wore his salt-and-pepper hair cut in a low fade, stylishly longer than traditional on top. He had a bit of a devilish air that made Hope think he might be an actor.

No. I can't put my finger on it...

"I must say, I never expected to find such beauty at a stuffy old investment conference."

Hope smiled at the handsome stranger. She passed a quick glance to her father, but to Hope's surprise, her father didn't seem too fussed about Jack's blatant flirtation. Strange, she thought, because he would normally find that sort of behavior unprofessional—and comment on it. In any other situation, she might have thrilled at Jack's attention. But she was still, despite her efforts, preoccupied with thoughts of Slater.

"Mr. Allen, are you staying at the resort for business or pleasure?" Annie asked.

Jack released Annie's hand and explained, "I came specifically for this event. You see, my current financial manager isn't really doing the best job, and a friend of a friend of Alexandra Brent-Collingsworth—one of the owners—mentioned that Beacon Financial was having a big get-together here. I was overdue for a little R & R away from the tech scene, so I thought—two birds! It was really very spontaneous."

Tech scene? That's where I know him from!

"You're Jack Allen, the owner of Pacific Tech."

The roguish grin stretched wider. "The very one."

Her father cleared his throat. "Jack will be joining us for the conference this week as our VIP. It's last-minute, but I expect that you'll see to it that he has everything he needs—seats at all the speaking engagements, a table at all the dinners, and, of course, a front-row seat at the awards ceremony."

Hope nodded. "Annie and I will see to it."

"And if you have any questions about the way we invest, our client strategy, our services, anything at all, Hope is absolutely the person to ask."

Hope warmed a little at the praise. "Thank you, and, Jack, of course, I'd be delighted to tell you all about Beacon Financial at any time."

Her father gestured toward the podium. "Come on, Jack. Let's find you a seat in the front row and save it for the speech. And how about a drink?"

With a polite smile, Jack followed her father toward the front of the room. As they made their way through the copse of cocktail tables, Hope realized that she hadn't asked her father why Ralph Murphy was running late.

CHAPTER 4

"MAYBE WE SHOULD RESCHEDULE THE whole thing." Wyatt made a nervous circuit around the lobby of the Cabins in the Pines. It wasn't as grand or sizeable as the lobby of the executive resort, but he made up for the lack of distance by upping the laps. Though he looked as though he were trying to seem casual—he even had his hands in his pockets as he paced—if Wyatt wasn't careful, he was going to break a respectable sweat and ruin the starch in his Cabins in the Pines camp shirt.

So this morning meeting is going well. Slater surveyed the campground family, who were gathered, as usual, to do a morning rundown before business got bustling. The reception area at the Cabins wasn't as fancy as the one at the resort, but the renovations here had made it cozy, inviting, and comfortable. The whole crew were either on or gathered around the overstuffed, L-shaped blue sectional. Rachel, however, had her legs hung off over the arm of one end of it. She was engrossed in her phone, a sight that Slater knew was bound to drive Delaney crazy.

"The summer's going to be over fast," Del would chide Rachel. "Go! Seize your days!"

Slater stared at the cold fireplace, zoning out a little. The topic at hand was now the contested ballroom. The conversation was stretching past the time they'd all planned to leave for a wedding-not-working outing.

Delaney's eyebrows practically disappeared into her hairline as she gawked at her husband-to-be. Her dark ponytail swung as she whipped her head around to look at him. "Do you mean the wedding party outings today, or are you saying that we should stop the whole wedding?" Though she looked a little taken aback, Slater knew that calm-and-steady Delaney would tame Wyatt, who'd started to pace again. The thing she was good at—aside from what her General Manager's nametag said, pinned to her own Cabins in the Pines shirt—was soothing her often-anxious fiancée.

"Yes. I mean the wedding—"

Ursula gasped. Beside her on the sectional, Maisie put an arm around her. Charles, who was standing behind Maisie, put up a finger as though he were going to jump in, but Maisie looked up at him and shook her head, and her husband curled the finger back, dropping his hand.

Delaney looked too shocked to reply.

Rachel's phone let out a series of sounds that Slater could only associate with *Charlie and the Chocolate Factory*. He was pretty sure she was too engrossed in her game to notice what Wyatt had just said.

"We could, you know. I'm sure there will be a full week with no conflicts come September."

Slater spoke up before anything else could come tumbling out of Wyatt's mouth and get him into more trouble. "Hey, hey, now. Come on. We've been through way worse than this. We all pulled together when Alex tried to sabotage us on national TV and sell us off to the highest corporate bidder."

"That is most certainly not what happened!" Alex stood up from her chair, eyes wide. At Slater's grin, she sputtered and sat down. "You're not funny, Evans. I'm reconsidering your promotion."

"You can't. You can only reconsider forty percent of it."

Alex threw a couch pillow at Slater, which he easily caught. He tossed it over to Rachel, who lounged on the other half of the couch where he sat. Rachel caught the pillow without looking up from her phone, tucked the soft square behind her head, and continued playing her game with one hand and petting a sleeping, snoring Duke with the other. Neither dog nor teenager seemed perturbed by the wedding chaos that was swirling around them. Rachel kept methodically running her fingers through Duke's cream-and-russet fur as Alex dropped a question that Slater knew was going to open up a whole interrogation that he didn't want to participate in.

"Besides, Slater, aren't you old friends with that lovely young woman from Beacon Financial?" Alex said. "Can't you talk to her about the ballroom? She seemed intractable when I spoke to her, but if you *know* her."

Every head—including Rachel's—swiveled toward where he stood at the back of the room. Slater felt his face flame, but he tried to keep his voice as emotionless as possible.

"I don't know her anymore. It's not an option." There was a beat of silence. Slater cleared his throat and forged ahead. "Now that I have most of your attention, I'll make my point again. We've been through way worse than this. This is nothing but a hiccup. I liked Alex's suggestion to have the reception down at the lakeside, here at the Cabins. After all, it's where you two spent most of your time together as kids, where your whole relationship started, really."

"Didn't you think our wedding was nice?" Maisie asked Wyatt. "We thought having it here at the campground was perfect."

Delaney rose from her own seat in a nearby wingback chair to go to Wyatt, who ceased his pacing when she stopped beside him. She looped her arms around his neck and, grabbing the back of his head, brought their foreheads together. She stared into his eyes.

"Everything will be fine. This isn't about the location. It's about you and me—"

"And us!" Rachel piped up, shocking Slater with the fact that she'd been paying any attention to the conversation. In her lap, Duke twitched, chasing dream squirrels along the shores of Lake Fairwood.

The whole room shared a laugh. Delaney continued. "Yes, and all of *us* being together for a special day."

Wyatt huffed out a breath, his frustrated features relaxing. He wound his arms around Delaney's waist and pulled her in closer. "I just want everything to be perfect for you."

Delaney jostled him slightly. "Are you gonna be there?"

Wyatt looked at her, scoffed, and said, "Of course, Friday."

"Then it *will* be perfect."

All of the women in the room sighed. Charles kissed Maisie on the cheek, wrapping his arms around her from behind. Slater averted his eyes—not because the affection between his friends made him uncomfortable, but because in combination with his little blast from the past the previous evening, the reminder that love did sometimes work out was a little more than he could handle at the moment. He was thrilled for Wyatt and Delaney, but at the same time, the beautiful reminder of his own failed attempt at forever was somewhere across the lake, probably talking about yearly gains or shifting risk percentages or some such. And he wavered between being thrilled that she was there and angry that she was.

He hadn't even asked her last night if she still made music.

"And to Maisie's point..." Delaney moved to the big property map that was hung, framed, on a nearby wall. She pointed as she continued. "Why don't we switch the whole event to the lakeside? We can have the wedding there, too, the same as we did for Maisie and Charles. Remember, we even laid out that dancefloor by the pavilion." She tapped a spot right next to the blue expanse that symbolized the lake. Delaney looked around the room, and Slater added his nod to the group's general positive response to her suggestion.

Wyatt seemed to consider it. He slowly nodded, too. "We'd need more seating, of course. I don't think the folding chairs from the resort would do well in the grass. Mais, the benches from your wedding..."

"Rented," Maisie offered, apologetically.

"I'll build new ones," Slater blurted. Everyone looked at him again. He didn't mind, this time. He had a way to help. The feelings that rose at his swirling thoughts of Hope were decidedly unhelpful, and they weren't solving any of the problems currently being discussed. Slater rushed on.

"Alex, you'll be over at the resort to keep an eye on the Beacon seminar, anyway, so I could spend some time here getting things ready if we relocate the wedding."

"That would be amazing," Wyatt said, relief evident in his voice. His face relaxed. He smiled. "Yeah, that would be great. As long as it's okay with you, Del?"

Delaney ruffled Wyatt's hair. "I think it would be perfect. Now, we all have wedding party fun times today, right? No work until this afternoon. Everyone go get your fishing gear, and let's get out on the lake!"

Slater watched as they all filed out of the office. He brought up the rear of the line, and just before he walked out the door, he went to the map, tapped the place on the drawing of the resort where the ballroom would be, and pictured—for a long, wistful minute—Hope in that blue dress.

They all made it to the lakeside with plenty of time to spare. Maisie had sorted out life jackets and distributed them, and soon, a veritable fleet of rowboats launched from the dock and out onto Lake Fairwood. Slater, who'd managed to snag a boat on his own, could sort of see through the gaps in the trees as they all glided across the rippling surface of the lake. He spotted the cabins further into the woods as they rowed through the inlets and reeded coves, looking for prime fishing spots. This place still had a lot of wildness to it—some of these very coves still didn't have easy trails that led to them. Looking farther up, over the trees, Slater could make out the faint outline of the mountains in the distance. He tried not to look at the resort, which was clearly visible from the lake.

Soon enough, they drifted to that side of the shore. When they were about a dozen yards offshore, Alex, who shared a rowboat with Rachel, pulled up alongside Slater.

"Isn't *that* the woman you know from Beacon financial?"

Slater had been tipping up his water bottle when Alex spoke, and he choked a little on a sip. He shook his head, sputtering. The tears in his eyes cleared in time to catch the mirth in Alex's. "You know, you do need some date options for the wedding."

Slater could feel his ears growing hot. "I will find my own date."

"You should talk to her, Slater. She's just sitting there, all alone." Rachel's voice was wistful, and Slater suddenly saw the bad side to her obsession with teen romance dramas.

He looked over at the shore, and on the one of the resort docks, sure enough, Hope was sitting, dangling her feet in the water. Her high heels sat on the dock next to her. Wyatt and Delaney pulled up on the other side of Slater. Before Slater could make a case for diving into the bottom of the boat and just letting the lake water push him at whim, Hope looked up and spotted them. She raised a hand and waved. Everyone in the boats flanking Slater raised their hands and waved back.

Great.

He could still wave and go, right?

After a brief moment, Hope leaned back and planted her hands beside her on the dock timbers—promptly knocking one of her shoes into the water. Slater could see that it was too far from the dock to the water level for her to reach.

Slater, with a sidelong glance at his friends, grabbed his forgotten oars and began to row.

"Hold up!" he hollered, watching Hope try a reach off the dock. "You're going to end up in there with it."

In a few moments, Slater slid right past the bobbing high heel, which had dunked under and resurfaced, scooped it up, and maneuvered the rowboat beside the dock. He tied off to one of the dock posts and held up the dripping shoe. Hope padded over, barefoot, the other heel dangling from her opposite hand.

"I'm pretty sure Cinderella got a dry slipper," Hope quipped, taking the heel as Slater held it out. It was covered in lake muck.

"I'm pretty sure I'm not the prince you're looking for."

He'd meant it as a lighthearted joke, but the look of hurt that crossed her face made him instantly regret saying it.

"Nice. Thanks for the shoe," she said, her voice wavering. She turned abruptly and started up the dock.

"Hope! Hope, wait." Leaving all of his fishing gear behind, Slater scrambled out of the boat, acid rising in his throat. She had a head start, but his legs were longer, so at a slow jog, he caught up to her in a few strides. "C'mon, wait up. I didn't mean it like that."

She slowed, and then stopped, turning to face him. Her eyes were bright, and Slater felt doubly awful. "I was just getting some air, enjoying the lake before our sessions start for the day. I wasn't trying to interrupt your..."

"Fishing," Slater supplied.

She pursed her lips. "Catch anything?"

"Your shoe and a case of regret."

That got a small smile out of her. Slater squinted out across the lake, where his friends were waving again. He watched as they all began rowing back toward the cabins on the opposite shore. Shaking his head, he waved back, and then turned to Hope. "I'm sorry. As you probably remember, my mouth works before my brain sometimes. Can I walk you back?"

She studied him for a minute, and he would have paid a month's salary to know what was going on in her head. He thought she'd say no, but she nodded instead, and they both turned away from the end of the dock.

When they reached the point where the dock met the shore, Slater looked over at Hope's bare feet. There was a lot of ground—and a small line of trees—between the shore and the smooth pavement of the lodge parking lot.

"Let me pick you up," Slater offered.

"Well, that's a switch from the shoe comment."

He laughed. He'd almost forgotten about her quick wit, the way she could snap back with something funny in almost any situation. He also remembered how she used her sense of humor as a shield when she was nervous, or sad, or uncomfortable. The jokes deflected. Was she nervous being around him? Sad? Uncomfortable?

"You could just put on the wet shoe," he suggested. They both looked at the slimy heel, and they both grimaced in tandem. Hope sighed.

"Okay, but just to the parking lot. And don't drop me."

Slater bent and scooped her up, quick enough to cause a huffy little laugh to escape her. Her arms wound around his neck, and she bent her knees over his forearm. He braced his opposite arm behind her back and stepped out onto the shore. He tried very valiantly to not think about the softness of her hair against his collar, or how amazing her perfume smelled.

"This is not how I pictured our reunion," she admitted, a smile on her face. The smile was much larger than her small, earlier one.

Slater's heartbeat picked up a bit. He reasoned that it was the effort of carrying another person, but he knew that it was mostly to do with having Hope—literally—in his arms again. His voice was slightly hoarse when he asked, "Did you?"

"What?"

"Did you picture us reuniting? I wouldn't have thought it."

They neared the tree line. Again, she was quiet enough that he began to think he'd made another verbal faux pas.

"I can't say that I haven't."

Slater ducked under a low limb and shielded Hope's cheek from a branch. "That's interesting."

Slater had never read so much into such a clipped conversation. Then again, he hadn't really ever had a conversation while carrying the reappearing former love of his life to a parking lot. It was a *unique* situation. They reached the parking lot, and Slater carefully set Hope down on the warm pavement. She held both of her heels in one hand and straightened her skirt suit with the other.

"Thanks. And, listen, I'm sorry I got huffy back there. It's just a little embarrassing that we're forced together here after..."

"You broke off our engagement and left me?"

She blinked. "Okay, that's fair."

Slater reached out and adjusted the collar of her

jacket. He said, softly, "Listen, little songbird, it's a week. We can survive."

I've survived you before, he thought, but at least he didn't let it slip out.

She seemed to soften when he used his old endearment for her. "Yeah. It's just a week. But we shouldn't make such a big deal about it. We could get together. Catch up."

Now his heart was trampolining into his throat.

"Not right *now*. I mean, I have to go. We're starting soon." As if to reinforce her point, her phone dinged from the pocket of her suit coat. She dug it out and silenced the reminder alarm. "So, maybe dinner?"

Before Slater could reply, his phone chirped from his pocket.

"Oh, you have a digital leash, too?"

He nodded. "Ruff, ruff."

Slater swiped to read the text. His slightly giddy mood dropped to the same heavy worry that he'd been carrying at the morning meeting.

"What is it?" Hope must've been able to see the disbelief that surely filled his face.

Slater shook his head. "The wedding singer just cancelled."

The day's sessions were going well, and Hope watched from a table at the back of the darkened room as the last speaker before the lunch break wrapped up, dividing her attention between the soon-to-be-exiting attendees and her laptop. The packed session was only one of three with similar attendance today, even with the varied topics being offered. Despite how much she had to do over the course of the seminar week, she'd also brought some work with her, hoping to stay on top of things while they were gone from the office.

But she couldn't keep her mind on the seminar or her work. Her mind kept drifting back to Slater and how she'd blurted out that dinner invitation.

Ugh. He called you on basically breaking his heart, and you were like, "I hear the bruschetta is great here!"

She was so intent on her mental drubbing that she didn't notice her father come over to her, not until he was standing right beside her and had spoken.

"I just saw your young man in the front lobby," her father said, his voice soft but sharp, causing Hope to jump. When she looked up, he was adjusting his tie, straightening his tweed jacket, his expression as terse as his tone had been.

Hope put a hand to her chest. "Yeesh, Dad, could you give me a little more warning before you scare the wits out of me? What young man?"

"Skater, your old boyfriend. Did you know he was here? Is that why you chose this place?"

"*Slater*, Dad, and, yes, it was him. He's a manager here." Hope pursed her lips. She did not want to have this conversation. As much as she was still drawn to Slater, she was still resolute that nothing would disrupt her plan to flawlessly execute the seminar week activities. "But Annie chose this place, and so your theory is just that—a theory. And running into Slater is a coincidence."

He must have caught her expression, because his softened slightly. "Oh. Well, that's good. At least he isn't out chasing that music pipe dream. Almost roped you into that crazy sche—"

"Dad."

His lips pressed together into a thin line. She knew from his expression that he wanted to keep speaking. But she wouldn't have this derailing her day.

"I didn't pursue my music degree, did I?" she asked.

He shook his head, looking momentarily uncomfortable.

"And did I graduate with my business major *and* honors?"

He nodded.

"Then that's all that needs to be said." She turned back to watch the speaker up at the podium.

Her father opened and closed his mouth a couple times, as though he were about to unleash the old argument that they'd had surrounding Slater all those years ago.

There's no future there—in music or this relationship.

I raised you to be more practical than this!

That boy has his head in the clouds. He'll amount to nothing, and he'll keep you back with him.

Hope quickly changed the subject. "Hey, speaking of old friends, Ralph Murphy didn't make it in yesterday. Did he have trouble getting a flight? Is he coming in today?" She spun her laptop to show him the spreadsheet she kept of attendees; Ralph's name was highlighted as the only no-show.

At the mention of one of their oldest clients, his face darkened. "He's actually not coming this year."

"What? Why? He loves these seminars. I booked the guy speaking on Thursday specifically with Ralph in mind. It's a whole presentation on how to upgrade factory equipment for the greatest possible benefit in itemization." She gestured to her laptop. "It is really good material."

Her father waved her off. His face was flushing, the tips of his ears turning red. "He's not coming. I don't know. The juice king of Boston doesn't clear his schedule with me. But Jack Allen filled his spot, so attendance is still perfect."

Hope turned her laptop back around and looked sideways at her father. His face was starting to redden, and her mind flashed back to the argument she'd heard from her father's office before they'd left. He was certainly more on edge lately than she could ever recall. "He's busy? That's it? Nothing else you want to tell me?"

"No, why would there be?" He huffed and drew back his shoulders, his new posture challenging her.

"Should I call him?" Hope probed.

"No," he said sharply. "I'd prefer you stay out of it."

Hope was weighing the pros and cons of continuing to push him for more information when Jack Allen came sauntering down the rows of folding chairs that were still occupied by the audience. He was in animated conversation with Annie, who looked, Hope thought, positively *enthralled*. Hope couldn't blame her. The man was handsome, accomplished, and very suave. His toothpaste-commercial style was bright against his tanned skin. Today, his gray designer suit was paired with the barest hint of five o'clock shadow—something Hope felt sure was as curated as his forest-green pocket square. Annie looked lovely in her lavender wrap dress, and Hope wondered if Jack could see the extra sparkle in Annie's eye.

Hope's father immediately shifted focus as Jack approached, and his entire demeanor changed to a lighter, happier one. *Hmmm.*

"Jack! How are you liking the speaker?" he asked,

almost whispering, extending a hand toward the younger man.

Jack shook hands and nodded enthusiastically, throwing a look back over his shoulder at the man who still stood at the front of the room, clicking slides. "Wonderful, simply wonderful! So much expertise here." Jack looked over at Hope, even though it had been her father who'd posed the question.

"I love your suit, Hope. It's very power chic."

Hope looked down at her red skirt suit, and then back up. She caught Annie's eye, and Annie's grin turned into a small, sly smile. Her friend cut a sidelong glance at Jack and twitched one eyebrow. Hope took in the bespoke suit—he had to have them tailored—the neat haircut, and the polished good looks of the man in question. And then she pursed her lips and shook her head the smallest fraction at Annie.

Hope found herself thinking of someone even taller, a bit broader, with warm hazel eyes and the power to lift her off a dock and make her heart skip a beat even after they'd been apart for years. As Jack continued, Hope had to shake off the mental image of Slater standing under the portico last night. She had to purge the sound of him calling her songbird just this morning. She was sure Slater wasn't thinking of her right now. He'd been completely right—*she* had broken off their engagement and left *him*.

"I can really tell that you all know your stuff. Say, I was wondering if I could talk to you, Dan. Maybe over lunch? My treat," Jack said. "I know they include lunches with these things normally, but let's go to the steakhouse here on property."

Her father looked over at Hope, and she thought he

was about to invite her along. But then his eyes fell on her laptop, and the barest hint of his previous stormy look reappeared. It was gone in an instant, and he leaned in to give Hope a quick kiss on the cheek. "Honey, don't wait for me. I'm going to skip the speaker after lunch. Unless"—he looked at Jack—"it's something you're interested in? You don't seem like a 401k beginner."

Jack laughed and shook his head. "No, that's fine. Shall we?" He inclined his head toward the door. Her father started toward it. Jack gave Hope and Annie a warm smile as he followed. "Have a lovely lunch, ladies." But his gaze lingered on Hope just a hair longer than Annie. "Unless you'd like to join us?"

Annie seemed as though she would speak, but Hope answered for both of them, heading off Annie's words. "Oh, no, thank you. You go ahead." The lights came up, rescuing her with an excuse. "We'll stay here and be sure everyone gets to their lunch and next event."

And then the two men were gone, and Hope whirled to face her friend. "What was *that*?"

The attendees began to get up, mill around.

Annie's grin was back. "Oh, I'm sure it's nothing. He's a potential client interested in the company."

"In the company of who?" Hope forced a smile as people passed her on the way out the door to go to lunch. She waved to a few. She was aghast, but amused by Jack Allen. Maybe he was simply a natural flirt.

Annie burst into laughter. "I swear, you go from working so much that I don't hear a whisper of you dating for the past two years to suddenly being a man magnet."

"Jack Allen is not a plural," Hope protested. "Nobody else is flirting with me."

"Who was the 'nobody' that had you so flustered last night?"

Hope looked around to see that the room had cleared of attendees. The speaker was packing up his stuff, and a few resort staff were coming in to clean up. She had a sudden, possibly unwise idea. But she did need to eat. And she had heard that there was a great diner just around the lake on the other side of the property. They had plenty of time.

"Let's go get some lunch. I'll tell you all about him."

Annie's face registered surprise as Hope closed her laptop, tucked it under her arm, and linked arms with Annie on the other side.

"Well, that's an unexpected twist." But Annie came along willingly as Hope tugged her out the conference room doors and toward the exit to the parking lot.

CHAPTER 5

THE SMELL OF CUT LUMBER was somehow soothing to Slater as he worked in the midday heat. Dressed in a T-shirt and cargo shorts, he felt a bit more in his element today than he did in his deputy assistant manager getup—though the heat was starting to be a bit much, even in work clothes. He wiped sweat from his brow and daydreamed about a dip in Lake Fairwood when his work was done.

Being out by the lake with only his tools and the sound of the birdsong took him back to when this had been his sole responsibility—the Cabins in the Pines and keeping the old place running. It didn't need him much these days, and it made him just a tiny bit melancholy. But he had today, and despite the task in front of him, he was enjoying work—rather than stressing over it—for the first time in a while.

After they'd wrapped up their fishing trip, nobody catching a darned thing, they'd all split up to their various responsibilities, and Slater had headed here to get started on his promised benches. He'd take this job over entertaining Delaney's wacky Aunt Tildy any day.

He'd driven his Jeep right out to the lakeside and parked it, and the tailgate was now down, holding his water cooler and a canvas tool bag full of extra tools and cordless battery packs. Stacks of rough-cut lumber, the bark still on, were piled around him. He had a steady workflow going at the sawhorse station he'd set up, and the construction was going much faster than he'd expected.

He'd made sure to have enough staff on the resort side so that he didn't have to venture over for the day. Between the work he'd promised to do prepping the lakeside for the relocated wedding festivities and the emotional blow to the chest he'd suffered last night, he felt better being alone right now, working with his hands, using the distraction of methodical measuring, cutting, and hammering to keep his mind off of Hope Bergman. Plus, over here, there was almost zero chance of them running into one another.

Slater picked up a fresh piece of board and slanted it across his sawhorses.

Man, she's still so pretty, though. Prettier now than when they'd been together, and he'd been mesmerized by her back then. Time had only made her more beautiful—and all morning Slater'd had to shake off thoughts of her sweet, lilting voice accompanying his guitar. That had been a whole other life, a whole other set of dreams.

Slater wasn't sure what to make of her dinner invitation, and luckily—if you could call it that—the latest wedding catastrophe had swooped in to save him.

At the sound of his name being called, Slater looked up, his heart leaping, his throat tight. But it wasn't a pretty blonde coming down the embankment to where he was. It was the chestnut-haired Delaney, and she sauntered up and stopped to survey his progress. His heart stopped racing, and he tried to ignore that it knew the difference between his friend and the woman he'd been so madly in love with once.

Great, now I have a nice, anxious on switch for when Hope's around.

"Wow, you are really working out here!" She went to sit on one of the completed log benches, smoothing a hand over the freshly-cut top. "Need any help? I'm dressed for work." She waved at her Cabins camp shirt and khaki shorts, the same outfit she'd been fishing in.

"Nah. I'm good. Some of the guys from maintenance made a bunch of precuts after I called this morning, so I'm really just assembling." He lifted up a second piece of lumber and showed her a notch that was already there. "See? Oh, and, careful," Slater cautioned. "Splinters." He smiled when she yanked her hand back.

"These are amazing. I can't believe you're doing all of this."

He set aside the set of legs he had completed and bent to flip the halved log that would become the bench top. "Well," Slater explained, "first, I'm happy to. I want your wedding to be the best it can be. You and Wyatt deserve the perfect day." He marked out where the legs would go and drilled some pilot holes with a cordless drill, shouting to be heard over the noise. "You went through a lot to find each other. Seems a few logs nailed together is a small hurdle to get you both to happily-ever-after."

Delaney put a hand to her heart. "Thanks, Slater."

"Second," he went on, picking up one of the legs and fitting it into the notch he'd made in the log's underside, "this solves more than one problem."

He didn't miss Delaney's bemused expression before

she schooled her features into neutrality. "Oh? You mean we get this beautiful setting, and your friend across the lake gets her ballroom?"

Slater efficiently hammered four nails into the leg of the bench at evenly spaced intervals, making sure to set them at slight angles. When he looked up, he cocked an eyebrow at Delaney. "Not you, too. Who sent you down here, Alex or Rachel?"

Delaney shrugged. "No one sent me. We're just curious."

"Ah *ha*! You said *we*!" He flipped his hammer in mid-air, grasping it by the head and pointing the wooden end at her.

"As if this entire family wasn't absolutely Jane Austening me and Wyatt when Alex first showed up!" Delaney protested, throwing up her hands. "And we only want you to have a date for the wedding. What harm could come of that?"

Slater let the hammer drop. "Fair enough. But I'm not asking her to the wedding. And I don't want to talk about her. It was a long time ago, in college, *as I said*, and it didn't end well. So it's not a story worth retelling."

Delaney's eyes softened. Slater leaned on the assumption that she was feeling compassion for him, rather than pity. "Oh. I'm so sorry. I know how that goes."

He dropped his hammer next to the in-progress bench and came to sit on the completed one with Delaney. She scooted over slightly to give him room, and he plunked down with a heavy sigh. He looked up and out into the air, where motes of sawdust from his work were still hanging in the sunlight, reflecting as they rode the balmy breeze.

Delaney didn't say anything, only sat and waited.

Slater felt a tightening in his chest, and he went with the sudden urge that pressed at him to tell *someone* about how seeing Hope had really thrown him for a loop. He knew Delaney understood heartbreak, and he trusted her with what he was about to say. Heck, honestly, he trusted every member of the Cabins in the Pines family. There wasn't any reason they couldn't know. They were always there for one another, and this time should be no different.

He cut his eyes sideways at Delaney. "We were madly in love, okay? At least, I was. We met freshman year, and we were both music majors."

Delaney frowned slightly. "I thought you graduated with an engineering degree?"

Slater smiled, but he didn't feel happy. In fact, the gesture felt hollow. "I did. Switched majors right after she bailed out on music—and me. You see, Beacon Financial? Owned by her dad. He had a cushy spot waiting for her after college, and I didn't really fit into that plan."

Delaney patted Slater's hand, and when he didn't continue, she said softly, "Well, plans change. People change. It's not always for the worse. Wyatt and I are proof of that."

"You two are the best proof," Slater agreed. He took a deep breath. "But you know how my dad and I were on our own while I was growing up?"

Delaney nodded.

"In a lot of ways, he was an amazing single dad—he taught me to be hardworking, to keep going even when things were tough. He made sure I had absolutely everything I ever needed."

"I'm sensing a caveat here."

"Never in the relationship between him and me, no.

But after he and my mom split, he seemed so intent on forgetting her. He never talked about her, avoided it when family would mention her..."

"He was hurt," Delaney said softly.

Slater nodded. "And maybe I took his example a little too much to heart. After Hope left, I did the same thing. I tried to cut her out of my mind completely. I stopped talking to her or about her. I thought that meant that I would be able to forget her. And I thought it would make seeing her—if by some miracle I ever did again—a nonissue."

Slater picked at the bark of the bench under him. "I've always been pretty embarrassed at how it all ended. I *thought* Hope and I were a perfect match, just like you and Wyatt. She was strong where I was weak, and I was brave when she was scared. We were a real team. But then she had to make some choices that affected us both. And she didn't include me. I mean, I knew it was young love, but I never expected to get dumped for a job."

Delaney wrinkled her nose. "As a woman who has past experience with the fallout of jumping to conclusions, I have to ask—if you never talked it out with her after the breakup, how do you know that the job was the only factor?"

Slater grabbed Delaney's hand and squeezed it. "I *don't* know, Del, and the past is the past, in this case. But it really sends me somewhere, seeing her. Somewhere dark and smoky, up on a stage with my guitar, too late at night. And Hope was right up there with me. We had all the time in the world, it seemed, but time just flew by, always going too fast when we were together."

"And lasting too long when you were apart?" Delaney offered.

"You got it."

"And here, I thought you were only a poet at the campfire," she teased.

Slater laughed, and it actually elevated his mood a bit. "Nah. I used to be a regular performer. You'd have thought it was something." He picked up Delaney's hand and flipped it over, pretending to examine her bare knuckles. "Enough about me. What's *going to be something* is seeing Wyatt put a big, shiny wedding ring on this hand. And everyone's going to cry tears of joy and jump to their feet. But they can't do that unless they have somewhere to sit first. So I've got to get back to work."

Delaney stood, and Slater did the same. She reached up to fold him into a big hug, squeezing tight. "Thanks for sharing that," she said. "And we're all here for you. Anytime."

Slater returned the hug. "I know, I know. Where are you headed now?"

"Bean Pot," Delaney said, skipping back a few steps before turning to start up the embankment. "It's lunchtime! Come with!"

"I got to keep working. Go on," Slater grumbled. "Carry the tale to the rest of 'em!"

"That's not my only mission, you know. Still have to figure out the wedding singer problem!" she called. She pulled out her phone and waved it at him.

"Or else Wyatt really will make us reschedule everything," he called back.

Slater turned his back to Delaney and, on the answering wave of her laughter, picked up his hammer to resume his work, feeling a little bit lighter. But, darn it, he still didn't have a wedding present figured out. And they still didn't have a replacement wedding singer. Two unsolved problems.

Three, actually.

Now that he'd brought Hope back up, how in the world was he going to stop thinking about her?

"You did *what*?" Annie practically choked on her root beer float, sputtering as Hope shushed her.

Hope swiveled to make sure no one in the bustling diner was looking at them. The Bean Pot was hopping, filled with chatter and the clink of glasses and the sizzle of the grill. But Hope was still nervous about being overheard.

"Shhh! Yeesh, Annie, we are not only at his place of business, but there are lots of employees here! I don't want him to have to chastise some kid for being late to work, and the whole time that kid is thinking about the time he overheard the story of how—"

"The boss got his poor, innocent heart stomped on by *you*?" Annie finished, punctuating the words with a long, slow slurp of the rest of her float.

Hope glared. "I didn't stomp on it. I only broke it a *little*." Hope held up her thumb and index finger, putting them a hairs-breadth apart. And she winced, hearing the obvious nature of the lie even as it slipped out.

Annie tapped an index finger on the black-and-white checked tablecloth to punctuate her words. "Hope. You just told me the man gave up music after you left him. You took the man's music. Our open mic nights are more like *love eulogies*. I am *shocked*."

Annie was really having way too much fun with this at Hope's expense. Hope pushed her empty plate away.

"We were young, and young love never lasts, Annie. I mean, is it even real? Or is it, like, a rite of passage that you go through, like your first painful breakup is the adult version of scraping your knee as a kid? It happens, it's sudden, there's some healing after, and you go on with your life. Everybody does, right?"

Hope looked past Annie and out into the diner. At the retro jukebox, an old couple were selecting songs, and Hope watched as the wife pushed a button and the husband held out a hand to her. A romantic oldie began to stream from the neon-flanked speakers. The couple began to dance, heedless of the waiters and waitresses zipping around them.

"Except your parents are supposed to kiss your scraped knee and help you up, and in this case, from what you're telling me, it sounds like your father was the pavement."

Hope tore her eyes from the couple, looking back at Annie.

"It wasn't exactly like that. And I'm never telling you anything again," Hope whispered. She snagged one of Annie's fries and chewed angrily, frowning the whole time.

She tried not to look at the cute, dancing couple, lest they make her think anything soft or fuzzy about running into Slater again, and instead looked around the diner. Their waitress was leaning behind the long front counter, her phone to her ear. When the woman saw that Hope was watching, she turned away quickly, pushing through the swinging doors to the back.

These fries are delicious.

Hope and Annie sat in companionable silence for the

next few minutes, Hope nibbling on fries and letting her mind drift out between the crisp, green pines.

I wonder where Slater is right now?

"Everything all right here?" The cute, petite woman who stopped by their table looked at them, smiling a little too wide. It was the waitress who Hope had just seen book it into the back.

How much did she hear?

Hope sucked in a breath, avoiding eye contact with the woman, instead letting her eyes sweep over the diner, which was a well-done pastiche of retro chrome and soft, teal vinyl. Hope let her eyes settle on the black-and-white checkered floor.

"Umm, yes. Thank you..." She braved a look at the woman's name tag.

Maisie. Manager. Oh, no, she must know Slater. They're both managers. Hope couldn't form any more words as her mind raced to recall exactly what she and Annie had said over the past thirty minutes. Thankfully, the woman moved on to the next table to check on them before it could become awkward—or Hope could faint away in panic, face-first into the basket of fries that Annie had scooted across. Hope reached for the ketchup, planning to take her frustrations out on the condiment.

Annie picked up the last of her cheeseburger and talked between bites. "Listen, sweetie, I get it. Everyone has regrets. Maybe you didn't treat the guy so nicely at the end, and now you're here, and it's awkward. But don't be a revisionist about it. You loved him back then. Otherwise, would you feel so bad about the breakup now? Would you even be talking about him? I mean, your face when you talk about him is—"

Hope waved a French fry at Annie. "Stop making sense."

Annie smiled and popped the last bite of lunch into her mouth. "You were nuts about him."

Hope swirled a fry in ketchup, sighing. She hoped the butterflies in her stomach were the type that were easily placated with simple carbs. "I was. I really was. But I had all this responsibility, and my mom was sick, and I can't entirely blame my dad for pressuring me. I felt like I had to step in. He was probably feeling uncertain, too. And he wanted my future to be a sure thing." Hope dropped the fry, her appetite suddenly gone. "It was hard, and I had to give up a lot, but I did. I did it for family."

Hope could feel Annie watching her, but she knew her friend wasn't judging. Bringing her hands up, Hope dropped her forehead into her palms, letting out a breath. "Annie, this is so dumb! I mean, we're adults. And I'm here for a week. There's no reason to be this worked up over something that's been done for years. Right?" She lifted her head to look at the woman across the table.

"Do you want my opinion on this one, or is this a nod-and-smile situation?" Annie asked.

"Nod and smile," Hope said, smiling to start things off. Annie grinned back.

The voice of the woman who'd stopped by moments ago—Maisie—broke the comfortable silence between the friends.

"Hey, y'all are from the Beacon seminar, right?" She stood by their table, holding a large, checkered paper bag and wearing that too-wide smile that made Hope suspicious that something was up. The woman pointed to the lanyards that still hung around Hope and Annie's necks, clipped to badges announcing their roles in the seminar.

"We are," Hope said, resuming her plunder of Annie's fries.

Maisie held out the paper bag. "You're headed back to the other side now, right? Would you mind terribly doing me a big ole favor? I just got a call from a friend. She said that one of our other managers is out by the lakeside doing some work today, and I'm afraid he isn't going to stop for lunch unless it's right there in front of his face."

Hope looked blankly at the bag. "Uh-huh?"

"Can y'all run this to him? If you could, I'll make sure your lunches are on the house."

Annie asked before Hope could even think to. "What's the name of the other manager?"

Hope knew before Maisie even spoke—and when she did, Hope didn't know whether to take it as a sign that fate was nudging her or an omen of impending disaster.

"Slater Evans. He's about yay tall"—Maisie reached up with one hand as high as she could—"Outdoorsy. Kinda rugged and sun-kissed. A real looker, but also has a good head on his shoulders. Steady, you know? Dependable. But not boring! Great with kids and dogs."

Hope stared.

"Well, he'll be the only one out there, anyway. I can get y'all a camp map for directions to the docks."

Annie reached out and snatched the bag from Maisie's hands. "Absolutely. We'll go right now," she said brightly.

"Fantastic!" Maisie turned to, presumably, get them a camp map, and Hope looked wide-eyed across at Annie.

"Are you *crazy*?" Hope whispered fiercely.

"What?" Annie said, dipping her head to look at Hope over the top of her glasses. Her expression was one of pure innocence. "You said you invited him to dinner—now you want the man to go without lunch?"

"I still don't know if this is the best idea," Hope said, holding the paper bag in her lap as Annie steered the rental car away from the Bean Pot moments later. True, Hope had invited Slater to dinner, but had she really intended to stick with that? What good could come of them just hanging out like nothing had happened between them?

Trees flashed past, a blur of green that was interrupted with bright flashes of gold at each break where the sun managed to get through.

Annie shrugged. "You said you were both adults. Take him some lunch. You can handle that. Besides, they already gave us ours for free because we *said* we would."

"You said we would! And you work in finance. You must know that there's no such thing as a free lunch. This one's going to cost me." Hope waved the bag. "How would you like to have to go pass off a casual sandwich to the ex-person-you-thought-you-were-going-to-spend-forever-with?"

"We're two turns away. And you thought you were going to spend *forever* with this guy? Oh, honey. And you broke up with him via *note*?"

Hope twisted in her seat toward Annie. "Text wasn't a thing back then, or I would have done it that way. I hate confrontation. And I reiterate that I am never telling you anything again."

Annie sat patiently in the driver's seat.

"It was the end of spring semester. I thought it would help soften the blow if we had the summer apart to get over everything," Hope admitted.

"And in the fall?"

"I had changed majors, and he had changed schools."

Hope's stomach did a little flip as her friend swung the sedan around the last wide turn before the lake. Their tires crunched on gravel as Annie rolled to a stop in the cleared parking area a bit shy of the lakeside. A copse of trees separated the parking area from the lakeside, but they were thinned enough that Hope could see the shape of someone just past the tree line. She clutched the bag in her lap tighter.

Annie put the car into park and reached out to put a hand on Hope's shoulder. "Look, if it really does bother you, I'll go give the poor guy his lunch. You know I don't want you to be actually uncomfortable. I'm only saying that maybe it would help you feel better—maybe both of you feel better—if you did what *you* suggested and talked to him. You said he thought it was nice to see you last night. He helped you this morning. I know you want to chicken out on that dinner invite. It might make your week here less awkward, and there is such a thing as needing closure."

Hope took a deep, steadying breath. She wanted to whine about how embarrassing it would be to have the talk she'd suggested, but there was some legitimacy to what Annie was saying. And maybe she did owe Slater an explanation—if he wanted one. He had seemed, or at least said, that he'd liked seeing her the previous evening. And despite his ill-timed prince joke this morning, he had been sweet and helpful.

"You're right. I'm going to talk to him."

Annie threw her hands up in a cheer. "Atta girl! Get your casual sandwich face on."

Hope opened her door and vaulted out before she

could change her mind. The trail through the small line of trees was well-worn and easy to spot, and she enjoyed the smell of the lake that tinged the air, relaxed a little at the sound of birdsong carrying through the trees on her short walk. Fingers of yellow afternoon sunlight filtered through the lacy canopy overhead, making patterns of gold on the shaded ground that danced as the leaves above moved. The early colors of spring were mostly gone, and almost all of the branches sported thick, dark-green pine needles or the flat, solidly verdant wings of the broadleaf variety. She was coming down the embankment in moments. Now that she was free of the trees, there was nothing blocking her view of Slater. And he hadn't yet noticed her.

She took the time of her short trek between the tree line and where he was working to really look at him. He really was even more attractive than he'd been years ago. He seemed to fit with his surroundings here. There was an ease to his movement as she watched him that she'd never seen when they were back in college. Well, unless he'd been playing music.

She was steps from him before he looked up from his work and their eyes locked. There was a moment where she wanted to turn on her heel and run, tossing the bag over her shoulder as she split in order to still fulfill her promise as she high-tailed it out of there. But he gave her a wary smile—one that didn't quite reach his eyes, but was not at all the stormy reception she'd expected. And so, instead of running, she stopped a bit short, holding out the bag.

"Lunch?"

Surprise was evident on his face. "What are you doing here?" He looked across the lake at the resort side, as though he couldn't fathom how she had crossed, and then he looked her over. His eyes settled on the bag. "You came all the way over here to bring me lunch?" Incredulity had replaced the surprise in his tone.

"Well, no," she said, relieved when he took the bag. "Sorry. I don't mean to intrude, but I was up at the Bean Pot with my assistant, and Maisie asked us to bring this to you."

His laugh was instant and full of pure amusement, and Hope had no idea what the joke was. "Did she now? Well, thank you."

"You're welcome." Hope looked at the detritus of his work, toeing at a nearby chunk of discarded bark. "What are you working on?"

He tilted his head toward a row of eight rustic benches that sat in a neat line behind him. "Seating for the wedding and reception. We're moving it down here. You can keep the ballroom, by the way."

"Oh. Oh, thank you. That will make—" She started to say *my father happy*, but she stopped herself. "Our clients will appreciate it. I appreciate it."

He nodded and sat down on a cut stump nearby, opening the bag and digging in. "And I appreciate the lunch. Did you get your shoe clean?"

"Sadly, no. And I really liked that pair."

Slater patted the stump next to him. "Sit, please. How's the seminar going, by the way?" He unwrapped the cheeseburger he found in the bag and took a bite.

Hope sat down next to him. "It's great. Better than great. And we've got lots more planned. In fact, I'll even be up on stage this week."

He raised his eyebrows and swallowed hard, coughing a little. He reached for a water bottle nearby and took a long swig. Then, still lightly coughing, he asked, "Your father's going to let you sing at a financial seminar?"

Hope felt the heat creep into her face, and she took a step back. *Bolt. The bolting plan was a good one.* "No, no, not to sing. I'm presenting on updated retirement tax law."

He didn't react, only replying smoothly, "That's great. You could always make a crowd fall in love with you. Voice like an angel who'd been through a few wild lives. Perfect pitch, but smoky. Man, you'd really draw them in."

Hope shifted, trying not to warm at the compliments.

"Listen, Slater, I feel like I owe you an explanation."

He stopped chewing. Hope felt her stomach tie in a million tangled knots. She rushed on.

"I mean, I never gave you one. That awful note. I mean, who does that? 'Dear Slater, it's not you, it's me.'"

"Hope," he said gently, "you don't have to."

"But I do. When my mom got her diagnosis, I felt obligated to go back home. And, it wasn't fair of him, but my dad put a lot of pressure on me to join Beacon. The two obligations—to her last months and to my father's business—they shouldn't have been tied together. But they were. And I went to do what I had to for both, no matter the sacrifice."

"I was the sacrifice." He dropped his chin slightly. It wasn't a question, and it didn't sound like he needed her to confirm it.

"I shouldn't have done what I did. And I'm sorry I hurt you. But I've rebuilt something now, even if it came out of a lot of hurt, and I'm *still* rebuilding. I don't know if that makes sense."

Slater looked over the lakeshore. "We were building something, back then."

"I know." She didn't know what more to say, in the moment. There wasn't anything she could offer that would change the past.

"I get it, kinda," he finally said. "I've done a lot of rebuilding here. I've seen others do it. Happy endings don't always grow from the best beginnings." The ghost of an implication—that there might be something beyond this chance meeting for the two of them—wasn't lost on Hope.

Slater nudged her knee with his. "You don't sing anymore?" He took another drink of his water, slowly this time, and turned his steady eyes on her. Hope had never been more aware of being at the very apex of a conversation's turning point.

"I don't. Not since, um, college."

"You mean not since us?" He was still looking at her with those steady, devastating hazel eyes. The color of moss on trees in summer sunlight. Like a sunset viewed through vintage green medicine glass.

She answered carefully. "Well, I do this open mic back in the city. My friend Annie comes with me. It's fun. The crowd's really mellow. And...I have a piano in my apartment. I play all the time at home."

"Alone?"

She nodded, but didn't say anything.

"It's a shame we quit when we did," he said, standing and crumpling the wrapper around what was left of his burger, and then placing it back in the bag. He set the bag carefully on the stump he'd been sitting on. "Thanks again for lunch."

She shoved her hands in her jacket pockets, and her watch lit up as she did so. It was her reminder that the next session was starting in twenty minutes. She swiped to dismiss the alarm. "No problem. I actually have to go."

It might have been a pure figment of her imagination, but Hope thought that disappointment flickered across his face. He nodded, though, and turned back to his project without saying anything else. She waited a beat, expectant, but when he didn't say anything else, she turned to walk back toward the tree line. He spoke when she was only two strides away.

"Hey, Hope?"

"Yeah?" She spun maybe a little too fast.

"Let's have that dinner sometime. What do you say?"

Hope looked at Slater Evans, backlit by the light glittering off of the surface of Lake Fairwood, and she could suddenly only see the younger man she'd fallen breathlessly in love with all those years ago—and hurt. But this new version of him didn't seem to hate her. There was a small rush of relief that calmed the jitters she'd felt as she'd walked away from the rental car earlier.

They didn't have to be best friends. They could just be nice. Pleasant. That was something.

"Okay," she agreed. Her watch buzzed again, a fifteen-minute warning, and her phone began to ring in her pocket. That would be Annie calling her. Their reminders were set the same.

With a little wave, Hope turned and walked back to the rental car—as briskly as her racing heart would allow.

CHAPTER 6

"Y OU'D BETTER TAKE THAT BACK," Ursula warned, waving a finger in Alexandra's direction. Seated at opposite sides of a long, sleek conference table, they could have been two rival business tycoons, duking out the terms of a merger. Each bore the same serious expression. "You never know what the universe is going to do with those words."

Slater took a quick, appraising look around the conference space closest to Alexandra's office as he entered. He'd always liked this room, with its wood-planked walls and room-length table surrounded by high-backed, nail head leather office chairs. It looked lush, comfy, not cold and sterile the way one would expect.

Slater didn't speak as he entered, trying to gauge the exact mood of the room. Balancing a bakery box and a drink carrier, he took a seat. He'd finished up at the lakeside, and with the way the light was waning, that was a good thing. He hadn't wanted to drag out any work lights—they attracted mosquitos like magnets. So he'd packed up his tools and sat on one of the benches he'd made to watch the fireflies come up around the perimeter of the lake. And as he'd done so, his foot had hit the bag that held the remains of his lunch—the bag he'd nearly forgotten about.

Staring out at the winking yellow-green of the fireflies, alone in the fading wisps of orange glow that had stretched across the sky to silhouette the trees, he'd allowed himself to sit in silence and think about Hope Bergman. He knew that it had to have been deeply uncomfortable for her to come find him, considering their past. And they had agreed to avoid one another. So why had *she* agreed to come to the lakeside? Maisie's matchmaking aside, he'd have never thought there was a power in the universe strong enough to compel the woman who'd cut and run without so much as an in-person goodbye to deliver him a friendly burger.

But it hadn't been unwelcome. The visit, that was. Or the burger. And his quiet moments hadn't brought him any closer to figuring out Hope's motives.

"Well, we'll all feel better if we just sit down together and hash this out. That's why I called you all here," Alex explained, pulling Slater from his thoughts. Alex, Charles, Masie, and Ursula all looked a little tired, but with the busyness of the business lately, it was a familiar sight. The two pizza boxes scattered on the conference room table told Slater that he'd picked exactly right with the box currently in his hands.

"Cookies," he said simply, sliding the box across the table toward the assembled group. "And what are we manifesting in here?"

Ursula put a hand to her forehead. "Alex said, 'What else can go wrong with this wedding,' and now I'm worried. It's out there now. You can't take that back!"

Slater sat down in the empty chair next to Ursula,

set down the drink holder he'd been carrying in his non-cookie hand, and popped open the bakery box. "These were fresh-baked at the café by the spa. Butter pecan shortbread. And this is decaf apple cinnamon tea with vanilla syrup and a touch of cream." Slater lifted one of the to-go cups from the drink holder and pressed it into Ursula's hands. "The universe wants your nephew and Delaney to get married and live happily ever after. After all, it brought them together. And nothing is going to change that."

Ursula smiled, her expression grateful. She patted Slater's cheek. "Oh, you're right. I'm being silly." She took a sip of her tea, hummed happily, and then selected a cookie from the open box. After she'd taken a nibble, she said, "Maisie says the universe sent you lunch today. Is that right?"

Slater sat back in his chair and cast a withering glance across the table at Maisie, who was flanked by Alex and Charles on the other side. Maisie simply grinned and popped out of her chair, reaching across the table for the drink carrier. "These all tea?"

Slater nodded, deadpanning.

Alex leaned forward on her elbows, accepting a cup as Maisie passed one. Alex popped the plastic lid off to blow on the hot tea. Charles lifted the last cup from the drink holder, and he caught the box of cookies when Ursula gave it a nudge to the side of the table where the other three sat.

"How *was* your lunch?" Alex asked over the rim of the paper cup.

Slater groaned. "Do you guys ever give up?"

"Nope. And thanks, Slater." Maisie raised her cup in salute. "Now, Wyatt, Delaney, and Rachel are out to dinner with Delaney's folks. We don't have much time. So it's back to the business at hand. Charles, what did you find out today?"

Slater felt a glimmer of hope. Charles, despite his quiet and unassuming nature, was one of the most efficient, tenacious people Slater had ever met. Surely, he'd found a solution.

Charles consulted a clipboard in front of him on the table. "I called thirty-two wedding singers in the tristate area. No luck. I even name-dropped Alex, the reality show, the network. Everyone is booked solid and not budging."

Slater's brief spark of hope sputtered out and faded. He grabbed a cookie.

"Wedding season," Alex said sourly, cradling her cup. "How is it that absolutely no one is available?"

"Well," Charles said, "there is *one* option, but I don't think you'll go for it. I got in touch with a band—they all come as a package deal—but they only do eighties music covers. Their name is Wed Zeppelin. They are available…"

The entire team shook their heads in concert.

"No, no, no," Alex said. "It simply won't do." They all sat in silence, and more of the cookies disappeared as everyone grabbed them, chewing and pondering at the same time. Suddenly, Alex sat straighter in her chair. "We can use the musicians who play at the restaurant on the weekends! They're fabulous and extremely experienced. I'll bet they're available."

"But we'd still need a singer," Maisie said, sighing. "Anyone sing?"

Slater's throat was suddenly dry. He'd been struck with a wild, improbable—no, *impossible*—idea. He could play, but he couldn't carry a true note if his life were on the line. But back when he'd been writing songs and playing, he hadn't *needed* to carry any tunes. His guitar had done half the work, and there'd been someone else to lift the words, breathe life into his chords.

Ursula sipped her tea. "Not me. And, no offense, but I've heard every one of us at the Christmas festival during caroling. I love you all, but we sound like a bouquet of dented-in teakettles when we sing."

Maisie waved half a cookie in the air, mock-offended. "We're enthusiastic."

Slater thought of the solution that'd been pinging around his brain all afternoon.

Voice like an angel who'd been through a few wild lives. Perfect pitch, but smoky. Man, you'd really draw them in.

His conversation with Delaney that morning came back to him; how he'd wryly said that he was solving two problems at once. If he said what he was thinking, would he only be creating more problems? *But what if Hope said yes? Then your best friends could have their perfect moments, and you and Hope could...* His heart lurched, and he extinguished the thought before it could finish.

"Wish we knew someone with a good voice," Charles lamented. "We're really running out of time."

Slater swallowed thickly, finding his own voice, which rolled out almost as if disconnected from every ounce of good sense he thought he had. He felt some force behind the words, like they'd been waiting to come out. Like the universe wanted him to find a way to bring Hope back into his orbit.

"Actually, I know someone who can sing really, really well."

The end of the day's sessions, capped off with the planned nightly group dinner-and-decompress, had taken their toll on Hope. They had days and days to go in the seminar, and already she was bone tired. But here she was, headed down the halls of the resort to an evening meeting with her father and Jack Allen. She at least had high expectations that it would be a positive meeting, since her father had come back from lunch in a fairly good mood, carrying the news that Jack wanted all three of them to sit down together after the scheduled events.

She passed several conference participants on their way back to where she'd come from. Hope rounded the corner, studying the resort map on her phone. It was guiding her through the maze-like halls to the meeting room. When a deep, warm baritone that she instantly recognized cut through the silent hall, she froze mid-step and looked up, expecting to see Slater standing in front of her. There was no one.

Now you're imagining his voice? Get a grip, Bergman.

But it came again, and there was no mistaking it this time. "...get married and live happily ever after..."

It was definitely Slater, and it was coming from a partially opened conference room door just a few paces down from where she stood. What was he talking about, and with who? The air conditioning above her head kicked on, and the conference room door creaked slightly. Afraid she might get caught standing in the hall, and lest that look like eavesdropping, she put her plan from earlier in the day into action and bolted.

Once she was well past and almost to her destination, she slowed. In moments, she heard another voice call out to her.

"Hope! Hope, you're two minutes late." Her father

was sticking his head out of the room she'd been on her way to. He was frowning. His reading glasses, normally tucked into the front pocket of his suit jacket when not in use, sat crookedly on top of his head. She hadn't even realized she had reached the right door yet.

She turned on her heel and slipped past her father and into the room, brushing by him as he countered her and stepped out into the hallway, presumably looking for Jack, who was not inside. Hope quickly took a seat, setting her bag beside her chair. She was relieved that Annie was seated in the chair to her left, and she reached out to squeeze her friend's hand. They waited, the room's only two occupants.

Hope looked around, pleased to see that, instead of a generic, gray box furnished with typical light-wood-and-neutral-cloth seating, this meeting area was walled in rough, multi-hued wooden planks, and the chairs and couch were of smooth, soft dark-cherry leather. The lighting, unlike other executive accommodations she'd been to, was soft, not fluorescent.

Hope could see her father appear in flashes in the doorway as he paced.

"Any idea what this is about?" Annie whispered.

"None," Hope replied.

"Hope, did you bring those quarterly reports I asked about?" He'd stopped pacing and was fidgeting in the doorway, practically vibrating with impatience. Hope's tired mind scrambled to recall him even asking.

"I, uh..."

"You mean these?" As Annie spoke, she passed her tablet over toward Hope. A neat row of files was displayed on the screen. "I should have confirmed when you asked me earlier, Hope, but I assumed digital was okay for format since Jack is a tech guy."

Her father looked between Hope and Annie. Hope tilted the tablet screen toward her father. "All set." There was a brief moment when Hope thought he might question her further, but he seemed satisfied.

When he'd exited again to resume his pacing, Hope passed the gadget back to Annie. "Oh my goodness, thank you. I honestly don't even remember him asking."

Annie stifled a yawn. "Girl, I'm exhausted, too. It's been a long day. And as cute as Jack Allen is, a hot bath and a good book seem way more appealing right now. I am ready for no reports and lots of R & R. Your father has called Jack three times without an answer."

Hope heard her father's phone ring. She heard him stop pacing, and the muffled sound of his conversation with whoever was calling came drifting back into the conference room. She couldn't make out any of the words her father was saying, but she thought about Slater's voice and what she'd heard in the hall. Hope felt an odd mixture of emotions grip her, and she held her breath for a moment, trying to sort them out. Curiosity, maybe a little completely unfounded jealousy, and a big heap of embarrassment. Who was he in there with? What if he had been talking about her and their breakup?

She was saved from too much speculation as her father came bustling back into the room. "Well, the meeting is called off. Jack made alternate plans for tonight, and he says we can discuss this tomorrow at some point."

"What is the *this* we were supposed to be discussing?" Hope asked, rising and shouldering her bag. Annie did the same, and they walked toward her father, who backed into the hall.

"Jack coming aboard at Beacon Financial, of course," he said. "He'd be our absolute biggest client, and would need to be a major focus of the firm. I need the both of you to be on your A game, showing him that we're the best and we can more than handle being his advisors." He stopped, seemed to think of something, and gestured to Annie. "Ms. Goodman, make a note: if Jack commits to Beacon, we can offer him a dedicated liaison within the firm. That fellow who always wears the nice ties, maybe. Brian?"

As Annie began tapping a reminder on her phone, Hope reminded, "Brian is already the client liaison for Ralph Murphy and all of Ralph's Sun Squeezed Juices accounts."

He nodded curtly. "Brian, it is. Good night." And then, with another nod and no explanation, he turned and walked briskly away down the hall. Annie and Hope exchanged a look.

"Well, that ended weirdly."

"Agreed," Hope replied. She sighed, now too tired to even try to sort out whatever was going on with her father. "You headed up to your room?"

Annie answered in the affirmative, and Hope said she'd be up after visiting the café off the lounge to grab some after-work goodies. Visions of cinnamon rolls and brownies came to her as she took off her heels and padded down the hall away from the conference room, opposite of the direction her father had walked. And, to her relief, it didn't take her back past the room that she'd heard Slater in. An even greater stroke of luck, she passed no one else on her way. She didn't have the energy for any more peopling today. She stopped and took off her right shoe, balancing on one foot to rub at a sore inner arch.

She tried to shake off the queasy feeling that the meeting had caused, focusing instead on finding her way to the café. The hall looped around to end near the front desk, and the last room on the right before the hallway let out into the main lobby was one painted in soft off-white, empty except for a stunning baby grand piano that took up the center of the room. Something about it called to her. Hope tried the door, and it opened easily. She walked across the cool tile inside, set her shoes and bag on the floor by the piano bench, and took a seat at the instrument.

She ran her fingers over the fallboard, wondering how often the beautiful keys beneath got played. She looked out the glass wall in front of her, which had curtains drawn across it. But there was a small gap where she could see out into the lounge that she had been impressed by when they'd first arrived. The window seemed designed to open, allowing those in the lounge to hear whoever was playing, but the glass was closed now.

Out in the room past the glass, through that small gap, people in suits and skirts mingled, holding drinks or setting aside briefcases to shake hands. They all looked at ease—unlike Hope, who was currently feeling all kinds of out-of-sorts. *They* all certainly looked as though they were in their element.

The fallboard lifted easily. Hope caressed the keys, remembering how her mother had sat next to her when Hope had been small and taught her to play at the small upright in their living room. Her mother had explained, after naming the parts of the brand-new piano for the start of Hope's musical education that her father had wanted a piano when he'd been a boy, and that after Hope could play, they could teach her father to play together.

Patiently, lovingly, Hope's mother had taken hours upon hours with a struggling little girl until the notes had clicked, the lines and symbols on the sheet in front of Hope had made sense, and Hope had been able to make music. She'd quickly learned other instruments, and had no trouble after moving to writing her own music. The fire had been lit.

Her mother had been so calm, so loving, so kind. She'd had always known how to teach. She'd even taught Hope's father to bake, which had been almost a necessity—her father had a notorious sweet tooth, and he loved fresh baked goods. He had become a pro under her mother's tutelage and used to delight the whole family with his creations. Hope's mother used to pack whatever he'd bake into a brown paper bag and make sure he had it in hand every morning on his way out the door to work. But since her mother's passing, her father hadn't created a thing in the kitchen. Instead, Hope stopped at Kahn's bakery every morning.

Hope had never had gotten him to sit and learn music, though she'd tried a number of times over the years. He'd become increasingly busy at the office, and then her mother had taken ill, and then...

Hope tapped a few keys, pleased by the richness of the notes that resulted. And then, she thought of Slater, pictured his broad smile and warm eyes, and remembered distinctly what it had felt like to be the sole focus of his attention. In a lot of ways, Slater's personality was like her mother's—steady, even, dependable. A brief snippet of song came whispering back into her mind. She was tired, and she didn't fight it. Her hands slid across to find the starting note, and she began to play softly.

"No matter where we start,
A million miles or breaths apart,
The stars might burn and all go dark,
But I would still find you."

Slater froze in the hallway near the front lobby of the resort, stopped at the edge of where the wall met the sparkling glass of the piano room. The door a few steps beyond was ajar, and he let the silvery, mellifluous words that came from the slim space between the door and the jamb flow over him. He could picture the next words in his mind before she even sang them. Without being able to see her, he could still picture her, singing as he strummed the simple, poignant melody on his old guitar. And the hurt that came with the words was so profound that he almost turned and walked away.

"If every old love leaves a mark,
A broken trail to lead our hearts
Then let this new love be the spark,
That lights the way to what's true."

He was at the door, and her back was to him. As she vocalized the words that had been only in his head moments before, he looked past her to the closed curtains at the front glass. She wasn't playing for anyone. So was she doing it for *herself?*

"I thought you only sang at open-mic nights." He tried to make sure his voice was soft so that he wouldn't startle her. But she jumped anyway, and fumbled with the fallboard, slamming it down a little too hard.

"Sorry! I'm so sorry. I'm probably not supposed to be in here, right?" She stood, and then sat down, and then stood again.

"No, no, it's okay." He held a hand up to reassure her. "I'm not here to bust you. I was coming back from a staff meeting. I saw the door open. I heard…"

She blushed. Even in the dim light of the room he could see the pink staining her cheeks. "Yeah. I just had a little bit of a rough day, so I was blowing off steam."

"I would think that anything to do with us wouldn't exactly be stress relieving. Can I sit down?" When she nodded, he smiled, pushing off of the door jamb to walk across to her. "Scoot."

He couldn't read her face, but he was hoping that she would hear him out when he dropped the question he'd planned to work up to—tomorrow, sometime. Or never, depending on how his courage went. She slid over on the piano bench, her eyes wide as he sat down and she watched him lift the cover from the keys. He still heard her singing in his head. Why had she been singing *that* particular song?

"I'm rusty at this," he joked.

He was all-too-aware of the big, summer-blue eyes trained in his direction. Those eyes, combined with the way hearing her sing had made him feel all sorts of nostalgic, took the edge off of some of the other feelings that seeing her again had brought up. There was a bittersweet element, the sour memories of how they'd left so much unsaid.

"Playing piano or talking to girls?"

He laughed, starting up the melody to the song she'd been singing. "Both."

She didn't sing any more, just watched his hands move across the piano keys. Slater found himself longing to hear her voice again. There was a way he could. And it would solve two problems.

He took a deep breath, and his hands stilled on the keys.

"What is it?" she asked, frowning lightly.

Here goes.

"Hope," he said, "I need to ask you a huge favor."

CHAPTER 7

HOPE LOOKED OUT OVER THE rows of people fanning out in front of her, all seated in the same conference room as yesterday, as she clicked to advance to the final slide on her presentation. The last hour had flown by, and she could only half attribute it to the dense information she'd been delivering during today's tax-law refresher.

"In summation, you as investors need to know that there are governmental taxes on many facets of investment income. You'll want to be sure that you're getting the proper amounts—taxed and paid—on any capital gains, dividends, earned interest, even commercial investments or real estate."

At the back of the room, Hope spied her father watching intently. Next to him sat Jack Allen, and to the other side of Jack was Annie. When Hope's eyes met Annie's, Annie gave her an enthusiastic thumbs-up. Jack Allen wore an easy smile, and her father's face was blank, neutral—which Hope took as a better sign than his usual scowl.

"And that concludes today's update. We here at Beacon Financial are always apprised of the latest revisions to these laws, so if you have any questions, feel free to find me after the presentation, or we can set up a meeting with any of our advisors at a later time."

Hope clicked the projector off, and there was a solid round of applause as the lights came up and she stepped down from the podium. Annie was already pushing through the dispersing crowd as Hope began to gather her things and tidy up for the next presenter. The schedule was tight today, and there was little dawdling conversation as the room cleared out and the attendees all left for the day's lunch break. Hope got a bit of déjà vu—but then, the days did tend to blend together on trips like these. There was usually little to differentiate between one seminar day and the next.

Usually. She thought of Slater, leaning in the doorway in the low light of the piano room.

"You rocked it! It was perfect. I didn't even see those PowerPoints before we left. Your bar charts were unreal." Annie clapped delightedly.

Hope grinned. "You just complimented my bar charts."

"Sorry, sorry, yes. I loved it." Annie lowered her voice. "And I heard Jack lean over and tell your father that he was very impressed with you, as well."

Hope knew she should feel delighted that the man her father was trying to woo to Beacon Financial had been pleased with the presentation—and she was—but it didn't hit the same place in her chest that she'd thought it would. It seemed, six months ago, that she might have swelled with pride at any compliment over her work at her father's firm. After all, she'd always felt she needed to prove that she could hack it. That she could shoulder things, strong, like her mother.

But the pleasant, tingly feeling that was making her especially buoyant this morning had nothing to do with tax law or the approval of Jack Allen. It had to do with a not-too-small secret that she'd carried back to her room the previous evening, clutched in her heart, making her thrill with a long-forgotten joy despite the *almost* equal misgivings that came along with it.

She couldn't wait to tell Annie about the conversation between her and Slater. She was sure her friend would squeal with delight at what had resulted from the chat. But Hope couldn't spill with Jack Allen and her father coming up to join them. Well, not in front of Jack, anyway.

"Hope, a perfect performance," Jack complimented as he stopped close beside her.

"Thank you," she said, looking at her father to try to find any clue as to why he was so intent on landing Jack. But her father was poker-faced today.

"I have to say that you really educated me up there. And I think there might be a lot more that I could learn from you."

Hope laughed. "This was my only session for the week, Jack, I'm so sorry."

"A pity," Jack chided, looking over at Hope's father. "Dan, you need to let the world see much more of this brilliant woman."

"Oh, I intend to," he said, grinning. Hope had to school her face into blankness. Why was he grinning so oddly, so...plastic and wide? "I have great things planned for my little girl."

Well, it *was* a smile, and Hope wondered if the small

show of effort on her father's part was the start of something that could grow.

"I suppose, since you have nothing else on the schedule that I can sit in on, I'll have to pencil myself into a little of your personal time," Jack said.

"We do need to reschedule that meeting we missed out on, the four of us." Hope had never been more grateful for a cancelled meeting.

"So we do," Jack agreed. He tapped a sheet of paper that Hope hadn't noticed before against his palm. She recognized it as the day's speaking schedule. "But if you'll excuse me, I'm going to pop out for a few phone calls before advanced strategies for international investing. Though I'm sure it will be nowhere near as engaging as you, Ms. Bergman."

Hope got the impression once more that his interest wasn't simply in investment taxation.

As soon as Jack disappeared, her father grasped both of Hope's hands in his and actually *smiled* again. "Darling, you were wonderful! Now, I don't want to press too hard, but you brought up a good point just now. I'll be asking Jack to another sit-down soon, and I know he'll love to have you join us."

His enthusiasm was real, and Hope felt a spark of elation. Her plan just might be working.

Annie chimed in. "I'm sure Mr. Allen will be thrilled with how you've built Beacon Financial into a premier firm, Mr. B. Jack came from a small startup, himself."

He squeezed Hope's hands. "Oh, the work hasn't come from only me, dear. After all, once I retire, I'll be handing Jack Allen and every other account over into Hope's capable hands."

Hope felt suddenly lightheaded. *Every other account?*

Hope laughed, but it felt humorless. She pulled her hands free of her father's grasp and patted his hands. "That's a discussion for another time. What's next on the agenda, Annie?"

Take over Beacon? Hope had never been sure that was what she wanted. And, like many things, she and her father had never discussed the reality of her replacing him.

Annie consulted her tablet, scrolling. "It looks like you're clear for the rest of today."

"Oh, should we try to press Jack for an evening meeting, then?" he asked, excitement edging his voice.

"No," Hope said. "I actually promised to help Slater out tonight. I'm meeting him after we're done for the day."

If Hope could have had a picture of her father and Annie's simultaneous reactions to the announcement, she was pretty sure it would have been a perfect recreation of the classic comedy/tragedy dichotomy. Annie grinned from ear to ear, looking as though she'd won a prize—or, at least, their earlier debate over whether or not Hope would be seeing Slater again.

Her father's face, however, drew into a deep scowl and stayed there. "Hope, you must be joking."

Hope leaned over and kissed him on the cheek. "No, Daddy, I'm not."

"But that boy—"

"Is not a boy anymore, and I'm well past the age of adulthood, remember?"

Hope waited for the eruption. Her father searched her face for a long moment and then looked up at the podium she'd been behind moments ago. Hope must have gained some of his favor, because he relented—though there was a split second where she feared he might not. "You're right. You're not a kid anymore. But promise this…this… blast from the past isn't going to distract from your work obligations. I need you to help win Jack Allen over. It's *vital*."

There was such a look of seriousness on his features that Hope reached out to link their hands again. "Dad. I will be here whenever you need me."

He smiled. It was weak, but it was something. She wouldn't let Slater become too much of a distraction. She had to keep—and improve—on whatever tenuous bond was reforming between her and her father.

"Good. Now, I hear there is a café in this building that bakes some amazing sweets. Shall we?"

"And so, she said yes."

Slater stared straight ahead as they hummed along the road, afraid that another volley of questions and advice about Hope would bombard him from all angles now that he'd dropped the news. But there was nothing but silence, aside from the sound of Alex, in the driver's seat, flipping on her turn signal. He fidgeted in the passenger's seat.

Slater swiveled his head slightly to take in the shocked faces of the entire Pines crew—minus Wyatt and Delaney, who'd opted not to ride in Alex's late-model luxury SUV to the day's wedding-party activity. Ursula and Norman sat in the seat directly behind the driver and front passenger, and the third-row bench seat was occupied by Masie, Rachel, and Charles. When no one said anything, Slater turned back around and studied the flyer in his hand, pretending a level of extreme interest—that didn't really rise to the level he applied himself at—in the classic movie double feature they were headed to.

Then Rachel, Alex, and Maisie all spoke at once.

"Oh my gosh, my mom and Wyatt are going to be so happy!" Rachel bounced in her seat.

"I'm just as pleased as punch. She was so adorable. I wonder if we should get her a dress in the same color as the ones the bridesmaids are wearing." Maisie turned to Charles, looking across Rachel, who sat between them, to do so. Maisie continued, "I think we should."

Alex looked at Slater in the rearview mirror. "Well, that solves two problems, doesn't it? We needed a singer, and you needed a date for the wedding. Slater, I'm telling you, it would look dreadful if the best man showed up alone. Dreadful."

When all three had finished speaking, Charles spoke up. "We should we make sure she's on the guest list."

"Wait, no." The silence fell again. Five pair of eyes settled on Slater.

"No?" Norman parroted. "Why not? Everyone knows the whole sordid tale of shattered dreams and heartbreak by now. You don't have to hide the poor girl."

Slater's head was spinning. As they pulled into the parking lot of the movie theater, he gently shushed everyone. "What if we didn't tell Wyatt and Delaney who the wedding singer is?"

Alex put the SUV in park. Confusion was written across every face that was turned toward Slater.

Slater thought back to his discussion with Hope in the piano room at the resort. "I have a surprise planned. But if we tell Wyatt and Delaney who the singer we found is, it might spoil it. I'll tell them we've found someone so that they won't stress out—"

Rachel giggled. "So *Wyatt* won't stress out."

Slater turned pleading eyes on the group. "But can we keep this one little detail under our hats until the day of the wedding?"

Everyone nodded. Slater breathed a little easier. "Thank you. Hope's going to practice with me tonight. If any of you want to stop by, we'll be in the same conference room that we all had our meeting in yesterday."

Maisie unbuckled her seat belt and opened the door of the SUV, throwing back over her shoulder as she slid out, "Oh, I think we can leave you two *old friends* alone to practice."

There it is. Slater smiled at the teasing. He heard the honk of a horn as he got out of the SUV, and Wyatt's old truck slid to a stop in the parking spot next to Alex's vehicle. The window was down, and Wyatt leaned out to give a wave. Delaney was already out and coming around the front of the truck to meet everyone.

"Okay," she said, holding up a stack of movie tickets and fanning them out. "Pick a card. Any card." One by one, each of the crew took a ticket, and they all coalesced into a group, headed into the theater. Rachel walked with Wyatt and Delaney, chatting happily, her phone actually tucked away.

Slater studied the ticket. Back-to-back, black-and-white romances. He might have rolled his eyes at the sap before now, but it was sweet, the way Wyatt and Delaney were using the days leading up to the wedding to recreate memories from their life together. As though the signs had always been there that they were meant to be, and they were reminding themselves—and everyone else—that every small moment mattered.

Slater's step faltered a little. He thought of Hope and

how he'd felt the years melt away in the low light of the piano room the previous night. It had certainly been a *moment*, but if it was one that would matter for the future, he didn't yet know.

"You okay, man?" Charles clapped Slater on the back lightly. Everyone slowed to a stop.

"Yeah," Slater said, smiling. He looked up at the marquee above the theater. It read, "Welcome Andrews-Phillips Wedding Party!"

"This place used to be the only theater in town?" Fairwood had grown so much even in the years Slater had been here, but he appreciated that the main bustle still centered on the old-fashioned downtown.

"Yes," Delaney said. "Wyatt and I saw *His Girl Friday* here at a showing like this years and years ago. It was the first time he was allowed to drive without one of his parents in the truck. He was…a novice at smooth steering."

"Hey!" Wyatt protested. "That garbage can was out in the flow of traffic, I swear."

"Your first date with your future wife, and you demolished a trash can on the way?"

"It wasn't a *date* date," Delaney said.

"I thought it was a date," Wyatt supplied evenly.

"Is that why you wore a bow tie?" Delaney's eyes widened.

Wyatt grinned sheepishly. "My dad said girls like it when you dress up. Besides, it worked for Fred Astaire."

Slater's eyes widened. "There's a dent in your front left bumper that's been there since I can remember. Are you telling me that that dent is older than Rachel?"

Wyatt nodded solemnly, throwing an arm around Rachel's shoulder. "Adds character."

Delaney grinned and wrapped her arm around Wy-att's waist on the opposite side. "Just like this place." She nodded toward the theater. "It was reopened as event center, and they've let us rent it out for the wedding party to show the same double feature as our first date."

"Well, everyone else is inside. Del, I think your parents are saving us seats by them. No telling where Aunt Tildy will want to sit, but she steals all the popcorn, so everyone be warned."

Delaney gave Wyatt a squeeze, and then let go and hung back with Maisie as they all started walking to-ward the door. Rachel and Wyatt reached the doors of the theater first. Rachel made a show of opening the door for Wyatt, who made a show of walking through. Slater smiled. He knew how happy Wyatt and Delaney made each other, and he'd seen how much closer Rachel and Wyatt had grown since the engagement. And in less than a week, they would be an official family.

The rest of the gang repeated their own version of the grand entrance, each pair sillier than the last. Charles carried Maisie over the threshold bride style while Nor-man held the door. Delaney and Alex waltzed through with linked arms and faux-haughty expressions. When Slater got to the door, he held it for Norman, shaking his head.

"You're all something else." But he chuckled as he said it.

Norman grinned at Slater as he did a few tap-dance moves into the theater. "You think we're all too much now? Wait until you show up with your girl to the wed-ding. What else is family for but embarrassing you in front of a date?"

At the mention, Slater thought about the practice to come that evening. "I can handle it," he assured Norman. But his stomach was suddenly full of nervous butterflies.

CHAPTER 8

THE AFTERNOON WAS PERFECT AND golden. Hope plopped onto the shore, ignoring the dampness that lingered in the grass. She was glad she'd changed into jeans. They seemed better suited to this side of the property, and they were certainly easier to lounge in at the edge of the lake.

She checked her smartwatch. Thanks to an opportune speaker cancellation, she had over an hour to kill. And this—she looked out over Lake Fairwood—seemed the perfect place to do so. The wind had died down this afternoon, and the towering pines weren't rustling the way they had when Hope had first arrived. Instead, their still images were reflected in the dark, placid surface of the water, with the mirror image of the sky stretched out above. It gave Hope a bit of vertigo, looking out across the glassy surface to try and find where the two worlds met.

She ignored the little voice in the back of her mind that nudged her to explore *that* line of thought.

Small birds hopped in and out of the reed-fringed edge of the lake. The occasional trout or turtle broke the water's surface, only to disappear as quickly, sending ripples through the reflection. Taking in a deep inhale of the fresh lake air, she dug into the small bag she'd brought with her and pulled out the pencil and notebook she'd stuffed inside.

She'd written down as many lyrics as she could remember, but had blanked a few lines past what she'd sung in the piano room the previous night. It was possible that Slater still remembered, but Hope was bothered that she didn't. She could rattle off a million types of financial modeling techniques, but she couldn't bring up the words that had once flowed so easily. Closing her eyes, she hummed a few bars of the melody, rolling the lyrics through her mind.

No matter where we start,
A million miles or breaths apart,
The stars might burn and all go dark,
But I would still find you...

If every old love leaves a mark
A broken trail to lead our hearts
Then let this new love be the spark,
That lights the way to what's true

Behind her closed eyelids, she could see every detail of the stage where she and Slater had first performed together. That night, one of the boards at the edge of the last stair had been cracked, and she'd tripped on it. He'd caught her before she'd fallen, and, after steadying her, had wrapped her hand in his as they'd gone up together. Hope had felt protected, safe, solid—even though, moments before, she had been terrified.

She'd been singing since she was young, but doing it

in front of a crowd was at the very least nerve-racking. With Slater by her side, though, every fraught emotion melted away. He had a quiet, easy way of making everything that weighed on her lighter. Stress over classes, the storminess after she'd argued with her father, her deep worry over her mother's illness—he kept it from seeming like it would overwhelm her. But Slater had not been without his own struggles and complications back then. He shared in her burdens, and she in his.

And when he played and she sang, there was no better magic than that.

> And I know this love can last
> The storms that may...

Hope's eyes popped open, and she scrambled for her notebook. She added the lyrics to the first two stanzas she already had on the lined, yellow paper. Nearby, the birds in the reeds began to bicker. She stared down at the paper, willing more words to come.

That first night, once they'd started—Slater's fingers drifting over the strings as easy as breathing—she had simply lost herself in the moment. Her confidence had built as her voice and his music had reverberated off of the worn brick walls. It had been exhilarating. She could remember all of that, but the rest of the words faded out.

"Mind if I join you?"

Hope turned and squinted against the afternoon light, looking up at the person who'd spoken. She didn't know who she'd expected, but the woman standing a few steps behind Hope on the lakeshore was definitely not it.

"Hi. Ms. Brent—"

"Please, call me Alex."

Alex seemed to take Hope's momentary silence as permission, and so she sat down next to Hope in the grass, crossing her legs in a yoga-like position. Alex was dressed casually, quite different from the suit-and-heels look that Hope had admired when they had met the night of the welcome mixer. The other woman's khaki shorts and breezy linen shirt fit perfectly in the current weather. Her ponytail made her seem less intimidating than the usual sleek updo.

"How did you convince your father to book time over on the wild side of things, hmm?" Alex asked, putting her hands behind her and stretching back slightly.

Hope put her pencil and notepad down, finding herself smiling. "How do you know that I convinced him?" It was true, but there was no way that Alex could have known.

Alex shrugged. "Well, as you may be aware, I know a lot of folks in business."

"Mmm-hmm. Before *The ABCs of Business* even aired, you were a force in the venture capital world."

Alex looked surprised but pleased. "That was very early on, but yes. And to answer your question, I don't know many upper-crust businessmen who'd willingly shed their suits for an in-the-trees adventure course. But I know many who would do anything for their little girls."

Hope pictured her father in a climbing harness, inching across a rope that was suspended high above the ground. "Is he actually doing it?"

"Nah. But he did seem interested. We had a great talk about the cost versus profit of installing the course."

"That's very much like him. Did he remind you to factor in the extra insurance premium you likely carry?"

"Indeed," Alex said, sitting up and stretching forward

to put her hands on the grass in front of her. "So if all of your attendees are out in the playground of the pines, and even your father seems interested, what are you doing out here by your lonesome?"

Hope could feel the warmth that crept into her face, and she flipped the top page of her notepad, which was blank, over the lyrics, resting her pencil on top. "Relaxing. It's so beautiful here."

Alex hummed in agreement. "It is. It has its own sort of enchantment that pulls you right in." Alex pointed to the notepad. "You know, I used to be driven by my career, taking work with me absolutely everywhere. But I discovered that passion for work and passion for life aren't always the same thing."

"Oh, it's not..." Hope trailed off, thinking better of revealing what she and Slater were working on. He had said it was a surprise for the bride and groom, and she wasn't sure who it was safe to reveal to quite yet. "I do take a break now and then," she finished, hoping that it was enough of a deflection to keep Alex from questioning.

"Well, there's lots to enjoy in your leisure time here. A bike ride, a nice campfire, a walk around the lake with someone special."

Hope, flustered, opened her mouth to respond, but she was saved by a low, smooth voice from having to come up with something from her suddenly blank brain.

"Alex, please leave the poor woman alone. She isn't used to the competitive matchmaking league on this side of the lake." Slater, his hands in his shorts pockets, stood behind them, in the place where Alex had been earlier. He was dressed in a soft, dark-green V-neck T-shirt and dark-brown shorts. He almost blended with their surroundings. Hope smiled at that, thinking back to when she'd brought him lunch and really got to see how relaxed, how at ease he seemed in this place.

"Matchmaking?" Alex scoffed. "Please, I haven't even told her yet about the pool."

Slater shook his head vehemently. "Nope. Also not happening." He sent Hope an exaggerated apologetic look. Hope couldn't hold back the smile that she felt forming at his helpless expression.

Alex *tsked* and stood, brushing the grass off of her shorts. She pouted slightly, patting Slater on the cheek as she passed him to start up the path behind. "You're no fun anymore, Slater." Alex turned and looked at Hope. "You know, when I first met him, back when we were filming my reality show here, he was so breezy and care-free. But he's seemed tense the past few days. Hmm."

Hope couldn't resist joining in. "He used to be fun when I knew him, too. Too bad." She took in Alex's little tidbit of dropped information, though, and filed it away for later thought. Could Slater be tense because of *her*?

Slater rolled his eyes. "Yes, well, some of us have responsibilities, Alex. Which brings me to the reason I'm here. The front desk would like to see you about the set up for tomorrow night." He seemed to be avoiding a response to what *she'd* said.

"Ah, yes. Speaking of *The ABCs of Business*, we're doing a little show-themed recreation here at the Cabins in the Pines tomorrow night. A private party, as part of the wedding week festivities. You should come, Hope."

Slater rushed to cut in again. "You don't have to. I know you have the seminar, and—"

"During the day, yes. But my nights are free. And I think I should at least meet everyone before the wedding, right?" She picked up her notepad and pencil, holding them in her lap, schooling her features to be as innocent as she could. She waited to see how he would react.

Now, it was Slater who looked like a fish out of water, mouth opening and closing on air.

"Absolutely, dear!" Alex beamed. "That's a splendid idea. The more, the merrier. Now, I must be off. You two have fun at song rehearsal tonight."

Slater watched as Alex marched purposefully toward the office. He lifted a hand to run over the back of his neck, and Hope could almost feel his discomfort. "Sorry about that."

"It's kind of sweet, actually," Hope said, watching as Alex disappeared from sight. "They seem very interested in who you might be interested in." She traced a finger over the upper edge of her notepad, averting her eyes as she let the next words come out despite her better judgement. "I guess you told them about us."

He stood in silence for long enough that she looked up, afraid he might have adopted her in-hall technique from the previous night and bolted. But he walked slowly toward her and sat down next to her, in the spot Alex had vacated. He stared out at Lake Fairwood.

"I shouldn't have asked that, it's really none of my bus—"

"It's okay. And they all know. Not everything, but that we used to be a thing."

"They all?"

Slater grimaced slightly. "Well, Wyatt and Delaney— the bride and groom—Rachel, their daughter. Maisie, you met her at the Bean Pot, and her husband, Charles. Charles is Alex's assistant. And Alex, of course, and the reality show's director, Norman."

At Hope's shocked expression, he held up his hands,

palms-up. "This place is like a small town inside of a small town. Everyone knows everything. But they all mean well. They're family. You know how that can be." As he realized what he'd said, he dropped his hands and winced again. It was her turn to let him off the hook.

"I do know how that can be," she said plainly. "And speaking of..." She checked her watch again. "I have to get back."

He stood up, offering her a hand up. She grabbed her notebook and pencil in one hand and accepted his offered palm. She tried not to react to the warm close of his fingers around hers, but goosebumps ran up her arms at the first touch of their fingers. Slater pulled her up to standing. "You always seem to have somewhere to go when we run into each other," he teased.

"Yes, well, tonight, I'm all yours," she reminded him. The unintended meaning registered as soon as the words left her lips. "I mean, tonight. The practice. I never got the time?"

His wide, rust-and-emerald eyes locked on hers just a second longer than was casual. Was he remembering late-night open mics and the hushed, dark streets of their walks back to campus, hands entwined as they talked the whole way? Grilled cheese and tomato soup for breakfast in that diner near campus, after they'd stayed up all night practicing? Or was he thinking of the day she'd left?

"Tonight, then," he said. "Seven o'clock? My place isn't too far. I mean, if my place is okay."

"Seven is great." She managed to keep her voice even. She turned to leave, and their hands slid apart. She hadn't even noticed that, since he'd helped her from the grass, they hadn't let go.

She flexed her hand in the warmth of the air, but even the soft breeze that had started up wasn't warm enough to erase the cold that she suddenly felt without Slater's hand in hers.

Slater was determined to keep things professional. Tonight, there was no way he was going to repeat that nonsense from down at the lake. No, sir. He hadn't known what he'd been thinking as he'd offered Hope his hand, but she'd looked so pretty in the sunlight, at ease for the first time since he'd seen her again, and he had felt like no time at all had passed. He thought about Alex's teasing. Slater had to admit that maybe, just *maybe*, the offered hand had been because he'd wanted to be close to Hope for that fleeting moment.

But tonight, all business. They had a song list, the sheet music, and not a lot of practice time before the wedding. Everything was going according to plan. In fact, he'd even gotten Wyatt and Delaney's—surprised and delighted—blessing to trust him with the wedding music when he'd told them he'd found a singer. Wyatt hadn't fretted once when Slater had asked them if he could keep the singer's identity under wraps until the wedding.

Now, Slater paced in his living room, which he'd made sure was clean, well-lit, and completely uninviting. The modest kitchen, which was open to the small living room, was cozy in and of itself. The open floor plan, with only the bathroom and two bedrooms closed off, allowed the central space of his house to feel bigger. The southwestern theme of his decor was all soft, woven wall hangings and amber-shaded lamps, and the artful arrangement of dried cholla and pottery on the bookcase in the living room only made the place feel more like home. What *had* he been thinking, inviting her here?

He hadn't lit a fire in the stone fireplace. He had removed both of the cozy plaid throws that were usually draped over the couch, and he'd set up for their practice by placing two hard, wooden chairs—no cushions—in the kitchen and propping his guitar against one of them. He felt safer under the fluorescent light.

Unlike the night he'd found her in the piano room looking a little lost and playing a song he hadn't heard in what felt like a lifetime, tonight there would be no soft longing for the way things used to be. Hope was helping him with the wedding singer problem, and that was it.

It was five minutes until they'd agreed to meet, and with each passing one, he grew more and more nervous. He'd texted earlier to tell her that the front door was open, that she should just come inside once she arrived. What if she didn't show? He watched through the open front door, peering out each time he paced by.

His fears dissolved at the *snick* of the screen door opening. She stepped in, dressed in the same faded jeans and button-up shirt that she'd been in by the lake. Her hair was back in a ponytail, but a few sunny wisps escaped to frame her face. She leaned in the door and scanned the inside of the house, her eyes lighting on him. He really didn't need much convincing, but he studied her for long moment, fully believing now that she was more beautiful than she'd ever been. She reminded him of the old Hope—carefree, fun-loving, and his.

"Hey," she said brightly, "I almost drove right by. It's so dark here at night. I'm used to a zillion street lights and signs on every corner."

He swallowed thickly.

"What's wrong?" Her hand went to her cheek. "Do I have something on my face? I just ate dinner at the Bean Pot, and Maisie gave me a huge box of chocolate chip cookies after. They're still in the car. Want one?"

He smiled, refusing to ask about the rapid-fire line of questioning she might have had to suffer under as she ate. "No, and it's nothing. I was...come in, come in. Those mosquitos out there love to nibble on city girls."

She was inside quickly, letting the screen door close a little too hard behind her. He chuckled and came to ease the wooden entry door closed as well, pointing to the small kitchen. "Can I, uh, offer you some water?" On the kitchen island, he'd put two bottled waters. He had removed the labels. They looked very neutral sitting there, and not at all romantic. She looked over, and her eyes settled on the chairs he'd placed earlier.

Slater watched as Hope walked around the main room, taking in the warm, terra-cotta-painted walls and rustic décor. She ran a hand over the rough stone of the mantel and looked at him across the dark leather sofa. Her lips pursed.

"Are we really going to practice in the kitchen? Wouldn't it be nice if we moved in here and lit the fire?" She pleaded with a wordless flick of her big, blue eyes.

Slater crumbled instantly. "Yes, let's do that." He pointed to the small oak chest that sat by one end of the couch. "There's some throws in there if you want one. I also made some fresh-squeezed lemonade, which is in the fridge. And did you say Maisie gave you brownies?"

"Cookies," she corrected, her face lighting with a bright smile that hit him with undeniable force.

He was in big, big trouble.

The last few chords of the first-dance song vibrated from the guitar strings. Hope's voice slowed and quieted as they did, and Slater smiled as the song ended.

"Man, that felt good. And you sound great," he said sincerely. "I can't thank you enough for helping me out with this." He lifted his guitar strap over his head and set his guitar at the end of the couch. He looked back over in time to catch her ducking her chin shyly.

"It was nice," she agreed. She stretched, her feet poking out from under one of the cozy throws, and looked at the clock that hung over the mantel. "Oh my goodness! Look at the time!"

"You always do," he replied. When she cut her eyes his way, he worried for a moment that there would be anger in them. But there was only amusement.

"As you told Alex today, some of us have responsibilities."

"But that doesn't mean that's *all* you have."

She snorted softly, making no move to get up from her cozy-looking spot. "You seem pretty wrapped up in *yours* here. Which, actually, is something I don't get. You still play, sound great, and you still love music. So why this place? Why this job? What happened to music for *you*?"

He stared at her for a moment, gathering his thoughts. He leaned back against the couch and looked into the dying flames in the fireplace. He swallowed back the reply that was at the tip of his tongue, instead drawing a steadying breath and explaining, "You know, I don't know what drew me here. It was after I finished my engineering degree. I had a job in the field, but—"

"Engineering? You switched majors, too?"

His smile felt forced. "It seemed like something I could do. It interested me."

"But you don't use any of that here, right?"

He got the distinct feeling that they were dancing around discussing their past, and that was fine with him. He didn't really want to revisit any old hurts, despite the fact that their being here, together, singing and playing, brought up all kinds of memories. Slater pressed his lips together and then said, "I used to. I started here as campsite maintenance, and then managed the maintenance staff after we grew post-reality show. Something always needed fixing or figuring out around here before. It's only recently I've been promoted to where I'm at now."

"And you like it?"

"I've chosen it," he said evenly. "And you? I know it's your father's firm and all, but are you making your mark in finance at the co-helm of Beacon Financial?"

Slater watched the interplay of emotions across her face as she considered the answer to his question. A log shifted in the fireplace, sending up a shower of sparks that glittered against the grate. A small burst of heat hit his face, and he watched as the firelight that had previously been bright dimmed to a soft, burnish glow.

"I get along there. My father trusts me with a lot. He had to after my mom passed."

Slater nodded. "I'm so sorry you lost her, Hope. I remember seeing the condolences in the alumni newsletter."

"Thank you. She was really special." Hope smiled, and there was a tinge of sadness behind it. "You kept up with our old school?"

"A bit. Enough to have seen you in the graduation

photos in that same newsletter." He looked at her out of the side of his eyes. "Your cap was a little crooked."

The sadness vanished when she grinned. "It was a windy day. Totally not my fault."

He grinned back. "I'm kidding. You looked perfect. And top of your class."

They lapsed into a silence more comfortable than Slater had anticipated, and he didn't want to break it with his next question, but he had to.

"Hope?"

"Hmmm?" She was staring at the fire now, as he had been. He watched what remained of the flames reflect in her eyes.

Leaning forward, he picked up his guitar and stood, walking to place it in the open case that sat on the kitchen counter. "I haven't gotten a wedding gift for Wyatt and Delaney yet."

She rested her head on one hand and twisted to look at him. "You need help picking one out? My online shopping game is strong."

"No, no. Everyone else is doing something special for them. Planting pancake gardens, and I think I heard Alex say that she and Norman are cutting pieces of the extra footage from filming the reality show together to make a video that shows how it was obvious they were in love."

"Wow," Hope looked impressed. "I don't know what a pancake garden is, but I want one."

"I want to make them something special, too. They're the heart of this place. I was wondering if you would help me write a song for them."

She didn't respond right away, but she sat up, and he could see the distance creep into her features. What had he said? He started to panic a little on the inside.

"I, uh, don't know if that's a good idea. Maybe we should stick to what's on their music list."

For some reason, despite her gentle tone, the refusal still stung—hard. "Okay. Okay, that's fine." He fumbled with the latches on the guitar case, managed to close them and heft the case off the counter to set it by the door.

Hope stood and folded the throw she'd had across her lap, wiping her palms on her jeans when she was done. The fire had dwindled to almost nothing behind her. "Well, great practice. I really had fun. It's late, though, and tomorrow we start the week, so..."

Slater leaned back against the wall by the front door. "Can't keep the big career waiting. Trust me, I get it." There wasn't any real malice behind his words, but he was all too aware of the flicker of hurt in her eyes when he spoke them.

"Yeah." She walked over and gave him a small squeeze on the arm. "Well, goodnight, Slater."

Her eyes were wide and still uncertain. There was tension now between them, the easy atmosphere and familiar comfort gone, replaced by an exhaustion that suddenly weighed on him.

"Goodnight."

Slater stared at the kitchen island, at the two empty lemonade glasses and the bakery box that Hope had retrieved from the car. He heard a cacophony of crickets when she opened the front door to the heavy, humid night. The faint buzz of the front porch light was the only other sound as she silently, quickly slipped out.

CHAPTER 9

THE LATE-AFTERNOON LIGHT FELL THROUGH the skylights after another long, hectic day at the seminar, but Hope found herself oddly energized as she walked down the hall toward her room. And despite the trepidation she'd been pushing away all day, she was still looking forward to meeting Slater again, across the lake. She hadn't seen or heard from him all day—not that she'd expected to, but a friendly run-in might have eased her worries about the way they'd parted the previous evening.

"Why in the world did you tell him no about the song?" Hope asked herself.

"What song?" Annie asked, and Hope stopped short, causing Annie to bump into her from behind.

"Oof!" Annie fumbled, and then nearly dropped her tablet as she ran into Hope's back. "Hope! What in the world?"

Hope steadied her friend. "Oh, Annie, I'm so sorry. I was just thinking out loud apparently."

Annie looked pointedly at Hope. "You're daydreaming about Mr. Tall, Bronzed, and Handsome?"

"Shhh! I was not *daydreaming* about Mr. Tall, Bronzed, and—Slater. I was thinking about how last night's practice ended all sourly."

Annie tucked her tablet into her bag, and the pair of women started walking again, their heels making no sound on the plush carpeting that led to their suites. "I was dying to know why you've been quiet about it. I thought you were too busy. I saw that your father and Jack were practically *glued* to your side all day. But you're still going tonight?"

They reached their rooms, and Hope dug out her keycard, swiping it to open the door. She motioned Annie to come inside with her, explaining, "Oh, yes. Dad's still laying it on thick with Jack. There's something going on there, something Dad won't talk about. And of course, I'm going. I agreed to it. I made a commitment..."

As they walked inside, Hope couldn't help but admire the room for what must have been the hundredth time. Up here on the upper floors, the rooms had amazing views over the tops of the trees and the lake. Hope's room was absolutely massive, with double queen-sized beds piled with luxurious linens that made her feel, climbing into bed, like some kingdom's lost princess, coming out of a long exile in the wilds of regular-people bedding to be bestowed with a new, magical level of sleep nirvana. The place also had a high, heavy-beamed ceiling, and gorgeous, rustic décor that never strayed into cheesiness. The bathroom was like something out of an architectural magazine, and Hope would have happily spent all week in the massive jetted tub.

She doubted her father appreciated the rooms the way she did, and the way Hope was sure Annie did. At least, Hope didn't think he shared the princess feeling.

Hope dropped her bag on the bed beside where Annie had offloaded her own and put up a finger at Annie's wry smile. "Nice try. Zip it. He wants to do something special for his best friends, and I clammed up and made it weird."

"Was it weird?"

"Hmm?" Hope unfolded a suitcase stand and hefted her suitcase onto it. There were still a few articles of clothing she hadn't unpacked. Everything she had was for business. She didn't need a power suit tonight. She needed to be casual, approachable. She started sorting through the clothes she'd brought along, mentally trying on outfits for practice, which was in two hours. Maybe she had enough time to grab a bite to eat. Maybe Slater would want to come with her.

"Did he want you to learn fire juggling, or perform a routine where you roll quarters across your knuckles, both hands at once?"

Hope laughed. "No, nothing like that. He wanted us to write a song together."

Annie's face went soft and faraway. "Aww, like you used to when you were together? Hope!"

"I know, I know!" And she did. She knew exactly that it was the emotion his request was tied to that had made her shut down. Slater wanted her to go back to the thing that had always brought them the absolute closest. Hope didn't know how he could do that and not feel everything he used to claim to feel when they were in love. She didn't know if she could go back without the worry of falling all over again. And *that* simply couldn't happen.

Annie sat on the edge of the bed, kicking off her shoes and looking seriously at Hope. "So you're really going to go? And you'll be okay?" Before Hope could answer, Annie flopped back and sunk into the covers.

She reached for Annie's hand, and they both squeezed. "I'll be fine." Hope took a deep, steadying breath. Everything was going smoothly so far. She really had no reason to believe that Slater's songwriting request was intended to dredge up the past. Maybe she'd been silly to give in to her knee-jerk reaction last night. "You know what? Maybe I will write that song with him. After all, what's a little music between friends, right?"

Annie nodded from her divot in the duvet. "You're mature, levelheaded, and can platonically appreciate spending time with a rugged, attractive, intelligent man who writes love songs."

After an extended moment of trying to hold back, they both burst into laughter. "What would I do without you?" Hope said, wiping at her watering eyes.

"Keep your own schedule, which would be a disaster," Annie answered, sitting up.

"No, I mean without you as my friend." Hope leaned in and gave Annie a tight hug. When they parted, Hope turned back to her open suitcase. "Now, what should I wear to my *non* date?"

Slater was surprised to see that Hope was already at cabin six when he arrived. He'd almost sent her a message through the front desk earlier in the day to cancel their meetup, but as he'd been writing out the excuses on a pad of stationery at his desk, the words had all read wrong. Half a dozen sheets of paper later, all of which ended up on the floor by his wastebasket, he'd just given up and texted her to switch their meeting location to more neutral ground—and cabin six had been luckily open. It was silly to be so hyperaware. Of course, there would be moments of tension between them. They had a deep and important history, one that had never really gotten the epic happily-ever-after that so many stories did. It was natural that they would suffer some awkwardness.

But he hadn't expected her cheery greeting as he'd stepped through the cabin's front door. Nor had he expected the rich, welcoming smell of basil and cheese. He paused by the door and set down his guitar case. Hope was dressed in a breezy gray sundress, the cut vaguely retro, the flowing fabric scattered with cheerful sunflowers. Her hair was half down, falling between her shoulder blades in waves. Slater, just like the night before, couldn't catch his breath for a few heartbeats.

"Hi!" she said, waving a soapy hand from the sink area, which he could easily see off to the right from the front door. In fact, he could see from where he stood the entirety of the main gathering space, and he looked it over, now questioning his new choice of meeting place. There was a fire lit in the aged-brick fireplace. "I hope it's okay that I used the kitchen. I promise to clean everything up when we're done."

"It's fine," he said, a little shell-shocked. The small bar-height table that was butted up against the end of the kitchen counter was covered in dishes. "What's all this?"

"Well, I was so busy today that I didn't get a chance to eat dinner. And the resort has the cutest little market, like a whole mini grocery store. They have everything! I figured if you hadn't had the chance, either, then we could eat together."

Slater crossed to the table and lifted the lid on one of the dishes. It was the source of the delicious smell he'd been hit with on entering. Sauteed chicken, perfectly browned, topped with almonds and...rose petals? A second dish held a pile of garlic bread covered with a clean kitchen towel. A third, covered bowl revealed a Caesar salad, and his mouth watered at the sharp smell of lemon and ground pepper and more parmesan. "Wow. You really didn't have to do this."

"Oh, it was easy. And I'm dying for you to taste this chicken. You've already eaten?" He couldn't help but notice that she was trying to keep the disappointment off of her face.

"No, I haven't. I'm saying you didn't have to go to all of this trouble. I could have ordered something and brought it. But, honestly, I wasn't even sure you were coming."

He watched her dry her hands for what must have been the third time before settling for wringing the cloth between her fingers. That had been an old tell of hers. He always knew when she was nervous because her hands could never be still. "Do you want wine or iced tea with dinner?"

He smiled a little. "Do you want to tell me what's on your mind?"

"Yes," she blurted. "Yes, we can write a song together." The towel was almost in knots.

He walked around the table and took the cloth from her hands, laying it on the counter. He hesitated a second, but then put a hand over hers. "I'm not sure it was fair of me to ask. I only did because I know how beautiful your voice is, and I know how great we are at writing music. I wasn't trying to bring up bad feelings."

She puffed out a little breath that made the loose

wisps of hair around her cheeks drift upward. "It *did* bring things up. But I should have just told you that. I know you only want to make the wedding special."

She closed her eyes and slipped her hands out from under his. She busied herself with taking plates out of the cupboard and setting them on either side of the collected serving dishes on the counter.

"Hope," Slater said, watching her make tall glasses of iced tea studded with thick slices of orange, "We haven't talked about what it feels like, seeing each other after all this time. Our breakup wasn't the best, it's true. I never got a lot of answers I felt I needed. And I was an absolute mess after you left." She stopped in the middle of tearing mint, her fingers poised over the cutting board, eyes nearly as round as their dinner plates.

"But we don't have to relive the bad stuff. I mean, we don't have to pretend it didn't happen. But fate brought us back together for this one week. And it can be nice. For this week, we can let it be what it is."

"Okay." She garnished each of their glasses with several mint leaves and reached for the towel to untangle it and wipe her hands.

"Okay?" he parroted.

She nodded, handing him one of the glasses.

He set the tea aside and reached for the empty plate nearest him. "Thank you for this. It's very thoughtful."

Once they'd both loaded up on chicken and salad, they carried the bounty to the small sectional and feasted.

"This is amazing," Slater said after his first bite. "What do you call this?"

Hope's eyes sparkled, and she stabbed a bite of salad, hesitating with the fork halfway to her mouth. "It's called

Chicken a la Rose. My mom's recipe. She said it was so good that whoever you make it for immediately wants to marry you. I thought it was fitting, since we're practicing wedding music."

Slater laughed, ignoring the tightness in his chest at those words—*marry you*—coming out of Hope's mouth. They brought up way too many feelings, half warm, glowy, and romantic, and the other half painful and unwelcome. If she hadn't left the way she did so many years ago, would he and Hope have really ended up married? Who knew?

Just focus on the now.

Slater dug into his dinner with gusto. It tasted as heavenly as it smelled. The mood eased, and they spent a good deal of their dinner brainstorming lyrics, with Slater suggesting outrageous rhyming pairs while Hope scrolled through an online thesaurus to try and "save the entire wedding from abject embarrassment."

"You want to talk about embarrassment? You should have been here during the filming when Alex and her reality show invaded. Man, there were bloopers every day."

She laughed, sipping a glass of wine as she sat next to him on the couch, her bare feet tucked under her. Her boots sat discarded on the floor, and he didn't miss that it was a sign of how comfortable she was here. With him. "I can't believe I missed this episode! I'm dying to see it. I'll be sure to stream it when I get back home."

Those last five words hit him a little, but he brushed them off.

"Tell me the best story you have from filming the show."

"The best?"

She nodded. "The absolute best. What was the part you really, really liked?"

"Hmm. Let me think about it. It has to be the very last night, when the plan was hatched to get Alex to build the resort."

Hope leaned in a bit to listen. He caught a hint of her perfume—mellow vanilla and sweet peach, with some hint of spice he couldn't place. He had to swallow past his suddenly dry mouth.

"Basically, the entire staff did a *group version* of the rom-com airport run to try to save the Cabins from being bought out completely *and* finally get Wyatt and Delaney together. I mean, we had an army of people, a kid up past her bedtime, and even the dog came along. You haven't met Duke, yet, but he's a good boy. Loves belly rubs from his Uncle Slater and finding his owner true love."

Hope was giggling. "So you're a dog *uncle*? No loyal, devoted pup of your own? I didn't see a hint of dog dish or squeaky toy at your place."

"Nope. Only an adopted canine nephew. Oh, but every summer I get about a hundred seasonal *human* nieces and nephews when the Pint-sized Pines summer camp is in session. So that's always fun."

"Are you the uncle that gives rambling life-lesson lectures, or are you the uncle that lets the kids eat cake for dinner and teaches them how to make slingshots?"

Slater considered, narrowing his eyes. "A little of both."

Hope's next round of giggles ended in a gasp. "Wait. You said *save* the Cabins? What was Alex going to do with it?"

"I think it involved bulldozers and a lot more glass

and steel than the resort you temporarily reside in," Slater said.

Hope shook her head sadly, seeming to be thinking about the Pines being razed. She looked around the cabin. "That would have been awful. I'm glad you all saved this place." She laid her hand on his forearm, smiling. "We would have missed out on a good place to practice."

He hummed in agreement. "And Chicken a la Rose."

"It's nice having dinner with you."

Slater had to stop himself from saying that he wished they could have dinner together every night. He looked away, and his gaze on the clock over the kitchen window. Perfect timing.

"Hey, since you're so interested in the show, do you want to come with me to the wedding event tonight? They're doing a little show-themed party. It's part of recreating some of the moments that led to the bride and groom finally falling for good."

He let his eyes drift back to her as she replied.

"That sounds amazing! I would love to. Do you think anyone would mind?"

"Not at all. In fact, I think it would be the icing on a very sneaky matchmaking cake that my friends have been cooking up since they learned about us. You would thrill them."

Hope laughed again. Slater found that he liked hearing it as much as her singing.

"How about you? You got any stories from your swanky financial career that you want to share?" Slater reached for his wine glass, taking a sip as he waited for her to respond.

But instead of regaling him with any hilarious tale, she actually frowned. "It hasn't been all power-suit fun and luxe corporate amenities, actually. When I first came to Beacon, my mom was sick. And she passed shortly after. Even though I'd switched my major, I still struggled to keep up at first, at work. It was daunting, and I was grieving. I don't know if I was ready for all of that. But I had to handle it, y'know?"

Her eyes dropped to her plate and he knew she was hiding unshed tears from him. Slater wished he'd been with her then, able to support her. But he didn't bring it up. He just reached out to take her hand and sat in silence with her.

He avoided asking about her father, too, though he worried what Dan Bergman thought about Hope spending time with him again. Not that she'd given any indication that she was sneaking off to see Slater—she was, after all, a grown woman—but Slater had to push against the memory of what had separated them all those years ago.

Just focus on this week.

After a few moments, Slater got up and added a fresh stack of firewood to the fireplace. Once the logs had caught, he helped himself to seconds of dinner and returned to his spot on the sectional, cradling his plate. After a slow, thoughtful bite of salad, he shot Hope a curious glance.

"What?" She poked him with a toe.

"You know, you used to go days without talking to me when we were mad at each other. And you never made me dinner. This is…different." He bit into a slice of bread, humming appreciatively.

Hope lifted a forkful of chicken to her lips, and before she ate it, she shrugged, her eyes sparkling. "I wasn't *mad* at you yesterday. And things can change."

Once they were finished eating, Slater helped Hope with the dishes, and then into her cardigan, picking up his guitar case and following her out into the cooling night.

Slater could hear Delaney's voice in his head, and the words she'd said at the lakeside came back to him as clear as Lake Fairwood on a cloudless day.

Plans change.

People change.

It's not always for the worse.

CHAPTER 10

"AND THE RESORT WAS BUILT that fast?" Hope looked wide-eyed at Slater as they pulled up and parked at the Cabins in the Pines.

"I know," he said. "It's amazing what Alex accomplished. And the resort *is* spectacular. But I can't wait for you to see more over on this side. This...this is more like home."

Hope looked out the open passenger's side of Slater's Jeep. The night had fully fallen, and it was slightly cooler tonight than previous nights. She drew her cardigan a little tighter around her shoulders. Here, where trees were cleared, Hope could look up into the dark, velvet sky and make out a million twinkling stars. She leaned out and tipped her head back, marveling at how she could have forgotten that such natural beauty existed. Back home, the light bubble of the city obscured the stars. Here, they were on breathtaking display.

"You know, they're even easier to see out here." Slater was standing at her door. Hope had been so awed by the expanse of night sky that she hadn't even heard him get out of the Jeep. He popped the door on her side and held it open for her. Once she had climbed out, he closed it behind her and inclined his head toward a path of tiki torches that started at the edge of the tree line, leading back past the main office and deeper into the woods.

"Remind me of what they're recreating here?" Hope's view of the stars was blocked as they entered the torch-lit path and the trees arched above, closing out the rest of the world. Wondering at how the simple setting of the sun could turn this place into something even more enchanting, she turned to look at Slater. His face was lit by the vibrant paper lanterns that danced as far as she could see, strung on invisible wires, enticing them toward the smell of a bonfire. Hope could hear faint music and a distant smatter of laughter.

"This is actually set up like the 'big reveal' of the changes at the Pines, for the show. And everything was beautiful that night. But Alex tried to pull a fast one on Wyatt, and it almost caused a *big* rift between Wyatt and Delaney."

"Oh?" Hope put out a hand to let the pine branches that hung over the sides of the path brush against her outstretched palm as they walked. "And they want to recreate that?"

He laughed lowly. "Wyatt says that when he danced with Delaney that night, it was one of the moments that made him realize he truly loved her."

"And they concluded this romantic evening..."

"With her not speaking to him."

Hope felt her brows knit. "And now, they're getting married."

Slater's smile quickly gave way to a dry, short laugh. "Yeah, it doesn't always end that way, but it did in this case." He slowed, and then stopped. "Here we are."

Hope followed his line of sight to the clearing they'd reached. There was a large, rustic fire pit, blazing from the center of a circular seating area made up of cobblestone. Heavy Adirondack chairs were arranged around the fire, and barrels sat between the chairs to hold drinks and plates. On the far side of the bonfire, away from Hope and Slater, stood a long table laden with baskets of graham crackers, marshmallows, and various chocolates. A bouquet of long wooden skewers erupted from a hollowed-out tree stump that sat at the end of the table, acting as a vessel from which guests were enticed to pick the perfect roasting implement.

Hope didn't know many of the people who stood chatting, clustered in groups or around the fire, but she recognized Alex from the resort, talking with a couple Hope assumed were Wyatt and Delaney. Beside them, a girl, who looked to be in her mid-teens, was coaxing a lively, stocky, rust-and-cream-colored dog into doing tricks.

Slater stepped forward, but Hope hesitated. She looked around at the happy gathering, at the people who Slater called family. If they knew about what had happened between her and Slater in the past, then they would know that she was the one who'd left him. The one who'd hurt him. She crossed her arms and rubbed the sleeves of her cardigan.

"What is it?" Slater's eyes were on hers, golden-green in the firelight, full of concern.

"I, um, are you sure you want me to meet everyone?" Hope wasn't sure she did. They all looked nice enough, but she suddenly burned inside, glowing with a shame as hot as the fire lighting up the faces of the gathered celebrators.

Slater took two steps back, putting him even on the

path with Hope. He seemed to stop and think for a moment, but then he reached out and grabbed her hand. Warmth ran up the back of her neck, making the small hairs there stand on end. The burn of shame turned into a pleasantly radiating delight.

"Of course, I do. But there is something you should know."

Hope waited, expectant, vacillating between dread and giddiness. Slater tugged her forward, and when she was beside him, he leaned down and whispered close to her ear, setting off another bout of unexplainable elation.

"If anyone asks, you're my date for the wedding."

The bonfire was burning low, and the waist-high stack of wood that had been neatly arranged this morning to fuel the festivities had dwindled as well. Slater picked up the last two pieces of pine that remained, setting his cup of punch on the wide stone edge of the fire pit as he leaned over to add the logs. Many of the party guests had left, but the main Pines crew remained.

Slater looked back over his shoulder to where Alex, Ursula, Maisie, and Delaney sat with Hope, in a cluster of Adirondacks that had been repurposed from fire-viewing seats into a conversation group. Duke was curled up at Hope's feet, his head on her left shoe. Rachel and Norman were packing up the abundance of marshmallows, graham crackers, and chocolate still left from the side table. Some time had passed, and Slater wondered if Charles and Wyatt would need a hand loading up everything from the party to return to storage, once they came back from retrieving Wyatt's truck.

Slater let his eyes sweep over to Hope again, watched

her laugh at something that Delaney said, and followed the line of her smile up the delicate slope of her jaw and to the crinkled corners of her eyes. The blue of them struck him even from this far away. She caught him watching her, and her smile changed, grew warmer, more familiar. They stayed that way, looking at one another, until someone in the group spoke, drawing Hope's attention.

Cutting his eyes back to the fire, Slater frowned, remembering Hope's hesitation when they'd first arrived. He'd have to ask her about it later. The night had gone so well that he couldn't imagine what had spooked her when they'd arrived.

"Hey, you just going to stand there, or are you going to lend me a hand?" Wyatt's ribbing made Slater turn.

"You lose Charles in the woods?"

"Nah. Maisie has to be up early to coordinate with the caterers for tomorrow night's event, and so she snagged Charles from me a few minutes ago. They headed out."

"Pffft," Slater said. "Turning into an old, married couple. The first to leave the party."

"Hey, now," Wyatt said, mock-offended. "I'm about to be part of one of those."

Slater picked up his cup to toss as he followed Wyatt to the now-empty side tables. They made short work of folding everything, and Slater grabbed the handle of one of the tables in each hand, hefting the pair and walking with Wyatt toward the truck, which he'd parked at a wide spot up the path, rather than leaving it in the parking lot, which was a much farther walk.

As they loaded the tables in the back, Wyatt asked, "So, did Hope have a good time?"

Slater leaned on the bed of the truck, looking at his

friend across it. "I think she did. She seems to have hit it off with everyone. And everyone seems to have lightened up on trying to walk us down the aisle and stand us next you and Delaney this weekend."

Wyatt's laughter was a little too loud for Slater's comfort, and he waved a hand in Wyatt's direction. "Hey, man, keep it down." But Slater couldn't resist joining in a bit.

Wyatt propped his elbows on the edge of the truck bed, mimicking Slater's position. "Hope fits right in, seems to me. And don't be too hard on the rest. They want you to be happy, man."

"And I am. I'm happy here with you all, and that's enough. The way things are is enough."

Wyatt looked up at the stars, and Slater pictured Hope, the wonder in her eyes as she'd done the same thing earlier this evening. Wyatt nodded as he said, "You know, I used to think the same thing. And so I never took a chance with Del. And if I hadn't, if we both hadn't, we would never have known how beautifully, deliriously happy we could have been, all those years we never risked it."

"It's not the same, Wyatt. Hope and me, we were never meant to be. She has her big-city life and her family's legacy in finance. She chose her path a long time ago, and I was not a part of it. She made quick-and-painfully sure of it."

"Yeah, I know something about the influence of family legacy, too. And Hope's choice was *made* a long time ago, brother."

"I just said that," Slater groused, picking a bit of tree sap off of Wyatt's truck. He didn't like the way it felt when he thought back to the day he'd found Hope's note, pinned to his dorm-room door. And he certainly didn't want that memory getting its cold fingers into what had been a pretty nice night.

"But she still has her obligations now, right? And she's choosing *now* to spend time with you."

Slater nodded. "It's different. She—" he hesitated, but decided to spill his secret, so that Wyatt would understand that he held no illusions about Hope's reasons for hanging around, "—she's actually going to sing at your wedding. We're practicing."

Wyatt thumped the side of the truck lightly. "No way! That's awesome. Delaney will be thrilled. I know she and Hope have hit it off already."

"I wanted to keep it a surprise, so maybe we could still, for Delaney?"

"Sure thing."

Slater took a breath, listening to the crickets in the night air. "I only wanted you to know there's a reason. She's not spending time *with* me, we're spending time together *for the wedding*."

Wyatt narrowed his eyes at Slater. "Mmm-hmm. Where's your guitar?"

"In the Jeep, why?" Slater frowned.

"I didn't hear you singing at the fire. Did you guys practice the wedding songs tonight?" Wyatt replied.

Slater was confused. "Well, we didn't. We ate dinner together, and then we came here to meet you guys."

"So you had dinner and went to a party?" Wyatt lifted one eyebrow.

Slater narrowed *his* eyes at the grinning man across from him. "Yes."

"For the wedding?" Wyatt's question was said more slowly than it needed to be.

Slater didn't answer.

Wyatt threw up his hands, backed away from the truck, and turned toward the trail that led back to the fire pit. "Hey, hey, it's none of my business."

Slater let Wyatt get a few steps down the trail before he kicked at the dirt and followed after him. "Wyatt!" he loud-whispered after his friend, jogging to catch up, "Don't you dare tell the girls about this conversation!"

CHAPTER 11

HOPE WAS FINDING IT HARD to concentrate on the stack of papers in front of her. Sitting at the head of the conference table, staring down at the yearly numbers from Jack Allen's various enterprises, Hope squinted, trying to make the print form into anything she could make sense out of. She was, if she were being honest, getting sick of the monotony of the seminar and all of its related meetings, events, lunches, and—ugh, the awards ceremony. Hope had agreed to sit down with Jack—the previously cancelled meeting that she'd brushed off to meet Slater—but her mind wasn't here, not in the luxurious Pines Executive Resort, not in the lushly styled conference room, not even on this side of Lake Fairwood.

All Hope could think about was glowing, multicolored lanterns, the deep, rich smell of wood smoke and chocolate, and the way Slater's eyes had shined when he'd whispered to her right before they'd walked into the party.

She supposed she could be his date to the wedding since she was going to be there anyway. It wasn't as though she made any mistake in the intent; she'd be gone at the end of the week, and it was only another small facet of her helping him with the wedding music. Alex, Slater had told her, was pestering him to be accompanied on the day of the nuptials. And as sweet, warm, and welcoming as Hope had found Alex to be last evening, there was also a definite brook-no-argument vibe to the older woman.

So it was the only right thing to do, to save Slater from further lectures. That was it.

"And what do you think, Hope?"

She looked up from the stack of papers to find half a dozen pairs of eyes staring at her. Her father, Jack Allen, three of his people (had she caught their names, even?), and Annie, who was looking at Hope with an expression of half fear, half panic. Hope looked back down at the stack before answering her father's question.

"I'm actually not interested in the current line of discussion," Hope said, tapping the papers. She ignored her father's horrified look, holding up a hand to stop any immediate reply. "If we could table that and come back to it later, what I'd like to move to discussing is why, Mr. Allen, you aren't taking advantage of tax credits for specific energy-saving investments?"

Jack looked at her father, and then back at Hope. Her father sat forward and picked up his own copy of the file they were reviewing, donning a pair of tortoiseshell reading glasses and peering down through them to the packet.

"Page six," Hope said. There was a rustle as everyone turned to the page. "You have a long list of manufacturing facility upgrades that would qualify. And based on the square footage of your manufacturing facilities, those breaks could be significant."

Hope watched as her father scanned the numbers, his face tight with what she could only assume was worry—but she knew she was right. His features softened for a moment, and Hope knew that he'd likely found that her numbers checked out.

Jack Allen's brow furrowed. "I have a tax accountant. I'm not sure why this was missed."

"It's intricate," Hope supplied. "And if you remember from my presentation, Beacon Financial prides ourselves on keeping up with the latest in the laws. A lot of times, improvements like you've made aren't treated as infrastructure investment, but business expense, and that's not always the best way to classify things."

Hope caught Annie's eye, and the other woman was visibly relaxed. Her father, too, let the tension fall from his shoulders as he sat back in his chair. There was a proud glint in his eye that made Hope brush away thoughts of the previous night, sit up a little straighter, and focus for the moment on the group gathered around the conference table.

"You're right," he said. "This seems a much bigger issue than what to invest in for the next fiscal year." He seemed to be rereading the page she'd indicated.

"There could be a substantial amount here that could simply be applied to increase your investment capital for that very thing—next year's investments. It's found money."

"Money that you just found," Jack said, looking impressed. "I can have my accountant look into this."

Suddenly, a flurry of chimes erupted from Jack's side of the table. He picked up his phone and swiped the screen, rising when he saw whatever alert he'd received. "I'm afraid I have to go make a call. But it seems like this meeting is at a good stopping place, so we can reconvene once we've had a chance to explore the issue Ms. Bergman has brought up." Jack reached across the conference table and offered Hope his hand, and she stood to shake it. His handshake was firm.

"It would be our pleasure," Hope replied as Jack's people rose from their seats, following the lead of their boss.

After Jack and his companions had said their farewells and offered more handshakes all around, they'd left Annie, Hope, and her father alone in the conference room.

"Wow," Annie said, spinning slowly in her chair as she leafed through the financial statement. "Hope, what a great catch. I mean, there's so much cost here that Jack might recoup if they go retroactively."

Her father studied Hope as she gathered her papers and stuffed them in her bag. "Did you know that, coming in? That he was missing out on the tax credits?"

"Nope," Hope admitted. "I caught it on the fly." *And thank goodness,* she thought, shuddering a little at the thought of floundering in front of the client that her father was so insistent on landing this week.

Hope expected her father to be annoyed, to lecture her about being unprepared. And she did feel the very slightest bit guilty about being unprepared. But she was knowledgeable enough that she'd known, the second her eyes had fallen on the solar upgrades to Jack's manufacturing plants on the statement that she could brush aside her momentary inattention and show Jack Allen the kind of expertise he would get if he came to Beacon Financial.

But he wasn't annoyed. He didn't lecture. Instead, he smiled and slapped the conference table lightly. "I'll be doggoned. I agree, Annie. That was a fantastic catch, Hope."

Hope found herself smiling. She had caught his attention just as she'd wanted to—but what would that mean to them as a father and a daughter? "You know what Mom always used to tell me, right? 'If you don't have confidence in yourself, no one else will.' Jack simply needs to see our confidence. He'll be signing with us in no time."

Hope braced for his retreat into silence. Instead, at the mention of her mother, his face softened. "She was a wise one. A lot smarter than me. A real light."

When he wasn't frowning, it was easy for Hope to remember her father from back when she was young. He'd been quick with a joke and quicker with the sneaky before-dinner taffy he'd slip her at the end of his workday. She would dash out of the kitchen—where she'd been nodding over her homework at the heavy oak table—and sit on the large wraparound porch of her parent's house, letting the soft, sweet candy melt in her mouth as her father caught her mother up on the day's events. When Hope would return to the kitchen full of sugared energy, ready to tackle her neglected spelling words, she would also see her father catching her mother up in his arms.

Hope missed those days. She missed her father's smile. She missed her mom.

They all turned at the sound of the conference room door opening. Jack Allen stuck his head in. Her father stood. "Something else you needed, Jack?"

To Hope's surprise, smooth, sophisticated, designer-suited Jack Allen looked momentarily shy. "Actually, I was hoping that Ms. Bergman might want to join me for coffee."

Hope had gotten used to Jack's flirting, but she had never expected the outright ask. She was momentarily stunned into silence. Annie, who had been gathering her own things, paused and looked over at Hope and Dan.

Hope's eyebrows shot up, and she sputtered, "Umm, uh, I'm not sure if..."

"Go ahead." Hope was almost unsure she'd heard her father right. He wagged a finger at Jack. "As long as you aren't trying to win her to your company. She's too great an asset to Beacon Financial."

"I wasn't trying to win her over to any company I *own*," Jack assured. He stepped into the room and shoved his hands in his pants pockets, looking sheepish still.

Annie's smile started slow, but widened. Hope ignored her. Shouldering her bag, Hope shook her head slightly. "I've actually got a lot of work that I brought with me, Jack, and I'm a little behind. Can we take a rain check?"

Jack looked momentarily disappointed, but nodded good-naturedly. "Of course. Can't fault you for having a great work ethic. A rain check, then." With a small wave, he turned and left. Annie followed a few beats later, giving Hope a pointed look and making hand motions like two magnets attracting each other. For the second time in the past few minutes, Hope ignored her friend.

Hope's father reached for his own briefcase, motioning her to walk along with him. "I'm headed over to the afternoon workshops. I think everything's going well so far. Maybe you take the afternoon off, catch up on that work."

She nodded. "That sounds great. Except, I don't actually have work. But I'll call Slater and see if he wants to do something."

His expression soured. "You lied to Jack Allen?"

"I don't date clients, Daddy, potential or otherwise. And it's obvious he's looking more long-term than a coffee date. I saw an interview with him online last month that said he's 'looking for Ms. Right' now that he feels successful in his business."

"Of course, you're right. But this Slater thing—this reunion has turned social?"

Hope stopped short in the hallway outside the conference room. "I'm not sure. What would it matter if it had?"

"Slater caused you a lot of problems back in college, Hope. He was directionless, and he was pulling you off course."

Hope bristled. "Whose course?"

"You had responsibilities that you were ignoring because of him," Dan shot back icily.

"I also gave up a lot of things because of those responsibilities. What are you trying to say?" she said, exasperated.

"I want you focused," her father insisted. "It's of the utmost importance."

"You keep saying that, but you won't explain why."

At his stony silence, Hope relented. A sudden tightness between her eyes told Hope that, should she continue, she'd only be contributing to the headache that was forming. "Well, when you're ready to tell me what's going on, I'm here. Or, rather, I'll be across the lake."

Her father heaved a big sigh.

Hope reached out and squeezed his arm. "Daddy, look around you. Whatever's bothering you, you're missing out on a beautiful place. And I heard you had a good time over at the Cabins yesterday. Did I hear wrong?"

Her father was quiet, his face thoughtful. "No, no. You heard right. This is a lovely place. There's something about it that does charm a person, don't you think?"

Hope let the same distracting thoughts that had pulled her focus from the meeting rush back in. Firelight, rustling pines, and Slater laughing in the flickering glow. "There is."

"Have fun over there, Hope."

She narrowed her eyes at her father. "But not too much fun, right?"

His thin smile left her even more curious about what he was hiding. What was causing the worry behind his eyes?

Hope dashed a quick kiss across his cheek and strode down the hall. She dug her phone out of her pocket, but her finger hovered over the screen. The call she'd been planning on making stayed unsent.

It had been a long day, and Slater's attention had been pulled in a thousand directions. Unfortunately, none of them had been Hope's, and he'd been so overwhelmed with tasks that he'd lost complete track of how he ended up dragging his exhausted self toward the parking lot nine hours after walking through the resort lobby that morning. What a day.

He'd headed for cabin six and relaxed on the couch, waiting for Hope, drowsing a little. As he waited, Slater felt a new excitement fill him at the thought of seeing her. Something had changed last night in the time they'd spent together.

It was seven o'clock on the dot when Slater heard the front door ease open. He could tell that something was off, even before Hope spoke. Where she'd been dressed casually the prior day, now she'd come to their practice still in her work clothes. She still looked stunning in the understated burgundy skirt suit, but he couldn't help but notice that it added an air of detachment to her that he found curious. He looked down at his short-sleeved button-down and chinos. He felt underdressed.

"Hey," he said, standing. "How was your day? If I could boil water for pasta without burning it, I would have fixed you something, but did I bring the to-go menu from the Bean Pot, if you want to get some takeout."

"I've already eaten, thanks," Hope said, settling on the couch. She was carrying a notepad, the same one she'd had at the lakeside.

"Everything okay?" he asked, sitting back down next to her. His guitar was already propped against the couch arm, and he picked it up, slinging the strap over his head. "Bad day?"

"It was a little stressful, actually, and I'd rather not discuss it. Can we just get to practice, please?"

Slater was taken aback, but he didn't press her. Maybe it was the stress of the day. Maybe she was spooked after he'd grabbed her hand last night at the party. Maybe she'd been thinking all the same things that he'd said to Wyatt at the truck last night, and her distance was a reflection of that.

She doesn't really belong here. She has a life to get back to. She's only doing this as a favor.

"Sure." He turned to grab a book of sheet music from

the end table nearest him, flipping it open. "Want to practice the first-dance song again, or some of the later songs? Or, we could work on that original…"

She held up the notepad that she'd been holding in her lap. "I wanted to show you this. I thought we might be able to adapt the lyrics, or, you know, use it somehow."

Slater reached out for the notepad, meeting her eyes for the split second that she allowed it before she looked away. "You're writing music again?"

She laughed, short, dryly. "No. This is one of our old songs. It's the one I was singing in the piano room the night you asked me to help you. You said that Wyatt and Delaney sort of found each other again, and this seems to fit…"

A tingling feeling began at the base of his skull. He looked down at the neat, flowing handwriting on the lined yellow page.

No matter where we start,
A million miles or breaths apart,
The stars might burn and all go dark,
But I would still find you…

If every old love leaves a mark
A broken trail to lead our hearts
Then let this new love be the spark,
That lights the way to what's true
And I know this love can last
the storms that may

Slater ran his fingers down the words, his throat suddenly tight. He realized that she must not remember the circumstances surrounding this song. There was no way she could. If she did remember, but she'd been singing it in the piano room that night, and bringing it back up here, it would be a deliberate unkindness that he didn't want to believe her capable of.

"Do you remember when we wrote this song?" he asked thickly.

"No," she admitted. "I can't even remember the rest of the song. These are the only words that I could pry out of my memory."

Slater was able to draw a shaky breath. "Yeah, that's because this is all there is to the song."

"What?" Her eyes searched his face, her brow furrowed as she tried to sort out what he was saying.

"Hope," he said softly, "this is the last song we wrote together before we broke up. We never finished it."

Her eyes grew wide, and she bit her bottom lip. He could tell that she was holding her breath. Then, as she exhaled, her words rushed out, and her eyes were suddenly misting. "I'm so sorry. I didn't remember. How in the world could I not remember?" She reached out and took the pad from him, setting it aside, her hands fluttering in agitation as she turned back to him.

"You must think I'm being so cruel, to bring this. Honestly, I..."

"I know you didn't mean this as a jab. I know," he said, trying to soothe her distress. But he didn't reach for her—in fact, he stopped himself from it, though it was the very thing that he wanted. "And, let's face it, it was a long time ago. It wouldn't mean anything to you now."

He hadn't intended his words as a jab, but he could see by the way her eyelashes fluttered, the way she looked stricken for the briefest moment before recovering her composure, that she might have thought so.

"We can just work on the regular music tonight, if that's okay with you."

He nodded, strummed a few test chords on his guitar. Then, he launched into a twangy, fast, over exaggerated country tune. He bobbed his knee in time.

Hey there, pretty lady,
Let's turn this day around
Instead of getting dinner,
Let's get brownies by the pound

He finished with a fast flourish and grinned a silly *ta-da!* at her. "What do you say? I can have them brought from the Bean Pot. Maisie is the best baker."

Hope studied him for a moment, her eyes darting between the notepad—now on the side table by the couch—and Slater. Then, she nodded.

"Okay. But if we only get a pound, what are you going to eat?"

He was relieved to see her smile once again.

CHAPTER 12

NOSTALGIA NIGHT. WHILE THE IDEA for this wedding get-together was one that Slater had loved since its planning, the timing lined up poorly in reality. After last night's sharp reminder of everything he'd been trying to avoid thinking about in relation to Hope, nostalgia was the last thing he wanted to be steeped in.

But he was committed to being there for Wyatt and Delaney. So, giving himself one last look in the hall mirror that was in the small foyer of his house, Slater grabbed his keys from the set of hooks just to the right of his front door to start the trip to the Cabins. He slowed as he neared his Jeep, looking back over his shoulder at his small, ranch-style home. He was proud to own it, glad that the small nest egg he'd amassed before leaving his post-college engineering job had allowed him to buy the bungalow just two miles outside of Fairwood city limits. But something seemed different about the house, now. It felt somehow *empty*.

The drive took the same ten minutes that it always did, but Slater was so preoccupied that it seemed he'd arrived in no more than two. He parked in his usual spot around the back of the resort's main building, pausing and breathing deep for a few moments to try to shake himself out of his funk—a trick he'd learned from Ursula.

Once inside, Slater sat and watched as the guests at tonight's event milled around the central lounge, the same room where Hope's company had held their mixer the night he'd discovered that she was at the resort. Slater made the rounds, being social, and he talked with Delaney's old college roommate, Wyatt's high school football coach, and engaged in an interesting conversation with Aunt Tildy about how to properly season a pot roast—he really needed to learn how to cook—and he *still* wasn't free of constant thoughts of Hope. No matter where he turned tonight, he was *confronted* with thoughts of her.

Soft strains of old jazz filtered down from the speakers in the ceiling, and Slater admired the way the room had been transformed. With palm fronds tucked everywhere, heavy cream linen on the tables, and gold art deco touches, Slater could almost forget that he was at the resort. Almost. And he could almost get the image of Hope in that stunning powder-blue dress, looking like she'd stepped out of one of his heartsick post-breakup dreams, out of his mind. Almost.

Wyatt stepped up to the front of the room, raising a hand to get the attention of the crowd. He spoke into a handheld microphone, which made his voice carry all the way to the back of the large room. "Good evening, all!"

The murmur of conversation quieted and then stopped, and everyone turned to watch Wyatt. Slater, who sat at a back table, stood to make his way to the front of the room, shaking off his mood to join the rest of the group where they stood in a cluster near the front of the gathered guests.

On the way, he passed a variety of interpretations of the nostalgia theme—Delaney's parents were dressed in Ward and June Cleaver style, her Aunt Tildy was made up like a big-haired rocker straight out of an eighties MTV video, and other guests sported variations of every decade between. Slater had opted for a simple pair of dark jeans, rolled at the ankles, and a stark white T-shirt layered under a simple black leather jacket. As finishing touches, he'd tucked a pink bandana into his back pocket and combed his hair back with as much gel as he could. He hadn't had to fake the Kenickie sneer, with the mood he was in tonight.

Slater stopped next to Rachel, who silently held out her hand and offered him a piece of bubble gum. She had put together a Valley Girl costume, and he found himself grinning at her over exaggerated blue eyeshadow and neon legwarmers. He accepted the gum, popped it into his mouth, and watched as she blew a huge pink bubble of her own, letting it pop on her nose.

"Rachel!" Ursula chastised. The deco-dressed Ursula swiped back the feather that kept swaying forward from her flapper's headband.

"Whatever," Rachel said in a monotone, examining her nails. But she winked at Ursula, and Ursula swatted her playfully with a folded fan.

Maisie shushed them all gently as Wyatt started talking again. "First, I just want to say thank you for coming this week, and I hope you're all having a good time."

The assembled guests put up a cheer, and Wyatt grinned. "Good, good. Now, as you all may or may not know, Delaney and I—come on up here, sweetheart."

Slater laughed as Maisie gave a reluctant Delaney a gentle push toward Wyatt. Delaney turned and stood beside Wyatt, blushing slightly, looking pretty in victory rolls. Slater couldn't stay in his sour mood, not with two of his best friends standing up in front of the crowd, dressed in true Cary Grant and Rosalind Russell attire. They looked straight out of one of the classic black-and-white movies that the wedding party had seen over the weekend.

"Delaney and I would not be here if not for a lot of people, and many of those people are here tonight. But some people very dear to us can't be here."

The hush of the crowd went from ambient noise to complete silence.

"We called this nostalgia night so that we could take the chance to appreciate not only our pasts together, but also the people who got us here, who may not be with us any longer. My parents, for example—" Wyatt broke off, dropping the hand that held the microphone, drawing in a few deep, steadying breaths. Delaney slid an arm around him, hugging him close. Rachel was on his other side in the next heartbeat.

With a watery smile, Wyatt continued. "One of my biggest fears when the campground appeared on the reality show was that things would change so much around here that I wouldn't recognize the heart of the place anymore. That something would be lost. But that wasn't the case. I gained—we all gained—so much. And I know my mom and dad would be so proud of what we've created here."

The crowd applauded. Slater's chest felt tight. Despite his joy at seeing how happy everyone was tonight, he still carried an undercurrent of resentment from last night's unwelcome breakup reminder. How could Hope not remember that particular song? It made acid rise in the back of Slater's throat, and it had nothing to do with the sugary bubble gum that he was worrying between his molars.

He'd been pushing hard against all the old bitterness he'd felt after Hope had left—and wasn't this the very message that Wyatt had just delivered? Not in so many words, but Slater heard it loud and clear. *Time is precious. Take the chances life gives you.*

Slater watched as Iris and Larry, Delaney's folks, made their way up on stage. Wyatt and Del exchanged a look that Slater took to mean that they weren't expecting whatever the older couple were coming up to do or say. Iris grabbed the mic from Wyatt and stood next to him, while Larry slid next to Delaney, putting an arm around his daughter.

"Hey, wedding people!" Iris said, bubbly, bouncing on her toes as she waved out at the crowd. Someone even let out a loud, boisterous whistle. "I know that this is unexpected, but Larry and I have been talking, and..." Iris reached out and grabbed Wyatt's hand. Then, she teared up and started crying.

Wyatt's face registered immediate alarm, and he put an arm around Iris, drawing her to his side the way Larry had with Del. Before he could ask what was wrong, Iris raised the microphone back up. "Wyatt, you have been a blessing to our daughter, and we are so excited to have you as part of our family. We know that your folks can't be here, rest them, and so..." She heaved in a big breath. "I would love it if I could be your escort up the aisle on Saturday. I can't take the place of your own mama, but you should have *a* mama to take you up to that altar."

The celebrators went silent. Wyatt stared at his future mother-in-law. He lifted a fist to his lips, his forehead furrowing. Slater's heart squeezed in sympathy, empathy for his friend. Iris put a hand on Wyatt's cheek. He nodded, wordlessly pulling Iris in for a tight hug.

The crowd resumed clapping and cheering, a few people wiping at their eyes. Slater had to admit he felt a little misty himself. Delaney's dad pulled her over to Wyatt and Iris, and the entire foursome group hugged.

When they parted, Delaney grabbed the mic from her mother, sniffling and smiling.

"And now, the lovely and talented Alexandra Brent-Collingsworth will take the reins, as she is so good at, and lead all of us in some trivia. Remember that whoever wins gets a day at the resort spa!"

At Delaney's urging, Alex came up on stage. As Slater clapped and joined in on the cheering for Alex, who had gone all out on her disco dress and platform shoes, he wondered where Hope was. Could she possibly be as disoriented by the way last evening had ended as he was? Once Alex had taken the mic and started dividing the guests into teams, Slater took the opportunity to slip away.

He walked through the hallway where Hope had, coming to sort out the ballroom mix-up only days ago. It felt like a lifetime. He passed the front desk, waving to Amelia, who was checking in a guest, but still gave him a wave as he went by.

In the cool of the evening, Slater felt more clearheaded. Out under the portico, he took a few breaths of crisp night air and reached into his pocket for his cell phone. Pulling up Hope's number, he put his phone on speaker, hit the call button, and let it ring.

Out past the portico, in the dark beyond where he could see the familiar glow of the fireflies, he heard a ring. Then, another. A rectangle of light appeared, and he heard Hope's voice through his phone and drifting toward him, an echo that his brain couldn't quite make sense of for a few seconds. Then, once he understood what was happening—and that she didn't yet—he couldn't help but smile.

"Hey," she said, "I wasn't expecting to hear from you tonight. Don't you have another wedding party?" Her voice was light, but he could hear the edge to it, the uncertainty. Slater watched as the rectangle of light bobbed back and forth at the edge of where the parking lot met the tree line.

He took the phone off speaker and put it to his ear. "I do, but I wanted to call and make sure everything is okay after..."

She was silent on the other end. The rectangle of light stopped moving. Then she said, "Yeah, we're okay."

His heart did a little flip. She hadn't said, "I'm okay." She had said *we*.

"It hit me hard, Hope. And when you didn't remember, it felt like salt in the wound."

"I get it," she replied. "And I feel awful that I couldn't remember. I would never have done that to you, hurt you on purpose. Please know that."

He had to close his eyes for a moment, tell himself that she meant now—because he wasn't sure if he would have believed her, had she said that her leaving hadn't been intended to hurt. He wasn't quite over that heartache, no matter how much he worked to keep the tenuous truce they currently had intact.

He opened his eyes and took another deep breath,

stepping down off of the curb and walking out from under the portico toward her. "I do know that. It's why I'm calling. I can't make every single moment that we had back then matter to you. We might not have anything past this week. But we can make the days we have count, right?"

As he neared her, she turned and caught sight of him. After a brief moment of confusion, she smiled slightly and disconnected their call. "Have you been out here the whole time?" She swatted playfully at him.

Slater danced back, pocketing his own phone. "Maybe. It gets stuffy in those rooms with all those people. What are you doing out here, pacing around?"

She looked past him to the resort, as though she expected someone to come out the doors. "Same. Sometimes, these seminars get to be a bit too much."

"You have to be back anywhere?"

She shook her head. Before he could say anything else, she cleared her throat and said, "Slater, I want you to know that I never forgot you. I may have forgotten details, song lyrics, the way you took your coffee back then, but I never forgot you."

"Fair enough," he said softly, though what he wanted to say was, *Why didn't you come back, then?* But he knew the extenuating factors—and the passing of time, piled onto all the reasons she'd left in the first place, certainly made staying away easier. Their lives had become separate, to the point where, eventually, there was nothing they shared but fading memories.

"I knew this was going to be hard," she admitted. "But I don't think it's impossible."

"Apologizing?" he joked.

She snorted delicately. "Us being friends. Friendly. Spending time together."

"Nothing worth it is ever easy," Slater said—sagely, he thought. "Why don't you come in?" he offered.

She turned wide eyes on him, shaking her head fast. "No, I couldn't. I already crashed the party at the Cabins. Besides, is it a costume thing? You look—I mean, this look definitely works for you, but I don't have anything." She glanced down at her own outfit, which was a pair of dark jean capris and a gray tank. She wore simple white sneakers.

"It's perfect, actually. Here." He shrugged out of his jacket and swept it around her shoulders. She slipped her arms through the arm holes, her brow furrowing as she watched him. Reaching to his back pocket, he untucked the pink bandana. "Can you lift your hair?"

She paused for a moment, and her face was unreadable for a long second before she reached up and lifted the heavy blond waves from her shoulders. Twisting her hair into a makeshift bun, she held it with both hands and nodded at him. Slater unfolded the bandana, refolded it several times so that it was long and flat, and stepped closer to her.

It was only when he was leaning down that it occurred to him that the move might be a bad idea. As he slipped the cloth around the back of her neck and threaded it through her raised arms to tie it, kerchief-style, around her neck, his cheek nearly brushed hers. He could smell her perfume, something summery and sweet that reminded him of honeysuckle and peaches and long-lost, carefree days.

"There," he said, ignoring the hoarseness in his voice and hoping she would do the same. When he pulled back, her eyelashes were shuttered, eyes half-closed, and he could see a blush darkening her cheeks.

"Thanks," she whispered.

"Costume, check," he said, taking a few steps back and letting the night air intrude. "Plus one, check." He made six-shooter fingers at her, adopting his most swagger-laden Grease accent. "I think I'm ready to go back to the party, pretty lady. How 'bout you?"

Hope clutched at the edges of his leather jacket, which was many sizes too big. It made her look delicate—and the expression on her face added to her sudden air of vulnerability. The combination worked to convince him to reach out and draw her into him. But he resisted. The truce was back, but it was still tenuous.

"Wyatt and Delaney would love to get to know you more. And Rachel is wearing the most ridiculous eyeshadow. The rest of the gang is in there, and they are probably down a person on their trivia team..."

"I like trivia. Are there snacks?" she asked.

"So many snacks. All era-themed." He crooked his elbow and offered her his arm. She closed the few steps between them and wound her arm in his.

As they walked back toward the front of the resort, Slater added, "We skipped the sixties, though. They put too much strange stuff in gelatin molds."

His heart thrilled at the sound of her laughter ringing through the darkened pines.

CHAPTER 13

T HE FUNNY THING ABOUT RAIN checks was that people who asked for them often tended to cash them in. And the fact that Jack Allen was one of those people didn't surprise Hope. What did surprise her was where she ran into him—literally colliding with him while she took an early-morning jog around the resort.

It really was entirely her fault. She'd been caught up in the feeling of being outdoors before the rest of the resort was awake; though she'd passed a few staff members on her way out, the halls had otherwise been quiet, and the cool dew and slightly gray sky that had greeted her had added to the cocooned atmosphere. It definitely looked like rain, but she relished the chance to run, to think in solitude.

After stretching, Hope had started up her music and popped in her earbuds, taking off at a brisk clip through the trail she'd chosen from the resort map. The morning had been windless, but Hope had known, looking up into the leaden sky with its ominous colors, that she didn't have long before a summer storm moved in.

The smell of damp moss and pine needles had surrounded her as she'd entered the trees and made steady progress over dips and rises in the hard-packed earth. Concentrating on her breathing, she had checked the heart monitor on her watch and pushed a little harder, run a little faster.

The trail had opened into a meadow, and Hope had slowed and stopped, breath catching at the sight that unfolded on either side of the trail ahead. The sky above seemed endless. Minimal sunlight managed to get through the spectrum of dark clouds spreading in a billowing, ragged scroll across the sky as far as the eye could see, but Hope could still appreciate the shadowed beauty of the clearing. Knee-high grass waved at either side of the trail, and wildflowers dotted the carpet of dark green that flanked the path, all the way to where the valleyed meadow rose on the opposite side to disappear again into the woods. On a clear day, this place would have looked like paradise, something straight out of a painting, and she'd imagined the sky clearing into a crystal blue, interrupted only by the occasional cottony wisp of a cloud.

And then she'd imagined Slater beside her on this perfect, imaginary day.

When a slow, low rumble of thunder had rolled out across the expanse, Hope had hit the button on her earbuds once more, determined to finish the trail before the rain started. She'd made it quickly down into the dip of the meadow, and she had been coming up the other side, just at the edge of the forest, when she'd run into Jack.

The impact didn't seriously injure either of them, but it did send Hope tumbling over, falling backward to sit, hard, into a thick mulch of leaves, pine needles, and pinecones. Instinctively, she had put her hands out behind her to cushion the fall.

And in that mulch of forest bits was where she currently sat.

"Are you okay?" Hope looked up to see Jack hovering above her, his handsome features pinched with concern.

She sat for a moment, trying to feel if there was anything majorly amiss.

"Yeah, I think so."

He reached a hand down, and she took it. He pulled her up slow. "Careful. Easy. Are you sure you're not hurt?"

There was a stinging in the palm that he hadn't grabbed, and she looked down to see that her hand had been slightly abraded during the fall. And her knee on the same side was skinned. "I'll survive," she assured him, wincing slightly.

"I'm so sorry. I had my music going, and I wasn't looking up."

"Me, either," Hope admitted. "Are you okay?"

Jack patted the front of his blue T-shirt and down either side of his black running shorts. "All in one piece."

"Good." Hope let out a breath that she'd been holding. "My father would have killed me if I'd run down his favorite potential client." But she said it with a smile.

His laughter was low and easy. "Your father's? I was hoping I was your favorite potential client."

Hope floundered for a response, feeling her cheeks heat. "Mr. Allen, of course you are. Any firm would be lucky to earn your business."

"Is there a but there?" He put his hands on his hips and stuck a leg out, leaning to stretch his calf.

"But, if I can be frank with you, I get the impression

that your coffee invitation was more than just for business talk. I don't date clients, and I certainly wouldn't want you to think that I was doing so to get you to sign with Beacon." She flexed her scraped hand, feeling the sting again.

His wide smile revealed even, white teeth and a single dimple in his left cheek. Hope wasn't entirely unaffected by the power of that dimple. "I see. Well, I certainly wouldn't insult you by suggesting that you would use my interest in you to your advantage. And your father did hint that you'd be taking over Beacon Financial soon, so am I right that you won't be directly handling any of my accounts or interests?"

Hope couldn't find her voice for a moment. Clearing her throat, she replied, "If I were running Beacon, no, I wouldn't be handling any client account directly."

Why in the world would her father have told Jack Allen that she would be taking over Beacon soon? She recalled how evasive and mysterious her father had been in the past few weeks, and her heart squeezed. She would need to have a serious talk with him.

"Good," Jack said, "I trust that you would be ethical, regardless. You're obviously brilliant, beautiful..."

Hope looked down at her sneakers, feeling her blush deepen. "Mr. Allen."

"Please, call me Jack. And unless you have any objections beyond our potential future business relationship..."

Above them, thunder rumbled again, and a few heavy drops of rain fell.

"Come on!" Hope pointed back the direction she'd come from. "You're headed that way anyway, and I think it's a shorter run back."

The two of them took off to double back over the trail that Hope had just covered. In a few minutes, they were back at the front entrance to the resort, and they made it over the small bridge that led to the doors, slipping under the portico moments after the sky opened up. The bellhop, sheltered under the same awning, took in the drenched guests and hurried to get them towels.

Hope and Jack shook as much water from their hair and clothes as they could, and both accepted the towels that the young man who'd gone to retrieve them offered, momentarily. Once they were dry enough not to cause a mess, Jack draped the towel around his neck and held the front door for Hope. She looped her own towel in the same fashion and shivered slightly as she entered the air-conditioned interior of the resort lobby.

Jack stilled next to her and put a broad, warm palm on her upper arm. "You'd better go get into something dry before you catch cold," he said. Hope's skin tingled where his hand curved around her arm.

At the sound of a throat clearing, Hope looked up. Slater stood in front of the check-in desk, looking half amused and half disgruntled. Hope stepped forward, away from Jack's too-familiar gesture. She closed some of the space between Slater and herself, feeling rather than seeing Jack trail after her.

"Slater, hey. I'm glad you're here. Jack and I—"

"Jack?" Amusement was chasing away much of the other emotion in Slater's face, and Hope got the distinct impression that Slater was trying now to mess with her, ever-so-subtly. Slater stuck out a hand. "You must be Jack, then."

Jack Allen shook hands with Slater. "I am, indeed." Hope saw Jack eye the embroidery on Slater's polo. "Nice to meet you...Slater. You manage this place? It's impressive, I must say."

"Thank you. We try. Now, Hope, you and your friend here did what?"

Hope held up her scraped palm. "We had a little collision on the trail."

Slater closed the last two steps between him and Hope and gently took her hand, flipping it and examining her palm. He stroked a thumb over the place where her wrist started, just short of where an angry red scrape marred her skin. Despite the fact that she'd warmed at Jack's previous attention, Hope instantly forgot that Jack Allen was standing next to her.

She tried not to focus on the long, dark-gold lashes that were half-closed over Slater's eyes as he examined her hand. He blew out a breath, looking up through the same lashes to catch her staring at him. The ghost of a smile that edged the corners of his lips let her know that she'd been busted.

"Yikes. I've got a first-aid kit in my office. Why don't you let me disinfect it?"

Hope could only nod dumbly. She turned to look at Jack. "So, I'll catch you later?"

Jack's eyes ping-ponged between Slater and Hope, and Hope could only guess that he was trying to work out the dynamic between the two of them.

"Absolutely," Jack said smoothly. "I would say you owe me a rain check, but that might be a little too spot-on." Outside, as if at the command of the tech mogul, thunder rolled sinuously. Jack nodded politely at Slater and headed toward the elevators at the far wall of the lobby.

Slater crooked an eyebrow at Hope. "Come on, kid, let's get you cleaned up."

Hope followed Slater to a hallway she'd not noticed before that sat to the left of the front desk, all the way down to the end, where a heavy oak door opened up into a spacious, light-filled office. He waved her to a set of leather wingback chairs that sat flanking a small fireplace, and she sat down, sinking into the butter-soft seat and surveying the rest of the office. An antique-looking desk took up the far side of the room, backed by a wall of bookcases with the appropriate thick leather books and tchotchkes lining the shelves. There was even a little replica of one of the cabins from across the lake that sat at eye level.

Wow," she said. "My office isn't this big, and my dad owns the place."

Slater chuckled as he sorted through a desk drawer. "All Alex's doing. This office was built before I was promoted, and she has grand-scale taste. I'm rarely in here. I like to spend most of my time out on the property, when I can."

The light here was dim and gray now, raindrops making a serious effort against the picture windows, but she could imagine the room lit with warm, afternoon light—much the way she had been able to see some idyllic future summer day in the meadow on the trail. An idyllic day spent with the man who was currently pulling the other wingback chair close, a small first-aid kit in hand.

"So, your friend Jack..." Though Slater's tone was soft, Hope could hear the ever-so-slight edge to it. She titled her head to look intently at him, but his head was down, and he was opening the small red zipper case, giving it an inordinate amount of attention.

"Hmmm? What about my friend Jack?"

"Seems like a nice guy. You work together?" There it was again—the very slight-but-obvious strain that told her he was trying hard to sound as though he were making casual conversation. He bit his lip, apparently intent on deciding between two square, sterile packages.

"Slater." Hope matched her volume to his. Now they were both speaking low and a little slow. It fit, she thought, with the cloistered feel of the office, the way the rain made everything seem close and profound. His eyes flicked up, locked on hers.

"Jack Allen is a potential client. My father is dying to win his business."

"Oh."

"Were you jealous?" She dipped her head to meet his eyes again when he dropped his at the question.

His short, soft laugh belied his embarrassment. "No, no, not at all."

"A little," she challenged.

Slater nodded almost imperceptibly. "A little. Let's have a look, then."

She turned her palm over, and he ripped open a packet of antiseptic and used the small cotton square inside to dab at her hand. She cringed at the contact. "Sorry," he said, grimacing. "Looks like you'll live, though. Your knee is way worse."

He rifled through the first-aid kit again and unearthed two Band-aids and another antiseptic wipe. He opened the antiseptic, and the strong smell of it reached Hope's nose. Slater lifted her calf onto his knee and took out the cotton wipe. He held it up for her to see.

"Okay, this might be rough, but we can get through it together," he joked.

"You always did stick by that motto," Hope teased back.

Slater's free hand stilled, resting on her shin, and he looked at her, his face suddenly serious. He swallowed before saying, "You know, I wish we could have found out if it held true."

He looked so wistful in that moment, so utterly and hopelessly melancholy that Hope wasn't sure what to say. She reached for him, putting a hand against his cheek. He didn't drop his eyes. He didn't break their gaze.

Time seemed to still. The gray light dimmed a bit more, and the sound of the rain pelting at the window grew even harsher and more insistent. But here, in the shelter of Slater's office, Hope was only aware enough of the outside world to know that she was safe from the storm. She wasn't too sure about her inner turmoil, though.

Slater's breath, like their speech, had slowed. Hope could hear it, even over the contrasting increase of her own heartbeat. He seemed to be thinking, but whatever decision he was laboring under didn't trouble him for long. Hope couldn't take her eyes off of him as he began to lean closer to her in small degrees, his eyes on hers, giving her lengthy seconds to turn away. And she didn't pull away. Her hand slid to the back of his neck, her fingers threading in the soft hair at the nape of his neck.

"I never stopped caring about you," he whispered, so close that she could feel the words in a rush against her cheek. "And no matter what would have happened, I would have stayed by your side."

She could only nod in small, jerky movements, too caught up in the spell of his moss-gold eyes, their pupils dark and wide. "I know," she whispered back. And then, she gave a degree from her side. They were so close now that all she had to do was turn her head a fraction more, and all he had to do was meet her, and their lips would touch.

Hope held her breath. She turned her head a fraction more.

A sudden, sharp sting at her knee made her jerk back.

"Ouch!"

Slater sat up straight, looking confused. He glanced down at his hand, at the antiseptic wipe that he still held. Realization dawned. "Oh no. I am so sorry. I must have brushed your knee." He bent over and blew on her still-stinging kneecap. Her eyes watered.

She met his apologetic look with one she hoped would reassure him. Patting his wrist, her heart still racing, she said, "It's okay. Let's, um, let's get it over with, anyway." She pointed to the Band-aids that still lay on the arm of his chair.

He nodded and held out his free hand. She took it in hers and squeezed, turning her head away to avoid knowing when the next sting would come. He was gentle, but the antiseptic was even harsher on full contact. He followed quickly with the two Band-aids, covering her scrape.

"Thanks," she squeaked, still waiting for the throb under the bandages to subside—and still waiting for her heartbeat to slow.

"No problem," he assured her. Then, he was packing up the first-aid kit and standing, and with the distance between them, she was able to regain some of her composure. She did feel chilled again, though, as if the dark and gloomy sky was reaching chilly fingers through the glass, invading the warmth that they'd created between them.

After he'd stored the first-aid kit, he came back over and studied his work. "Prognosis is good," he said simply, smiling.

"Thank you. I was worried for a minute there." She had been afraid that, after the moment that had just passed, he would withdraw again, or she would, and they'd have to walk on eggshells, on repeat, until the week ended. But he seemed fine. And she felt fine—not even like bolting.

"So what are your plans for today?" he asked, leaning back in the chair across from her.

"Well, there's seminar chaos all day long, but I think I'll be meeting up with a pretty special guy tonight for this music thing..."

The shine in Slater's eyes reassured her that he didn't regret whatever had been about to happen moments before. "Oh? Do I know him? Is he cuter than me?"

Hope stood, shaking her head. "Definitely not."

Slater stood as well, stepping close and grabbing her uninjured palm. With his free hand, he brushed her cheek with the backs of his knuckles. "Hope, I don't know what we're doing here, and I don't know what happens beyond this week, but I know that it's meant the world to me to see you again."

She nodded. "You, too."

He leaned forward and kissed her softly on the cheek. "And I'll see you tonight?"

She nodded, untangling her fingers from his. "Cabin six, seven sharp."

The alarm on her watch rang out, signaling that she

should be dressed and on her way out of her room to the seminar's breakfast meet and greet. With one last look between Slater and the sheeting rain at the window, Hope turned and left. She had to fight hard not to look back.

CHAPTER 14

THE SPA AT THE CABINS in the Pines Executive Resort rivalled any that Hope had ever been to in the city. There was soft music playing, and she leaned back in the soft pedicure chair, her eyes rolling with pleasure as she sunk her feet into the warm, massaging foot bath. After all the time she spent in heels, she was always ready to jump at a little pampering. So when Annie had decided to catch a nap rather than accompany her, Hope had come alone.

She had found the Cabins in the Pines ladies already at the spa, indulging in early-morning wedding nail prep, and they had insisted she join them. This was the perfect treat before she had to jump back into her day at the seminar—something that was getting increasingly hard for her to slog through as the days rolled on.

"Isn't this place the best?" Delaney sighed beside her, seated in an identical chair.

"The absolute best," Masie agreed.

Hope opened her eyes to look lazily around the room. Much like the rest of the resort, it was impeccably done and looked more akin to a spa one would find in upscale

Los Angeles or New York than something that would operate out in the middle of the woods. The walls were muted, painted in a matte color that was soothing to look at. The lighting was low, and the room was kept slightly warmer than the outside resort.

The group sat in a row, feet all bare and submerged in foot baths. Across from where they sat, on the opposite wall, a row of big-screen TVs were mounted, and they showed a rolling assortment of naturescapes. Aside from the soft music that was playing over the ceiling speakers, there was also a white noise machine humming lowly on an occasional table at the back of the room. Hope thought she could have stayed the whole trip in the luxurious bathroom of her suite, but she was about to change her preference to the spa.

"This is pure heaven," Ursula crooned.

Alex, a few chairs down from Hope, leaned forward and spoke down the line to Ursula. "You didn't even want to come," she said, mock-accusatory.

"I did!" Ursula protested, wiggling deeper into her seat and turning up the massage with the remote in the chair arm. "I told you not to poke fun at me because my feet are ticklish."

Rachel plopped into the empty chair between Hope and Delaney. "If you really want to laugh," she said, "watch me get the *Lovestruck High* logo painted on my big toenails." She waved the three bottles of nail polish that she'd selected from the rack—bright blue, red, and lightning yellow.

"What's *Lovestruck High*?" Hope asked, picking up her coffee cup and peering over at her own pinky-peach paint selection and suddenly feeling pretty boring. Collectively, Alex, Maisie, and Delaney groaned.

Delaney answered first. "It's a reality show. Set in a high school. It's not even on the air anymore."

"Rachel was obsessed with it," Masie added, shaking a bottle of pale lilac polish. Then, as though she were purposefully changing the subject, she said, "Hey, do you guys want to get cinnamon rolls from the café delivered over here?"

Yeses rang down the line of spa chairs, and Masie picked up her cell phone to call.

Hope grinned and looked over at Rachel. "Who was he? The guy you crushed on in the show, I mean."

"Why would you think...?"

"There's always a crush," Hope sing-songed.

"His name is Scott. Scott Campbell." Rachel seemed to be looking at some spot far beyond the walls of the spa.

"Pretty dreamy," Ursula agreed, giggling. Maisie shushed everyone softly, talking for a moment with whoever picked up on the other end of her call.

Alex slapped the leather arm of her chair. "Okay. Sorry, girls, but I can't keep it a secret another minute. Not that I'm pleased that you put any reality show above my own—" she looked pointedly at Rachel "—but we have that actor's workshop this week at the resort, and it's called Camp Campbell. The young man who checked in as the organizer was rather handsome. Tall, blue eyes?"

Rachel had gone as white as a ghost. She fumbled at the side pocket of the spa chair, coming up with her phone and tapping at it frantically. When she'd found what she was looking for, she turned her phone, thrusting it out toward Alex. "Is this him?"

Alex squinted at the phone. "That's him. And we were going to wait until you had your spa day to surprise you, but there's an open Q and A he's holding in the ballroom later."

Rachel's eyes shot to Delaney. "*Mom.* I have nothing to wear. I need to...I..." She ended on a squeak.

"*Walk* to the resort gift shop and get that dress you've been eyeing. I had Amelia set it aside in your size last week. Go on," Delaney said, sitting up and grabbing for the polish bottles that Rachel practically flung at her while splashing out of the foot bath. Rachel jammed her feet into a nearby pair of sandals, and was through the door faster than Hope could figure out what was going on.

"Don't ask all the questions," Delaney shouted at Rachel's retreating back. When Rachel was gone, Delaney relaxed again, setting aside the nail polish. "So much for walking to the gift shop."

Hope looked over the group as they all chuckled, and she marveled at the closeness that was evident between them. She felt a pang in her chest at how wonderful the relationship was between Delaney and Rachel especially; it made Hope think of her own mother, and how much she missed her.

"She's a great kid," Hope said warmly.

"She is," Delaney agreed. "Though not so much a kid anymore. Before I know it, she'll be off to college, and all I'll have is memories of summers at the lake and her forcing Wyatt and me to watch the Scott Campbell show."

Ursula hummed. Her eyes were closed, and it didn't appear to Hope that she was at all ticklish as the pedicurist began to massage her feet. "She'll always come home," Ursula assured Delaney. "This is where her family is."

"She made you and Wyatt watch *Lovestruck High?*" Hope grinned.

"More than once," Delaney said, eyes flaring wide. "And there are many seasons. I guess that was one of the signs that Wyatt was really falling for me. He tolerated bad reality TV. In more ways than one."

Alex pursed her lips. "This girl's day is turning a bit too sassy for my tastes."

"Calm down and get your nails done," Delaney said. "Or I'll tell Wyatt that one of the bridesmaids won't match the others on the wedding day."

Everyone laughed at that.

As the laughter faded, Hope said, "I'm sure there were many more signs that you and Wyatt were in love."

"That they both ignored." As soon as Maisie spoke, Delaney picked up a cotton ball from a nearby open container and tossed it at her friend. Maisie easily caught it.

"But how do you ever really know, right?" Even as she spoke, Hope's mind was drifting back to Slater's office. The soft gray walls of the spa were turning into cold glass with sheeting rain pattering against it. The way her heart had sped up in the moment right before she'd been sure Slater was going to kiss her had been the exact way it had always sped up in the past when he had kissed her. Years had gone by, but she was realizing that nothing had changed about the way Slater made her feel. And if she believed what he'd said today, nothing had changed about the way he felt for her.

But what was that supposed to mean at week's end?

"You don't," Delaney said simply. "Sometimes, you have to take a leap of faith and believe that it will all work out."

Silence fell, and after a while, more casual conversation took the place of the words that had sent Hope's mind spinning. She allowed herself to be pulled into discussion about the wedding, whether the weather would clear in time for the outdoor ceremony, and whether or not she had ever travelled to Hawaii, where Wyatt and Delaney were planning to take their honeymoon.

There were no windows in the room where they all sat, but though Hope chimed in on the lively chatter of the women around her, even offering some college-fund advice to her pedicurist once the talk turned to what Hope did for a living, inside, all she could hear was the low roll of thunder and the soft, swishing sound of the rain.

Slater watched through the window of the barber shop as Fairwood's Main Street ran with rainwater. At the corner he could see from the barber's chair, the rain ran so heavily that the drain at the curb seemed barely able to keep up, and water pooled at the edge of the street. Even though the weather outside was gloomy, Slater couldn't help but smile. There was a warm summer glow that had lodged itself in his chest this morning, and he hoped it wouldn't go away anytime soon.

Inside Joe's Barber Shop, the scent of Barbacide, leather, and sandalwood permeated the air. Wyatt and Slater took up two of the four chairs in the place, and Norman and Charles sat in the waiting area, next in line for pre-wedding haircuts, each engrossed in reading.

"What are you grinning at?" Wyatt asked from the chair opposite Slater, looking across with a confused expression on his face. "You really like a rainy day?"

Slater shook his head. Joe, who owned the place, was

trying to trim the back of Slater's neck, and when Slater moved, Joe tutted. Slater stilled, chastised. "Sorry!" Cutting his eyes to Wyatt, Slater answered, "I was thinking about the wedding, actually."

It was only a small fib. He had been thinking about the wedding, about Hope and how she would look in the soft, mint green dress that he'd had delivered to her room not an hour ago. Now, when they sang together, she would match the wedding colors—her dress would match his tie, too, and the prom-yness of that wasn't lost on him. It made him feel giddy in a way that he fully embraced.

"You were thinking about your wedding date," Wyatt corrected.

Slater threw up his hands—cautiously, in case the barber was coming in for another swipe. "True, true."

"So things are going well with the lovely Ms. Bergman?" Norman asked from his seat in the waiting area. "Don't tell Alexandra. She'll want to make a whole new episode out of you two. Second Chance in the Pines."

"I'd watch it," Joe said, bemused.

"Maisie really doesn't want to be on TV again," Charles said, looking up from his newspaper. "She said the months after our first Pines show aired were the most chaotic she's ever worked. I think the expression she used was, 'busier than a moth inside a mitten.'"

"Well, we have plenty of staff now," Norman said. "Why not?"

"No, no, no," Slater said, "I think we're jumping the gun here a little. It's nice to see Hope again, and it's been great spending time with her, but don't go planning our wedding here anytime soon. We've already had Charles and Maisie get hitched lakeside, and now you and Del."

"Three's a nice number," Wyatt said. "Great things come in threes. *Musketeers, Amigos…*"

"*Stooges,*" Joe chimed in.

"*Men and a Baby,*" Charles finished.

"Good ones." Wyatt looked impressed. "Tell him, Joe. He's missing out. The life of the married man is a good one."

Joe tipped his client's head to the side and trimmed expertly around one of Slater's ears. He paused, thoughtful, and then shook his clippers as he spoke. "It's not a bad gig," Joe agreed. "Got a beautiful wife and two awesome kids. Wouldn't trade them for anything." Joe's smile was soft and sentimental, and he paused for a moment. Slater knew he was picturing his family.

Wyatt pointed at Joe. "See? Joe has got it made. But, Slater, you're right. It's unfair of us to foist immeasurable happiness upon you. Guys, let's not wish him undying love and matrimonial security for his heart of hearts. That would be wrong."

Joe snorted with laughter and resumed cutting Slater's hair.

Slater squinted at Wyatt. "Cool it, Groomzilla. I see how you're up late fretting over the particular green of the chair ribbons. If that's what it takes to get to undying love, I might skip it."

Wyatt shrugged. "There are many shades of green. And I see one of them in your eyes, my friend."

Norman guffawed and went back to the magazine he'd been reading. The barber working on Wyatt finished with his haircut and leaned his chair back, applying a steaming towel to his face. Slater closed his eyes as, moments later, he was put into the same position.

As Slater was enveloped in the steam of the towel, he let himself relax, let himself drift back to the morning and how close he'd come to kissing Hope. He let the scene play out in his mind again, examining every detail, reliving the widening of her cornflower eyes, the softness of her hair as it had brushed his jaw when he'd been a breath away from her lips.

If he was being honest, he was a little envious of what Charles and Wyatt had found with their wives. And he could imagine himself with Hope—but forever? He was afraid to think about it, afraid to let his heart get tangled up in her too deeply again. He had been telling the absolute truth this morning, that he had never stopped thinking about her, wondering where or how she was, though he *had* deliberately avoided seeking her out, knowing that if she had rejected him again, the pain would be tenfold. He had never stopped loving the woman who'd cut him so suddenly out of her life.

So why had he let himself almost kiss her? Had it been a mistake on his part, something that would only cause more hurt when she left—which she would. He had no illusions about that. Her departure was in black-and-white on the booking screen at the resort.

So why was it not equally as stark in his heart?

Something in him wanted so desperately to fall right back into the rhythms of who he and Hope had been together that he'd felt powerless, unable to stop himself from leaning in close in the intimate atmosphere of his office. But they couldn't be. They couldn't ever go back, of course, and it was unlikely that he would see her again after her week was up.

Despite that truth, as the towel was lifted from his cheeks and light flooded his closed eyelids, Slater decided to hold onto the time they had left. He conjured an image of Hope in a soft, mint-green dress, and the warm summer glow returned.

CHAPTER 15

THE RAIN HAD EASED SOMEWHAT when Hope returned to her room. Out the sliding glass door that led to the small balcony, she could see that the sun was starting to filter more and more through the wisps of gray that remained. She could see larger patches of late-afternoon light making it to the wet ground, and what had been a downpour was now a light, sporadic mist.

She turned from the balcony and eyed the black garment bag that hung on the bathroom door. It had been delivered while she'd been at the spa, and she had been delighted to open it and find the dress inside. But she'd been even more thrilled by the note that had come along with it.

To Hope.
From your date to the wedding.

Something about seeing the word *date* made it all seem real. Of course, it was real, and Wyatt and Delaney would be getting married in two days' time. And then they would be beginning their official personal happily-ever-after. Though Hope had known them a short time, she could see the love reflected in their eyes when they looked at one another. They had the real thing.

Hope reached into the unzipped garment bag and worried the soft, silky fabric of the dress between her thumb and forefinger. What would she and Slater have, after the wedding week was passed and she headed back to her life, leaving him here to live his? Had they had the real thing back in college, and she'd let the pressures of life pull her away from it? The thought made her feel strangely empty inside.

Hope drifted over to her bed, sat down, and picked up the notepad that she'd set aside the previous night. She flipped the pages of scribbles, getting back to the page she'd left off on. She traced the words, much the way Slater had when she'd shown him the lyrics. She wanted to tell him that she'd continued working on them, but she was afraid to bring it up again.

Hope set the notepad on the nightstand again. There would be a time to tell him.

A knock sounded at the door, and Hope crossed her room in silent, bare feet to peer through the peephole. Annie stood outside, suited and ready to go. Hope looked down at her own casual clothes and knew she'd have to get a move on. There was no way that jean shorts and a T-shirt would qualify as work attire. This morning had been fun, though. She wiggled her freshly painted toes, admiring her new pedicure.

At the second knock, Hope jolted out of her distracted thoughts and opened the door, letting Annie in even as she turned to head toward the bathroom.

"Hope!" Annie's eyes ran over Hope head to toe, and

the resulting expression was not heavy with approval. "You're not ready! Your father is already grumbly because you've been so scarce the past few days. If we are late, he'll blow a gasket."

Hope yanked out her ponytail holder and grabbed her makeup bag, which was sitting on the bathroom counter. "I know, I know. I'll be ready in fifteen minutes!"

She was out of the shower and dressed in eight. With Annie's laser stare on her, Hope rushed through a quick messy bun and a swipe of lip gloss, grabbing her briefcase just before she was sure that steam was going to come blowing out of her assistant's ears.

Despite the rush, there was an extra skip in Hope's step as they entered the conference room where today's opening workshop would take place. She was, again, a little sick of seeing these four walls—even if they were stylishly done. She saw her father at a far table, deep in conversation with Jack Allen, and Jack's flirtation from this morning came rushing back. Jack saw them and waved, and her father turned to see that they'd arrived. He checked his watch, and his lips pressed together into a thin line.

Hope checked her own watch. Miraculously, they were five minutes early.

"Let's go make sure all of the printed materials are in order and ready to go," Hope said. Annie gave her a quizzical look, but didn't question her—about that. When they were on the far side of the room, though, Annie launched not-so-subtly into a line of questioning that Hope got the distinct feeling she'd been saving up over the past couple of days.

"Where have you been disappearing to around this

place?" Annie's voice was light, but Hope could read the mischief in her friend's eyes.

"Well," Hope said, "since I'm helping out at the wedding, I went and got my nails done early this morning—"

"You went to the spa without me!" Annie gasped and mock-glowered.

"I got you a gift certificate for an hour-long hot rocks massage, a full mani-pedi, and something they call the 'organic milk and honey facial.'"

Annie, who was counting stacks of printouts, heaved an overwrought sigh. "Okay. I guess you're forgiven. But one morning polish does not account for your whereabouts for all the other missing pockets of time. Not that you can't have your own time. I'm just curious."

"About who I'm stealing pockets of time with?"

Annie grinned.

Hope had to admit that it was unusual for her to be so socially active during a seminar. On many other business trips, and at Beacon's seminars over the last several years, Hope had always stuck with her father and Annie. She hadn't had any desire to do much socializing. It was all business, and so she never sought out any fun. But this year, all she thought about during the business bits was the time she could be spending with Slater and the warm, welcoming group across the lake.

"If you must know, I've practiced with Slater every night since he asked me to help sing at the wedding. And I've been to a wedding event...or two."

"Good for you!" Annie whooped, and, more quietly once Hope shushed her, "You met his friends? What are they like?"

"They're lovely. I can see why he wants to help make

the wedding perfect. Everyone I met is so nice. They're like a little family."

"And that garment bag in your room?" Annie prodded, marking a tally on the small notepad she was using the keep track of the handouts.

"Slater sent that over. It's so I'll match the wedding party." Hope felt the uncontrollable smile that spread over her lips—and she didn't even try to control it.

"Girl, you've got it bad," Annie teased. They'd finished counting, and Annie ticked her pencil down the paper. "Looks like we have plenty of paper packets."

The first attendees were trickling into the room, and Annie nodded toward the rows of tables and chairs that were laid out facing the semi-circular speaking area. "Let's drop these at each place."

"Good idea. That might keep me from having to talk to my dad or Jack right now. And remind me to tell you about running into Jack Allen this morning." Hope held up her scraped palm.

The two women made short work of distributing the workshop packets, and soon the day was underway. Thankfully, her father had meetings scheduled with some of the bigger clients who were attending the seminar, and so he slipped out of the workshop soon after it began. Hope wouldn't have to answer any questions about where she'd been spending her free time—yet.

But his meetings also reminded Hope that she had intended to question her father further about why Ralph Murphy wasn't attending. Usually, her father and Ralph had several long lunches at whatever swanky location the seminar ended up at each year, and Ralph's absence—as her father's friend, and not just his client—was even more apparent now that Hope remembered that.

Every evening, one of the things that she'd made note of was that her father didn't stay at the evening mixers, which used to be one of his favorite parts of the seminars. Instead, he would wish them all good night after the last event of the day and retire to his room. After the second night that Hope had returned to her own room, after practice with Slater, and her knock at her father's door had gone unanswered, she'd stopped trying. He was closing himself off for some reason, and they needed to talk.

And Jack Allen would be one of the topics of conversation. She was determined to ask her father why he'd spun the tale about her taking over Beacon Financial soon.

"Hope, I trust that you're okay after our little run-in this morning?" Flashing an engaging smile, weaving through the crowd, and dodging staff carrying drinks and platters of appetizers, Jack was the picture of debonair when he approached Annie and Hope a few hours later, at that afternoon's mixer.

Hope set her wine glass aside and, avoiding his gaze and focusing instead on his sharply knotted blue tie, she turned her left palm up so that he could see. "It's a small scrape. But I invest with my right hand, so don't you worry a bit, Jack."

Even Jack Allen's laugh was handsome—deep, rich, and commanding enough that several other people turned around at the sound of it. And a few of them gave Jack appreciative glances. She met his eyes, and she was right in her prediction. He didn't just look at her—he focused on her. Jack's brown eyes were warm and direct when he was near Hope. So why, Hope wondered, did she harbor so little romantic interest in Jack? He was obviously interested in her. And anyone would be thrilled to be seen on his arm.

He made a show of examining her hand, and once he deemed her okay, he folded her fingers back gently into her palm. Then, Jack took a sip from his own wine, swirling the red left in his glass as he spoke. "Now that I know you will survive, I was hoping to cash in that rain check. Tonight?" His expression was hopeful.

Hope shook her head. "I can't tonight—" His face fell. She felt awful, turning him down again. If he was going to be a client of Beacon Financial, at least she could extend a friendly gesture. As long as they were clear that it wasn't a romantic meeting. "Actually, what about something late this evening? I can't do dinner because I have plans, but would you like to grab some dessert after? I hear the cheesecake is fantastic at the steakhouse here. And I'm happy to answer any questions you might still have about Beacon."

Jack's face lit up. "That sounds marvelous. I can meet you there."

"How about nine?"

"Perfect." With a nod to Annie, Jack turned and left, but not before pulling aside a circulating staff member and snagging two fresh glasses of white wine for Annie and Hope. He placed them with a flourish on the table they stood at, and then, with a wink, he was gone.

Once Jack was out of earshot, Annie let out a low whistle, shaking her head. "Are we in a love triangle situation here? Because I need to know if I should be Team Slater or Team Jack. Or, if you're undecided, I could wait until the season finale and the dramatic conclusion..."

Hope scrunched her nose and shook her head. "I think this place has seen its fill of reality TV. And definitely not Team Jack. I mean, he's very cute, accomplished, wealthy, charming—"

"You're bringing me onboard the Team Jack train, Hope."

"And he's a client."

Annie wagged a pen at Hope. "Right. Smart."

"As for Team Slater, the jury is still out. I mean, it's been a fun week, and he's a really great guy, but—"

"Not sure if the past should stay in the past?"

Hope bit her bottom lip. "It's complicated."

Annie nodded, waving at one of the day's previous workshop attendees as he left. "It always is, honey. It always is. And can I come with you tonight, to this party thing? Or is it only for wedding VIPs?"

Hope's phone chimed, and she picked it up and swiped to notifications to see that Slater had texted. *See you at seven?*

"I'm not sure. I'd love it if you would, though. Let me ask." She texted back quickly. *How about six? Is that too early? And can I bring a friend?*

His reply came just as speedily, and she couldn't help but smile again. *I'll meet you now, if you miss me.* She watched as the trailing dots on her phone ran in a loop, waiting for whatever it was that he was about to send. *And, of course, you can bring a friend. Unless it's Jack.*

You are jealous, she shot back.

Nah. I'm very secure. Moonlight, a campfire, you and me under the stars. How could you trade anything for that? His text came with a moon, campfire, and twinkling stars emojis.

I don't think I could top that, she assured.

Unfortunately, duty calls. Six is great. And, yes, bring Annie. See you then, little songbird.

Same here. Off to work I go. Hope sent a disgruntled emoji and tucked her phone away. Her silly grin was back. She could feel it. After a moment's pause, she fished her phone out, opened the message app, and brought up their text thread. Her index finger hovered over the onscreen keyboard.

I do miss you.

She backed the words off of the screen.

I think we should talk tonight.

The text sat, unsent, looking way too benign to sum up what was going on in her head. Hope wanted to tell him that she still loved him, but fear of diving in that deep—and after only just reconnecting—stopped her for the moment. He hadn't said he still *loved* her. He had said he still *cared.*

Hope deleted the text and slid her phone back into her pocket.

"Team Slater?" Annie queried.

"He somehow knew *you* were who I was bringing. And...Team Wait and See."

CHAPTER 16

THE ENTIRE CREW OF THE Cabins in the Pines, along with two new additions that Slater found had quickly settled in rather comfortably, were gathered around one of the large campfire areas at the campground. In a cleared circle of smooth, soft sand, felled logs circled a stacked-stone fire pit, serving as seats around a roaring fire. Evening was falling, and the smell of burnt sugar and wood smoke filled Slater's nostrils as he bit into his second s'more since they'd arrived. The sounds of the birds and scuttle of forest creatures was quieting, and Slater could hear the crickets rising, at first in jarring nonpatterns, and then in mysterious, unexplainable synchronicity. He couldn't have asked for a better setting. Or better company.

The murmur of conversation around the campfire grew loud and more jovial, and Hope's voice rang above the others. "That was not how you proposed!"

Slater could tell that Hope was trying to keep the disbelief out of her voice, and he put up a hand before Wyatt could jump in to explain the story that had just been retold to the group. Slater's first instinct—after the urge to laugh—was to run interference for his friends.

"Now, to be fair, it was a group idea," Slater told Hope. He had to bite his lower lip to keep from laughing.

Hope's eyes were locked on Wyatt, who was also trying to hold in his laughter, and failing in short bursts. Hope waved her stick at him—complete with skewered marshmallow. "But aren't you obsessed with old movies? Couldn't you have pulled some grand gesture out of one of those?"

The whole group gathered around the campfire was in stitches. They all knew this story by heart, as it had been repeated many, many times—in a wistful, romantic manner by Delaney and in fits of laughter by the others as a way to tease Wyatt fondly. But they still wouldn't miss an opportunity to recount it to the two newcomers. Especially not on this last night of wedding festivities before the serious countdown to the walk-down-the-aisle began. The wedding guests were all off enjoying the property, and tonight's planned get-together—which was set up to mimic Wyatt's proposal to Delaney—included only the inner circle. To Slater, it felt like the last time they'd all be able to truly relax until the hectic hustle and bustle of the wedding was over. And it felt good to have Hope here. It felt right.

"Tell it again," Hope insisted, and beside her, Annie put a second marshmallow on her own skewer and examined the two treats closely.

"So, was the ring, like, between two marshmallows, and so she couldn't see it?" Annie asked.

Rachel was laughing so hard that she almost fell over backward off of the log that she was sitting on. Ursula and Charles, who sat on either side of her, caught her before she tumbled all the way back.

Wyatt looked over at Delaney pleadingly, and she only shook her head at him. "I'm sorry, my love. I was not in on the planning stages, so if your audience demands details, you're the one who's on the hook."

"Okay, okay." Wyatt relented, grabbing his s'mores skewer—one marshmallow—and holding it up for all to see. "There was one marshmallow per skewer, you see, but I had a bunch of them made up early. So they were already locked and loaded. The ring was on this one certain one, near the edge, so I could find it. I had the works set up, too. Champagne on ice, lights in the trees, these yahoos waiting in the woods to film the whole thing." Wyatt jerked a thumb at the assembled group.

Hope leaned forward, her own skewer still in hand, listening intently. Slater studied her—the soft, dark jeans and plaid button-up made her look relaxed, more approachable than a fancy dress or power suit. And the way her hair, down and loose, framed her face took Slater back years. So many, in fact, that he had to keep reminding himself of where and when they were.

Wyatt arced a hand in the air, setting the scene further. "Night was falling, the campfire was roaring, and the plan was to have Delaney choose one skewer—not the one with the ring on it. Then, I was going to pick up the one with the ring sitting gently on top of the marshmallow and say, 'I think this one is what you're really looking for.'" He lowered his voice on the last string of words, giving them a gravelly heft that set off another wave of hysterics around the fire.

Norman wheezed, trying to stop laughing long enough to catch a breath. Alex patted him on the back.

Wyatt looked wistfully off into the woods, and Slater thought he looked very noble, if a little put out, in the firelight of their current roaring campfire. "And then, I was going to get down on one knee and propose. And she would say yes. And we would have the video, filmed by Rachel, to remember it for the rest of our lives." Wyatt heaved a huge sigh. Delaney put a supportive hand on his knee.

"Oh, I have the video," Rachel explained. "And I will be showing it to future generations."

Wyatt looked pained.

"And then," Maisie prodded, looking extremely amused and anticipatory, even though she had both participated in and retold the story's ending over and over.

"Delaney, my only one, the keeper of my true heart, picked up the exact skewer where the ring was, and, without looking—I mean, who doesn't carefully examine their marshmallow before making a s'more? It's science!—she put it directly into the center of the fire."

"And the ring?" Annie was hanging on every word.

"It went, too," Delaney finished. "And that fire had been burning a while. I'm guessing that ring, when it fell off, plopped right down into the blue-and-white of those flames."

Hope slapped the log next to her outer thigh, mouth agape. "I don't believe it! What did you do?"

"I played it cool. I didn't say a thing. Luckily, the ring was insured, but the insurance people got a heck of a kick out of that claim report." Wyatt rubbed at the bridge of his nose, as though even the memory of the incident gave him a headache.

"And so you had to wait to propose again?" Hope popped her own skewer into the fire, and Slater watched the flames dancing in her eyes as she trained her gaze on the flaming confection.

"I did," Wyatt said. "But, you know what, no wait was going to deter me."

"And I would have waited forever for you," Delaney added. "Which I thought I was going to have to." Her eyes were teasing, like she was.

Wyatt and Delaney locked eyes, both smiled, and then leaned together for a sweet kiss. Sighs rose around the campfire—except for from Rachel, who made an embarrassed harrumph, but was still smiling.

"The best things are always worth the wait," Slater said, watching Hope as she pulled her stick out of the fire and blew out the flame. Her eyes flicked up and met his, and he thrilled inside when she blushed before dropping her gaze. If he'd asked, she would probably blame it on the heat of the fire.

The conversation turned from Wyatt's proposal mishap—to the obvious relief of Slater's friend—to discussion of the upcoming wedding. Rachel had a date to bring, which she was very closed-lip about, despite the cajoling from the circle of people around her. When the group gave up trying to pry the secret out of Rachel, everyone began detailing their attire and wedding-party responsibilities proudly to Hope and Annie, eventually ending with Wyatt and Delaney coaxing Annie to attend.

"Oh, I'm not sure," Annie demurred. "It's the night of our awards ceremony in the ballroom."

An answering cacophony rose, and they all passed the next stretch of time harrumphing over how Hope and Annie were working too much, and the beauty of the landscape was going unappreciated, and if they could only slip away for a few minutes...

Slater looked around at his gathered friends, and his heart warmed. He was proud of this small and eclectic family they'd created, and there was a deep, sure feeling in him that whispered for him to pay attention to how good it felt that Hope was—even if temporarily—a part of it.

When the marshmallows were gone, along with the last vestiges of the day, Slater tipped his head back to stare at the patches of night sky that he could see through the trees. Stars winked between branches, and the low breeze that was weaving through above swayed the pines, making Slater's glimpses of the stars an ever-changing palette.

Across the fire, Slater heard Rachel yawn. Delaney rubbed her daughter's back.

"Tired, honey? Why don't you go back to cabin eight? You can crash there until it's time to go home."

Rachel nodded sleepily. "That sounds great."

Maisie stood, jingling her keys. "I'll drive you, Rach. I think Charles and I are going to call it an early night." Charles stood and untucked a flashlight from his back pocket, flipping it on and miming a scary howl as he held the light under his chin. Masie gave him a playful bat on the shoulder, and then put an arm around Rachel's shoulder. They both followed the light-wielding Charles out toward the trail.

Wyatt got up and added a few logs to the fire. It blazed up, sending flickering orange-gold over the faces of every-one still sitting.

"So, who's up for ghost stories?" Wyatt asked, sitting down and wiping his palms on the knees of his jeans.

"Ohhh, love those!" Annie said, hopping from her

place beside Hope to sit next to the spot that Rachel had just vacated.

Ursula grabbed Annie's hand. "I'm not much of a ghost story gal, but I don't want to be a party pooper. I'll be sure to keep hold of some moral support." Beside Ursula, Norman offered his hand, as well.

"Not me," Hope said, standing. "I am a big ol' 'fraidy cat."

"That's true," Slater chimed in. "Back in college, she wouldn't even leave the dorm on Halloween night. We had a date in the food court, but only because everything between her dorm and the doors to it was lit with flood lights, and she ran to meet me."

"Well, why didn't you walk her from her dorm," Alex chided.

"I offered," Slater replied dryly. "She told me that we would draw more supernatural attention if there were two of us. She made me wait for her by the burger place on campus." When he saw that Hope wasn't sitting back down, he stood, too.

"How about that walk now?" Slater bent to reach behind the log he'd been sitting on. He picked up his guitar case and hefted it over his shoulder. "We can go down by the lake, and you won't have to hear any scary stories."

"That sounds nice," Hope agreed. "I wanted to talk to you about something, anyway."

Slater swore he could feel the laser focus of the six pairs of eyes that darted between them, sudden and intense.

"Okay," he said lightly, purposefully ignoring the others. "Let's do it." He gave a small wave, and managed only to have to look at Alex on his way out of the fire circle. Her expression was likely the same as that of every

196

other person still gathered—a mixture of curiosity, rapt interest, and encouragement.

As he and Hope left the campfire, she stumbled just outside the circle of dancing light that the flames threw onto the forest floor. He caught her with his free arm and regretted that he couldn't make out her face in the darkness as the move drew her close against him. There was a rustling, and a bright light suddenly shone directly into his eyes.

At his groan, she turned the flashlight on her phone away from his face. "Sorry!" she squeaked. Then, she put the phone under her chin so that the light shined up the way it had when Charles had used his flashlight. She made the same low, spooky howl that Charles had.

Slater grinned at her. "You know that's not scary at all, right?"

"I can turn off the light, then, if you want to walk to the lake in the dark." He let her go—slowly—and as they started down the path toward the docks, she waved her phone across the ground in front of them, lighting the way.

"You want the best man to fall and break a leg days before the wedding? That's all we need."

Hope shifted her cell phone to the other hand and reached for his free hand. She twined her fingers with his. "I won't let you fall," she assured him. "You're safe with me."

He was glad that the light from her phone spilled out in front of them. He knew she would tease him for the goofy grin that was plastered across his face.

Moments later, they were settled by the lakeshore. Here,

the moon was full and bright—and in combination with the soft lights that lined the dock, the area was lit enough that Hope had turned off the light on her phone. And just as well—she had *tsked* a bit at the sight of the low-battery indicator flashing on screen as she'd switched off. They sat in companionable silence on the grass shy of where it merged into sandy loam, both of them staring out across the ink-black surface of Lake Fairwood.

"You want to practice any?" Slater asked, looking over to study Hope's profile. He drummed his fingers in the surface of his guitar case.

"I think we have the regular music down," she said. Then, she cut her eyes over to him. "Still no new song, though."

"Yep." Slater grimaced. "I've been meaning to talk to you about that..."

She reached out and laid a hand on his knee. "Actually, that's what I wanted to come out here and talk to you about." He watched her as she reached into her back pocket and came out with a folded sheet of yellow, lined paper. Tentatively, she handed it to him.

"What's this?" he asked, almost afraid to open it. "You know, the last time you wrote me a note, it didn't turn out too well."

She laughed, but it was low and a little sad. "I remember. But this isn't that kind of note."

He started to unfold the paper, and she put up a hand, seeming momentarily nervous. "Just, before you open it, I want you to know that this week has been wonderful. Seeing you again, I thought it would be a disaster, and when you asked me to help you at the wedding, well, I honestly don't know why I agreed, at first."

Slater felt his eyebrows knit together. He was unsure

whether their conversation was about to take a turn for the worse, or make the yearning in his heart finally quiet after years without her. No, it was impractical. She wasn't staying. So why was everything in him hoping that she was about to confess she was falling for him again?

"It hasn't been a disaster, Slater. It's been really great."

With that, she dropped her hand, nodding for him to continue with opening the note. He was surprised to find his fingers shaking slightly as he unfolded the creased paper. The words swam on the page at first, and he almost reached for his own phone to add more light. But it wasn't the lack of light that was causing him trouble. He blinked a few times, taking a deep breath, trying to quiet his pounding heart.

"Hope, this is…"

"The song," she said. "I finished it." Her voice was tight, and even in the moonlight he could see that she was on pins and needles over how he would react. The last time they'd talked about this song, it had caused a lot of old memories and past hurt to resurface.

Before he could speak, she rushed on. "I want us to sing it at the wedding. It fits, you know? With the way Wyatt and Delaney came back together. And I thought that we should use it for something good. Something right. Rewrite all the things that it used to remind us of and make it into something that's a symbol of love. A gift, just like they are to each other."

Slater couldn't respond for a long stretch of heartbeats. His eyes danced down the page to the simple ending to the song. "I can't believe you did this."

"You don't like it?" she whispered. "It was a bad idea. Forget I even—"

"I love it." Slater could hear the thickening of his voice, and he swallowed back the emotion that was rising in his throat. "It's perfect." He blinked, finding that his eyes were stinging, and held out a hand, which she took. "And they'll love it, too."

His other hand was still trembling as he held the paper. She didn't let go of him, but scooted in close, so close that he lifted the arm on the side where they held onto one another and draped it over her shoulder. She leaned her head on his chest. Her elbow bent, and their entwined fingers rested on her shoulder.

The night sounds of the lake merged with the sound of Hope's slow breath, which fell in sync with Slater's—once his heart slowed down. He closed his eyes and listened, content in this moment, with this woman, and wishing it would never end. The crickets and bullfrogs sang a soft serenade, and the sound of the lake water gently lapping the shore kept steady time.

After a moment, Slater's eyes opened. He took the deepest breath of balmy night air that he could, and blurted the words that were swimming in his brain before he could think it through. "I don't want you to leave when this week is up, Hope."

Hope lifted her head, looked up at him. She seemed to be searching for a response, her eyes wide. "Slater, I don't know how that's possible. I mean, I told you that I have a life in a whole other city. My job, my father's company, responsibilities—"

"All of which pulled us apart before, Hope. But we deserve another chance, don't you think? You can't tell me that this week hasn't meant something."

He let the paper fall from his hand, distantly knew that it drifted down in the summer air to rest on his guitar case. He lifted his now-empty hand and placed it on her cheek, keeping her gently in place. Even in the wash of the moon, her eyes were huge, endless pools of summer. Like the sky above the trees, in full daylight—almost too bright to look at. Her skin against his fingertips was as soft as the down of a dandelion. He never wanted to let her go again.

She didn't say anything, but she brought her other hand up to curl her fingers around his collar. Her chin tipped up. Her lips parted the barest fraction—on a breath or a whisper, he couldn't tell. All he could do was be drawn in, closer, her name a rushed exclamation that he let out quietly into the night. Her lashes fluttered and fell. Just another half heartbeat, and his lips would be on hers.

"Hope!"

Slater jolted. Hope's eyes flew open and locked on his. The sound of Annie's shout came again, but this time she shouted two names.

"Hope! Hope, where are you? Jack Allen!"

Slater felt Hope stiffen in his arms. And then, she was scrambling away, fumbling for her phone, which had been forgotten in the grass. He stood, disoriented, his head spinning.

"Jack Allen!" she groaned, stabbing at the button on the side of her case. When the phone wouldn't power on, Hope shouted, "Annie, we're here!"

"Jack Allen?" Slater parroted. Not exactly the name he wanted to interrupt what had almost been the perfect dreamed-for moment with Hope.

"What time is it?" Hope asked, looking at her bare wrist. "I left my watch back at the resort."

Slater checked his own watch. "Nine thirty."

"No. No, no, no, no…"

"Hope, what is it?" Slater turned as Annie crashed

through the trees at the edge of the lakeshore, making a beeline for them, waving her own phone.

"I was supposed to meet Jack Allen at the resort restaurant half an hour ago," she explained.

Annie had reached them by this point, and she had skidded to a top, panting. Between gulps of air, she tried to get out words. "Your...father. Father...tried..."

"To call me? My phone is dead!"

Slater, behind Hope, put both of his hands on her shoulders. She turned into him, burying her face in his chest. "I just stood up one of our biggest potential clients. My father is going to flip his lid."

Slater's arms came around her for enough time to squeeze her reassuringly. Then, he set her away from him and turned to pick up his guitar case and the song lyrics, the latter of which he stuffed in his pocket, scooping his keys out in the same motion. He reached out and put a hand on Annie's shoulder. "You okay? You're awfully winded." At Annie's nod, Slater swung his guitar case toward the trail he and Hope had used to get to the shore.

"Come on. I'll drive you back to the resort."

Hope's horrified face said that she didn't want to go back, but Annie, texting rapidly with one hand, used the other to grab the hem of Hope's shirt. "Girl, we have to go."

In five minutes, they were in Slater's Jeep, buckled in, and headed for the resort. And even though it wasn't Slater who was headed into trouble, as he looked over at Hope's worried features, barely outlined but still visibly pinched in the dimness of the car interior, his own stomach twisted into sympathetic knots.

CHAPTER 17

HOPE'S PALMS WERE SWEATY, AND she rubbed them down the legs of her jeans, trying to sort her jumbled thoughts into anything resembling a plan for what to do once they'd arrived at the resort. Turning in her seat, Hope looked imploringly at Annie.

"What did my father say? How did he sound?"

Annie, who seemed still slightly winded, took a long drink out of a bottle of water before replying. It seemed to Hope ages before she did answer, but it was probably only a few seconds. Conversely, the ride to the resort was going way too fast—they were already pulling into the winding drive that led up to the front portico.

"He wasn't happy. Jack tried to reach you first, and then called your dad when he couldn't get in touch. To be fair, they were both worried, too. But your dad, after he asked where we were…"

Hope cringed. She never forgot her professional obligations. She prided herself on being punctual, on being prepared, on keeping the highest standards in her work. But she'd been too distracted, and she'd let her meeting with Jack—however impromptu the scheduling—completely slip her mind.

Slater parked off to one side under the portico and leaned down to wave at the valet who started to approach them. Recognizing Slater, the young man nodded and went back to his podium near the entrance to the resort. Annie popped the back door to Slater's Jeep and hopped out. Slater and Hope both unbuckled and followed.

"Okay," Annie said, strategizing. "We need a way to spin this. A cover story. We got lost in the woods. You fell into the lake. We—"

"Annie, no." Hope held up a hand to stop her friend. "I appreciate you wanting to cover for me, but it's okay. I agreed to meet Jack, and it was my responsibility to show up to that meeting."

"Hope, if I hadn't asked you down to the lake—"

Hope cut in again, smiling softly. "Then I wouldn't have gotten up the courage to give you the lyrics to the song in time for you to practice for the wedding. It's okay, both of you. I'm going to go in, find my father, and explain everything."

"I think we're both owed a big explanation." Her father's voice carried sharply through the night air. Not even the sounds of the crickets and frogs could have softened the edginess of it.

Hope turned. She expected to feel more nervous at the sight of him. He was red-faced and accompanied by Jack Allen, who was not. The younger man bore an expression of disappointment, but Hope didn't see any anger in his gaze. The same was not true of her dad.

Slater stepped forward, faster than Hope could stop him. "Mr. Bergman, let me explain…"

He cut Slater off with a withering look and a decided

thrust of a flattened hand. "I'll hear nothing from you. Before she ran back into you, my daughter had a level head on her shoulders. She was reliable. She was responsible."

"She's *too* responsible," Slater shot back. Her father's mouth fell open. Slater continued, the words rushing out. "Have you ever asked her what she wants, instead of telling her what she's responsible for? When I first saw her again, the night your group arrived, she was as beautiful as ever. She took my breath away the same way she did when we were not much more than kids. But she didn't look happy. Her eyes—her smile didn't reach them. But this week, I've seen light come back into them. And I don't think that's because of financial planning."

"I suppose it's because of you?" he sneered.

"No," Slater said. "It's because of us." He looked at Hope and held out his hand. Slater's words rang true, articulating what she'd been feeling the whole week—but she let his hand hang, and didn't reach back.

"Slater, I think you should go."

Slater looked at her for a long moment before he curled his fingers into his palm and dropped his arm. He nodded, his expression shuttering. All she needed was some time to sort things out with Jack and her dad, and then she and Slater could talk. She could explain. Now was not the time to rub their time together in her father's face.

With a short nod, Slater grumbled a goodnight and silently passed her father and Jack to disappear into the resort lobby. Hope didn't miss that, before he slipped inside, he leaned in to whisper to the valet, who followed him in, at least giving them some measure of privacy. As much as one could have, standing outside and arguing.

Hope was thankful that they were under the portico; otherwise, there were a number of upper-floor rooms who would have a great view of this confrontation.

"Mr. Bergman, if I may—"

"You may not," he said coldly to Annie, who raised her chin and shot him an icy glare.

"Well, I'm going to anyway." She turned and pulled Hope into a hug, which Hope returned tightly. When Annie pulled away, she looked directly into her friend's eyes. "I'll be upstairs in my room. Come knock when you get done, and we'll talk about how I can schedule some time away to go to the wedding."

Hope nodded, and watched as Annie, too, took her leave, leaving Hope standing alone under the scrutiny of her dad and Jack Allen.

"This wedding nonsense. It's getting out of hand!"

Jack, to his credit, stepped forward before her father could keep going.

"Dan, listen, this doesn't have to be hashed out now. As disappointed as I am in the situation, and as much as it casts doubt on whether Beacon Financial is dependable enough to handle my affairs, I think we'd all be better off sleeping on things before we say anything that can't be unsaid."

Hope's eyes met Jack's. She could see that he was troubled, but she appreciated that he was being levelheaded about the mix-up. If given the chance, she would prove to him that Beacon could handle him as a client. The thought of Jack walking away, of her father's disappointment, along with the professional embarrassment— she just couldn't let that happen. Not over one night of distraction.

"Goodnight, Jack," her father said.

"Fair enough." Jack gave a small wave and turned, jogging the short distance to the entrance of the resort. Hope could only imagine what he was thinking, now. Once he was gone, Hope and her father stood alone. She conjured a little of Annie, lifting her chin, waiting for him to say the first words.

"Irresponsible," her father spat out. "Irrational! I got a bad feeling the second you said you were going to spend time with him, after all these years!"

"Slater, dad. His name is Slater, remember?"

He began to pace. "I've been curious as to where you've been all week, but I haven't asked. You're an adult, and I have no claim on your time. But you were gone more and more, later each morning to the sessions."

"I was actually never late," she corrected, standing firm when he whirled on her.

"You were tonight, when it counted. Your priorities are wildly off. What if this costs us Jack's account? I told you it was vital that we gain his business. Important that we get him to commit this week."

Hope crossed her arms over her chest, feeling the pressure of indignancy rise under her breastbone. "And why is that, Dad? You keep saying it, but you never explain it. Does it have anything to do with Ralph Murphy cutting out on this year's seminar? I still haven't gotten the full story on that."

"I told you it's none of your business. And don't change the subject," he shot back. "You were off in dreamland with Slater, and you neglected your duties."

"Which I have faithfully performed for years. All the way back to giving up music and switching to a business degree."

"For the better."

"Was it? Because Beacon Financial doesn't seem to have made you happy, Dad. You're angry all the time. You argue with the staff back home. You're a million miles away from me. And remind me again of what is and isn't my business, when you're telling Jack Allen that I'm very soon to be taking over yours?"

"Beacon Financial is your legacy. You've always known that. It's what your mother and I wanted for you."

"And what about what I want?"

He paused, looking at Hope, silent and serious. She stared back, taking in the tired eyes, the lines in his face that were deeper than she'd ever noticed, and the dropped posture of his shoulders that spoke of a defeat that's he didn't know the source of. She loved her father, and it hurt her when he was upset—with her, at life, with whatever secret he was keeping about Ralph Murphy. And she knew that he loved her, and that whatever misguided intent was behind not only his secrecy, but his insistence that she step up to helm Beacon was borne from a place of love. The problem was that it was being twisted by fears that he refused to share with her.

"You're right, I'm not happy at Beacon. The truth is that I'm retiring, Hope. I had hoped to announce your upcoming promotion to head of Beacon at the awards banquet, to everyone assembled. I want all of our clientele to see me handing the reins to the person I know is most capable. If you don't want to step up, I'll explore my buyout options. But I can't guarantee that there's a place for you if new senior management takes over."

"So this is an ultimatum? Take Beacon, or get pushed out?" Hope's heart dropped.

"No," he said softly. "Take Beacon, or I'll have to let someone else take it. I can't do it anymore."

Hope watched as he sighed, turned, and followed the path that Slater, Annie, and Jack had, pulling open the massive doors of the resort entrance, which swung on silent hinges, and fading quickly out of sight into the lobby beyond. She stood for a solid five minutes under the portico, her temples pounding. The low the buzz of the mosquitos bumping against the glow of the hanging lanterns above her filled her head.

What had started out as a lovely evening had turned into one of the worst nights of her life. After she was sure she'd given her father enough time to reach his room, Hope trudged over the warm concrete and through the set of doors that she just couldn't find beautiful at the moment. She passed the impressive front desk without a second glance, afraid that she would see Slater there waiting for her.

She knocked on Annie's door, and her friend opened right away. Annie took one look at Hope and stood aside, letting her in. Without a word, Hope trudged over and sat down on the second queen bed in Annie's room, kicked off her sneakers and socks, and crawled under the covers. Annie propped up next to her, a book in hand, and dimmed the bedside lamp.

"I'll sit here with you until you fall asleep," Annie reassured, squeezing Hope's hand.

Though she felt like crying, Hope's throbbing eyes produced no tears. Within moments, she fell into a deep and dreamless sleep.

Friday morning dawned clear and bright, with no sign of the rain clouds that has plagued the sky earlier in the week. Hope had decided, after last night's argument, that she wouldn't attend any of the seminar events today. With the schedule winding down, everything that remained was pretty much on auto-pilot anyway. And she had a lot of thinking to do before the awards banquet.

After a long, hot bath in the very swanky bathroom of her room, Hope donned the same sundress that she'd worn the night in cabin six when she'd cooked dinner. She left her hair down to dry in loose waves, and, giving her still-tired face a once-over in the mirror, decided to forgo makeup anyway. No power suits today, no heels, no artful swipe of contour. Today, she just wanted to feel like herself.

When she was finished getting ready, Hope went next door to Annie's room. She slipped in as soon as Annie opened her door, worried that her dad would come out of his door—which was on the other side of Hope's—at any moment. Sure enough, five minutes after Hope had sat down on one of Annie's beds with the room-service menu, they both heard a soft knock echoing down the hall. Moments later, the same knock sounded at Annie's door.

Hope shook her head silently. She didn't want any more confrontation. She didn't want to rehash the same old sticking points, going round and round until she and her father were at the same impasse they'd started with.

No more knocks came.

"How about you go cash in that spa certificate, and I'll send word to my dad that you and I are both taking the day off?"

Annie was already taking off her heels and rummaging in her suitcase for a pair of shorts and a tank top. "Sounds like heaven to me."

Hope passed Annie the room-service menu and

picked up her phone, which was now, she thought dryly, fully charged—so at least there was that. She had unread messages, but she ignored them for the moment and placed a call to the front desk, having one of the staff run a note to her father, who would be in the first event room, about Hope and Annie's absence. Hope knew he wouldn't argue. She prayed he would give her the space she needed to sort things out.

Over an overabundance of room service breakfast, Hope told Annie all about the interlude with Slater at the lake. Annie sighed in the right places and pulled a face when Hope revealed what had interrupted their near-kiss.

"Well, it was my own fault. None of this would have come to a head if I had worn my watch!" Hope joked weakly.

"Not true, and you're being unfair to yourself," Annie replied, waving a fork laden with fruit salad at Hope. "Your father was—is?—still planning to announce you as the heir to the Beacon throne, as it were. I mean, what are you going to tell him?"

Hope sighed and rubbed at the bridge of her nose. "I think, honestly, I need to talk to Slater."

Annie's eyes widened. "About the future?"

"I don't know what I'll say. Because I don't know what the right choice is." She felt her eyes burn with unshed tears, and she inhaled through her nose to stop their progression.

"Do you want me to stay with you today? Or, if not, why don't you come to the spa with me?"

Hope shook her head. "No, you go on. I think I'll take a walk and think."

Annie nodded, putting down her fork and declaring

herself too stuffed to eat another bite. She stood and grabbed a pair of sneakers, sitting on the bed opposite Hope to pull them on. Hope started neatly stacking their breakfast dishes and clearing up the napkins and empty cups.

"Hope, you're fidgeting." Anne looked up from typing her second shoe.

"You're right. I'm going for that walk now." Hope grabbed her room key, which sat on the nightstand between the queen beds, along with her phone. When her thumb grazed the screen, the display lit up, and the little envelope signaling that she had new messages was still there, reminding her that she'd never checked them after her call to the front desk.

There were three messages.

The first was from Jack Allen, saying that he would be glad to talk with her whenever she was ready.

The second was from her father, and it simply said, Take the day. She deleted it.

The last was from Slater. She opened the message, feeling a mixture of elation and dread. She knew she should have called him last night, tried to ease some of the tension that asking him to leave had likely caused, but she'd been too thrown off about the whole night— another moment where they'd almost kissed, followed by the argument under the portico—to sort anything out.

Slater's text said, *Come find me when you get this.* It wasn't reassuring, but it didn't cause her the distress that just seeing her father's name on her screen had.

With a promise to meet Annie for lunch, Hope left the resort. According to her GPS, it would take only fifteen minutes for her to walk to the Cabins in the Pines, and so she decided to leave the rental car behind.

The day was as bright and clear as the first day she'd arrived, though Hope felt worlds different today than she had barely a week ago. Unsure of what she would say to Slater once she arrived at the Cabins, she tried to still her mind as she walked. She focused on the beauty that surrounded her, in hopes that it would clear the way for some epiphany that would solve the problem of how to hold on to the two disparate halves of her life—the one she'd committed to and felt responsible for; her father, her work, and the one that she'd left behind, unfinished and unrequited.

Where she'd only just begun to notice that summer was making an appearance back in the city, Here at the Cabins, it surrounded Hope, invaded her senses, snapped her out of her tunnel vision (which always, before now, had been focused on her job) and pulled her into the magic of wide-open space, fresh air, and the feeling of endless possibility.

She had reached the end of the resort drive. Consulting the map on her phone, she made the appropriate turn and left the cool shade of the trees for the trail that followed beside the main road, out in the full sun. Warmth radiated over her shoulders and arms.

Beside the trail, black-eyed Susans grew in abundance, and Hope picked a few as she walked, trying to avoid gathering any that were serving as landing pads for the numerous bees humming to and fro from flower patch to flower patch. She could see that some of the wildflowers had crept inward, under the trees, but she knew that, further in, the denseness of the overhead branches likely stopped any from growing. She thought back to the Cabins and the campfire of last evening, picturing the darker landscape under the trees, where things like moss flourished and small, quick forest creatures scuttled through the underbrush, often unseen. Here, on the trail, she saw two squirrels boldly bickering over a found piece of twine, a rabbit that darted, all legs and ears, across the main road when she passed where he was hidden, and a small family of ducks that loudly followed the same route as she neared the office at the Cabins in the Pines. She imagined she would see the duo of ducks and their three small ducklings gliding across Lake Fairwood momentarily.

It took her only a few more minutes to reach the end of the trail that weaved past the tent sites and cabins, ending in the gentle slope that opened onto the lakeshore. She wasn't sure how she knew that this was where he would be—she'd simply followed the feeling.

He hadn't seen her yet, so she stood, scrunching the fabric of her dress in nervous fingers, surveying the lakeside. Slater was alone, though there were heaps of things laid out between where Hope stood and where he was that told her that he probably wouldn't be alone for long. There was no way one man could tackle all of the projects that she saw—the poles and parts for a popup canopy, a few palettes of deck tiles that she could only assume were meant to extend the paved area off the pavilion, and coils and coils of lights, some of which he was stringing now.

Hope took a deep breath, stepped off the trail, and walked silently through the soft, green grass toward him.

CHAPTER 18

W HEN SLATER SAW HOPE MAKING her way down the slope of the lakeshore toward the pavilion, he offered her a wave and a grin from his perch on the highest step of his ladder. He put one last screw hook into the highest side beam of the pavilion and then looped the guide wire he was stringing over it, running enough out from the spool on top of the ladder so that he could climb down. He grabbed the wire spool and walked backward toward the lake, where a newly-erected wooden pole stood ready to be the next point to tie off. The wire unwound as he walked.

"Careful," he cautioned as she drew close. "Don't go falling over me." He gave her a wink as he set the spool of wire on the middle step of the second ladder he had set up next to the pole. When he looked back, and she didn't smile, his heart lurched.

Uh oh.

He had thought about calling her last night, but his feelings had been the slightest bit hurt when she'd asked him to go, and so he'd avoided reaching out—at first. As soon as he'd left the resort and made it back over to the

Cabins to meet back up with his friends, his rational side had won out, and he'd wanted to make sure that his outburst hadn't caused her any more stress than she looked to already be under when he'd gone.

He knew he should wait for her to broach the subject of last night, but he could give her a soft pitch to ease into the conversation.

"How's Annie? She looked like she was about to expire last night. I think she ran all the way from the fire circle to here."

"She's good. I sent her to the spa today to let the drama die down."

He nodded, climbing the ladder beside him and grabbing the spool of wire. She didn't speak while he hefted it up above his head, quickly wrapping it twice around the large metal cleat that was bolted into the pole, up high. He let more wire spool out before he climbed down again.

"So, are you going to tell me what happened, or do I have to guess?" He tried to keep his voice light and playful, but Slater was getting some "unsettling vibes," as Ursula would call them, from Hope. "Look, I'm sorry I stepped in last night. I didn't want you to get into any hot water at work or with your father because of me. I think that's some déjà vu that no one wants to experience again."

"My father is retiring," she started, ignoring his words. Slater noticed that she was twisting the fabric at the sides of her dress, worrying the material over and over. Her tell. The bad vibes got stronger.

"That's a good thing, right? More time to relax, pursue things he's always wanted to. And maybe you can take more time off of work if he's not there day in and day out."

"He wants me to take over. Step into his position, once he steps down."

Slater set the spool of wire down in the grass, dusting his hands against one another. He swallowed past a sudden rush of acid in his throat. This felt—sounded— strangely like another conversation that he and Hope had had, a lifetime ago, when she'd been trying to tell him that she was quitting music.

"I wanted to talk to you about—"

"Yeah, I'm sure you need my input." His voice was harsher than he'd intended, but he was seeing her in now the same painful detail that he had back then, all loose, soft hair and wide, blue eyes—eyes that had been begging him to make it seem okay that she was giving up what they'd built. Acting as though their "discussion" had any bearing on what she would decide. It had been a joke back then. There had been no choice. And now, he felt strongly that there was no way he was going to convince her that her happiness lay down a different path.

Her dedication to family, her love for her parents, he didn't consider those weaknesses. They spoke to the positive side of her, of the fierce and devoted part that held on. Maybe that was the part of her that he'd hoped was still holding on to him. But when it came to what she needed, what he wanted, and the fact that her life was, in the end, hers to live—Hope had a definite blind spot. And she *hadn't* held on to him, to them, all those years ago.

And, to think, he'd had a whole confessional speech ready, one to rival the words he would trot out at the wedding to pay tribute to the love of his best friends. Only, these words had been planned for Hope only, and they would have ended with the same ones he'd said years back, the ones he'd thought, stupidly, would change things. They hadn't back then, and he knew they wouldn't now. So he left them unsaid. At least he would have that comfort of knowing, when she left, that he hadn't laid his heart bare again.

"What does that mean?" she shot back.

"Nothing, except this feels a little too much like the past repeating itself."

"That's not fair," she whispered. "You knew this couldn't go anywhere. The second I got here, you knew I would be leaving. I never promised you anything. You chose to assume."

Slater could tell he was putting her on the defensive, but he couldn't help it. He felt defenseless, powerless, speeding down the same road to heartbreak that he had foolishly thought led to a different destination, despite all the landmarks along the way that had been exactly the same. And she was right—he *was* being unfair.

"Of course, I knew you would leave," Slater said, yanking the spool of wire off the ground. "You're good at it. It's part of your resumé."

Her sharply indrawn breath was the exact thing he expected to hear when his barb landed. It was her against him, now. He had the barest fraction of a second to consider why this had so quickly gotten contentious. And then Hope was firing back. "I wouldn't expect you to understand, Slater. I know that, back in college, you could just jump from one thing to another, not really caring about where you ended up, but I couldn't. I had to be focused. I had a duty to my family. And, after my mom got sick..."

"I didn't jump from one thing to another, Hope. I stopped music because it reminded me of *you*! And you think that I didn't care where I ended up? I did care. I *do* care. I ended up here, with people *who care about me*. And I was hoping that you cared. That you would again."

She shook her head, taking a few steps back. Every trace of softness was gone from her face, and she had the exact same closed-off expression she'd had when she'd told him that she was not only quitting music, but him. Them. He hadn't believed her then, not until her dorm room was empty of everything but the note that said goodbye.

"Then you were mistaken. We had a week. That was enough."

"It wasn't enough for *me*. And I'd bet money not for you, either." He dropped the spool of wire, whatever he'd been doing with it forgotten. "I mean, Hope, seriously? Can you look me in the eye right now and tell me that you're *happy*?"

They stared at one another, both breathing heavier. Without a word, she turned and started marching back up the embankment toward the trail. After few steps, she stopped and whirled back on him. She shook her finger at him every step back.

"Tell me what to do if Jack Allen walks, Slater. Professionally, that's something I don't even want to *think* of the implications of. But tell me, please, what to do in that instance?"

He shrugged, crossing his arms over his chest. "Move on. Get another client. Don't spend your *life* worried about when the next wave of wealth is going to come walking in the door, or what your father will think if the tide rolls out. Find your happiness in something else. When is the responsibility going to be to yourself and what you want, what you feel? How do you live every day ignoring what your heart wants?"

She was seething. He could see it in her clenched teeth, in her flushed cheeks. "You don't know me, anymore, Slater. Not enough to know what would make me happy. And *especially* not after a *week*."

"Yes, I do." He reached into his back pocket and took out a folded sheet of yellow, lined paper. "Because I see the same happiness now that I did back then. And you wrote it down right here." He tossed the page on the ground between them. "Why don't you take it? A little souvenir of your meaningless week in the woods."

"And to think," she scoffed. "That I came here to talk to you, to get all this out."

"We've talked," he said flatly. "I think this is where you get out."

With a wordless glare, she took two steps forward, bent, and snatched the yellow paper from the ground. Then she whirled and stormed up the embankment— and, this time, she didn't turn back around.

Night seemed to come slowly, and even the heaps of work that Slater had to do didn't seem to make the day go any faster. He'd turned down an offer of help from a parade of people who'd stopped by the lakeshore as he worked— thankfully, no one too soon after Hope's dramatic exit— and he'd soldiered on, using his frustration to fuel his way through nearly every last-minute set up chore that he had materials for. When he was done, he was tired, achy, and still thinking about the angry exchange. And the sun was setting over Lake Fairwood, reaching soft peach-and-pink fingers into the remaining blue of the sky, as though the day were trying to hold on.

Just set, already, he thought grouchily. *Nothing worth saving this day for.*

Well, almost nothing. Tonight was the rehearsal dinner, and Slater welcomed the chance to be surrounded by his friends again. Not that he'd use Wyatt and Delaney's rehearsal as a way to vent all of his romance woes, but it would be a comfort to be with them all when he was hurting.

And he was, he had to admit. Hope's words, though he knew they'd been said in anger—as had his—still reverberated through his chest, echoed in his ears, and made his heart constrict. What had he honestly thought, that she would come running back into his arms after all this time apart? That, after a week, all of the things that had separated them would have suddenly disappeared? Time hadn't worn down his feelings for her, but it hadn't worn down any of the obstacles between them, either. Both his feelings *and* those obstacles were as strong now as they'd ever been.

After gathering up his tools and packing them into his tool bag, Slater stood and watched the sun slip below the spot where the lake met the sky. It was time to go.

An hour later, Slater was showered, dressed, and walking into the ballroom at the resort. He'd been on pins and needles, praying not to run into anyone from Beacon Financial on his way in. As he entered the ballroom, he had to concentrate on forgetting that, tomorrow, Hope would be here attending her big awards ceremony, and he would be attending the wedding of two of the people he loved most in the world. His gut twisted, thinking of how he'd have to pull Wyatt aside and break the news.

Slater spotted Wyatt, Delaney, and the rest of the

gang near the front of the room. Squaring his shoulders, he walked toward them.

Dan Bergman sat beside Lake Fairwood in the evening twilight for the first time ever. He'd admired the lake when he'd visited the Cabins in the Pines during the unexpected free time earlier this week, but nothing in its wide, placid expanse or natural surroundings had struck him enough then to make him stop and look around. Now, however, he was staring up into the night sky, feeling lost and insignificant under the glittering wonder of the stars that spread out above him.

He put his palms flat on the still-warm surface of the rustic bench he sat on. It still held some of the day's energy, though that would be gone, soon.

I know how this poor old log feels, he thought wryly.

He wondered, sitting alone here and thinking back over the week, why he hadn't taken the time to explore this side of the lake more. Every chance he'd gotten, instead of finding out what charms this place held, he'd scurried back to his room, fallen asleep with the TV on, slept fitfully, brokenly, until it was time to get up, get dressed, and attend yet another seminar event.

And none of them excited him. And it wasn't that he'd lost the passion for his job, no, he was just as thrilled with seeing clients and industry pros alike engage during the week's events. It was that everything seemed duller, somehow, less important. Nothing, he realized, held the exact light that he used to feel—a light that rivaled the stars he was staring at.

Because you lost the light. No, you stomped it out.

Dan knew he could control many things. At his office, he *did* control many things. And he'd spent years cultivating a prowess and aptitude for planning that had netted him dozens and dozens of clients and great company success. And, when it came to his personal life, he'd always felt sure that he was capable of that same kind of savvy, that exact kind of control. He liked to think of it, once he was out of the office and walking through the doors of his home, *firm guidance.*

And he'd done it out of love. Never malice. His late wife had jokingly called him the "armchair administrator," and it was true that he often tackled life problems like work ones, but, this time, it had gone well beyond the usual spreadsheet comparing the qualifications of potential plumbers they could call to fix the leaky kitchen faucet. He'd crossed the line. Heck, he could admit it now—he'd crossed the line all those years ago, too.

And he was so, so afraid that his daughter had suffered, had lost too much because of it.

He'd done some deep thinking since that night under the portico, when he'd given her that atrocious ultimatum. What had he been thinking? His daughter's life, her happiness, was not something that he could calculate, plan, or direct.

He missed his late wife terribly. Hers was a loss that he felt deeply every day. But, more recently, he'd been pushing Hope further and further away from him, all while demanding more and more of her—and, now, he felt like he was shouting across Lake Fairwood, with Hope on the other shore, stomping his feet like a child and insisting that she take the weight of unhappiness—unhappiness that was his own doing—off of his shoulders. But leaving Beacon Financial would not address the real problem.

He'd messed up, big time.

"Oh, Rose, if only you were here." He sighed out into the warm summer air, flexing his fingers against the bench.

"Would an Alex do?"

The voice behind him was soft, and Dan turned to find Alexandra standing a few steps behind him, beside one of the other rows of wooden benches that were set up, but empty, on the shore. Alex gestured to the empty spot on the bench next to him.

"Do you mind if I join you?"

Dan shook his head before he thought about it; and once he'd indicated that he didn't mind, he couldn't very well tell the pretty co-owner of the resort that she couldn't sit. After all, the place was hers. Alex took a few careful steps—Dan noticed she was in heels—and smoothed the skirt of her mint-green dress before she sat down next to him.

"It's a beautiful night, isn't it, Mr. Bergman?" She tilted her head at him, smiling, and he found himself looking out across the lake now, instead of staring at the stars. He took in the blazing lights of the resort just across from them, the music that he could hear faintly from that direction, the rustling trees and the calls of a night owl that sounded so close by. Different worlds met here, and yet there was harmony.

"It is a beautiful night, Ms. Brent-Collingsworth. What brings you out to the lake tonight, so dressed up?"

Alex looked down at her dress. "Oh, we had the re-hearsal dinner tonight, across the lake." She pointed to the resort, and Dan could only assume that the faint music he'd heard was part of the event Alex had come from.

"Still some partiers over there. Surprisingly, Delaney's Aunt Tildy is an up-all-nighter. The moment her post-rehearsal party game suggestions started tending toward things like Twister, I was out of there."

Dan found himself chuckling. "Can't put your left hand on yellow in heels and a formal dress, that's for sure."

"I don't even want to try." Her smile was wide and easy. "Besides, I have so much to do tomorrow for the wedding that I wanted to make an early night of it. But after the daily hustle and bustle at the resort, plus the rehearsal, I wanted to catch a few moments of quiet. And this is the perfect place for it. I come here often at night, just to relax and think."

He nodded, silent.

"Is that what you're doing?" she asked.

His chuckle this time was sardonic. "The thinking part. Not the relaxing."

Alex seemed to hesitate, but then must have thought it better to say what was on her mind. "I don't mean to jump in with unsolicited advice, but Slater told us about his past with Hope…"

Dan hummed, his face flushing with embarrassment. "Did he tell you that I pressured her to give up something she loved—two things she loved—because I was scared?"

Alex shook her head, and then waited for Dan to continue.

"When Hope's mother died—Rose—I felt so out of control. I could always handle anything, make the best decision, and achieve the best outcome. But I couldn't corporately maneuver away my wife's illness." Dan felt his eyes burn, a stinging start up where his eyes and nose met. He blinked against the suddenly blurry vista of the lake.

"So I tried to tighten my hold on Hope. I felt like, if she followed the path that she chose, I might lose her, too. To music, to Slater...Oh, I was so *unfair* to them both!"

Wordlessly, Alex put a hand over Dan's hand. He clutched at her fingers, uncaring that they were practically strangers. He blinked back again against the tears he felt rising, focusing hard on the reflection of the moon across the water. There was a tranquility here that he couldn't remember experiencing anytime in the recent past. Dan wished he could bottle the feeling and carry it with him, so that he wouldn't twist his sadness, his worry into a force that pushed the people he loved away.

"This place is special," he said to Alex. "Hope tried to tell me that from the start, and I can see now how it could do a lot of good for someone."

"For a lot of someones," Alex said gently. "And it has."

A warm breeze was beginning to kick up. Dan stared out at the rowboats that were all tied up at the docks for the night. They bobbed gently with the lake water, jostling slightly against one another as the wind pushed the water into slight ripples. Somewhere nearby, there was the sound of several small splashes, as though some aquatic night creature was testing the depth of the water at the edge of the lake. Dan stood, shoved his hands in his pockets, and took a few steps closer to the edge of the lake, noticing now how the trees cast shadows in the moonlight across the surface.

He heard Alex stand behind him, and then saw her profile ease into his peripheral vision. "I'm going to tell you something that I also told your daughter."

Dan looked at Alex questioningly.

"I used to be so much like you," Alex said. Dan cut his eyes toward her to see her wagging a finger at him. "I lost myself in my work, in my success, and no matter what I lost because of it, I didn't stop to think how all of it was affecting my heart, my happiness."

"Did you lose someone?"

"No. I was so wrapped up in all of it that I never found someone—*the* someone," Alex admitted. "But you had a great love. And you have an amazing daughter. You have Hope."

"But we've gotten so far apart," he admitted. "And she hasn't even spoken to me since—well, we had an argument. It was about work, but it was really about everything else that isn't work."

"Family is a powerful bond," Alex said, patting Dan on the arm. "I think, if you talk to her, tell her what you've told me..." Alex smiled softly. "Well, let's just say that an apology is sometimes the first thing that's needed for healing. *Before* a beautiful escape into nature."

Dan looked at Alex from the side of his eye. "How'd you get so wise about all of this?" he asked, finding himself smiling, feeling a bit lighter.

"Oh, I've never been smart at affairs of the heart. But I've come to know people who are. People who taught me. Good people."

Dan looked down at his shoes, feeling his embarrassment return. "I see."

Alex's phone rang suddenly, and the noise was jarring in the hush of the night. She answered it with an apologetic gesture. Dan watched her eyes widen as whoever was on the other end launched into fast, loud speech, not even waiting for a greeting.

"Maisie, slow down," Alex said, and Dan didn't know

who Maisie was, but he could tell by Alex's expression that something was wrong.

After a few moments and a few reassurances that she would meet this Maisie at the Bean Pot, Alex hung up.

"Is everything all right?" She didn't answer right away. A fatherly instinct kicked in when he saw the worry on the younger woman's face, and he blurted, "How can I help?"

Alex shook her head, staring at her phone, despite the screen having now gone dark. "I'm not sure you can. Unless you can bake?"

CHAPTER 19

THE AFTERNOON SUN STREAMED DOWN at the Cabins in the Pines, and Slater sat in cabin six, watching Wyatt nervously adjust his tie for what must have been the tenth time. The wide, bay window opposite the fireplace let in enough light that Slater could see the dust motes that his friend was kicking up from the throw rug as he walked in circles between the couch and the mantel.

"Forever and ever, I pledge to thee...no," Wyatt puffed out a huge breath, raking a hand through his hair. "You are my light, my love, my shining star...arg!"

Slater leaned back on the couch. "Man, how in the world can you not have your vows down yet?"

"I don't know! I've been so worried over all the other details." Wyatt completed another circle. "I thought you were the man with the music. Can't you help me?"

"I can with a tune, brother, but not with the words. And, not to rush you, but we're running out of time. You kinda have an appointment to keep."

Wyatt stopped walking and seemed to be steadying

himself. "You're right. It will all come out naturally. I'll see Del, and I'll know exactly what to say."

Slater stood and went to stand in front of his friend. "You will. And, even if you don't, she'll still find you charming and sweet, and everyone will be there to bear witness to another example of your excruciatingly perfect love." Wyatt laughed at the gentle ribbing, and Slater grinned, grabbing Wyatt by the shoulders and shaking him slightly. "Deep breaths. Best-man orders. Wedding. Del. You know, the pretty one in the white dress waiting to make you happy for the rest of your life?"

Wyatt nodded.

"And the numerous guests also waiting?"

Wyatt clapped his hands together as though he were gearing up to start a race. "Let's do it."

They walked to the front door, and as Slater pulled the door open, Wyatt stopped.

"What is it now?" Slater said, smiling as he shook his head.

"Listen, Slater, I know this probably isn't something you want to talk about again, but I'm sorry about Hope, man."

Slater's chest tightened. "Nah, it's okay. And you have nothing to be sorry for. I should be apologizing to you—to Del—again. I thought I had the music thing figured out. It was going to be special." Slater looked back into cabin six, and his heart did another flip in his chest at the memory of the nights of practice here with Hope. Her laughter. The fire. How being with her had felt so natural, so right.

His eyes fell on a pad of yellow paper sitting on the side table by the couch, and if it was possible, he hurt even more deeply. The same paper that she'd used to finish their song. Across the top of the notepad, emblazoned on the blue paper band that held the pages together, the words *Beacon Financial Planning and Wealth Management* stood out starkly in silver, almost mocking him. Even from across the room, he could clearly make out the letters—as if he needed a reminder of the crux of his angst.

"It will be special," Wyatt assured.

"We'll make it special," Slater added as they started through the door. "Ballroom or lakeside, music, no music, singer, no singer, cake, no cake—"

"Wait, what happened to the cake?"

They came out into the same sunshine that Slater had been focused on, and Slater locked up cabin six, stalling for time to answer. Fortunately, he was saved from spilling the beans on the latest wedding complication by one of the two men who greeted them as he turned back around from the cabin's door.

"Alex tells me the cake situation is handled," Norman said, waving his phone at Slater and Wyatt. "So no need to worry there."

"And Masie just texted that we are all being"—Charles scrolled through a text—"'slower than the cream rising in buttermilk,' and we have fifteen minutes to get there."

All four men, dressed in tailored tuxes and groomed to the nines, piled into Slater's Jeep.

"Buckle up," Slater said, looking over at Wyatt in the passenger's seat. "I don't want you bolting out the side here when I slow down for a turn."

Norman and Charles laughed. Wyatt frowned. "I wouldn't dream of it. I'm not even nervous."

Two hands came from the back seat and clapped Wyatt reassuringly on the back. Slater looked over as

Charles drew his hand back, but Norman lingered on Wyatt's right shoulder, dusting off some bit of lint on the shoulder of his jacket. Slater suspected that everyone was nervous today—Norman couldn't possibly have found lint on Wyatt's jacket for the rest of the drive, but he seemed to be looking intently for it the whole way to the lake.

They made it to the lakeside with five minutes to spare. Slater, Norman, and Charles rushed to take their places at the altar. Delaney's mom stood at the back of the aisle, waiting for Wyatt. He took his place beside her, leaned in to whisper to her, and looked to be wiping a tear from her cheek. Processional music started, and Wyatt and Iris took a leisurely walk up front together. Slater's heart was still racing from the rush to get here.

When Iris and Wyatt reached Wyatt's spot in front of Slater and the other groomsmen, Iris kissed one of Wyatt's cheeks and pressed her hand to the other before taking a seat in the front row of guests, next to Alex. Wyatt stood stoically with Slater, Charles, and Norman all lined up at his back. Slater looked across at Masie, Ursula, and Rachel, who stood opposite them. Maisie mimed wiping her forehead in relief, and Charles blew her a kiss.

The entire wedding party of assembled guests faced Lake Fairwood and the view of the docks, the meandering ducks, and the sparkling water that lapped between the thick reeds. Slater looked out over the sea of faces, and tried very hard not to notice the absence of one in particular. Instead, he cataloged with satisfaction the layout of the lakeside ceremony, proud that what had been a last-minute no-plan-at-all had turned out so lovely.

The benches he'd made flanked either side of the aisle

that Delaney would walk down, and the lakeside breeze had taken care of carpeting between them with fallen leaves, making them seem part of the landscape. Bare, hanging Edison bulbs swooped under the pavilion and outward, veeing to the pole where Slater had been working just yesterday, and then the same stringed bulbs followed wire guides to tumble in a dramatic spill of light that attached to the wedding arch. Once the sun set and the reception was underway, the lakeside would look like a fairy tale.

The arch was covered in pine boughs, flowers, and sprays of baby's breath, and draped with soft, partially transparent tulle. At least, Slater thought it was tulle—he certainly wasn't going to risk asking Wyatt at this point.

The wedding march swelled from the musicians that were seated off to the left of the arch. At least the instrumentalists that Alex had suggested had come through. Violin strings swelled, the assembled guests rose from the benches, and Delaney appeared down the row that ran between them.

Slater's breath caught. He saw Wyatt raise a hand to his mouth.

Delaney wore a cream satin dress with a short train that barely brushed the ground. She held in her hands a bouquet of wildflowers, wrapped in the same fabric that draped the wedding arch.

A fairy tale, indeed. Slater's heart swelled with love for his two best friends.

Delaney's father wound her arm around his and they started toward the front. The bride's walk down the aisle seemed slow and speedy all at once. Larry's eyes were filled with tears as he let go of his daughter and took his seat next to Iris, who patted him reassuringly. Slater was sure that Wyatt was feeling just as—if not more—overwhelmed.

The pastor, who had been silent until now, addressed the crowd.

"Dearly beloved, please be seated." The gathered crowd sat in unison.

He continued. "First, thanking you all for coming to be with Wyatt and Delaney on this most special of days. As many of you might not know, this wedding almost didn't take place here. We were almost all gathered under the roof of a ballroom, instead of out in God's nature to celebrate the truly destined love of these two people."

Slater thought of the night of the mix-up, of how the very mistake that had led them to such a beautiful alternate setting had also brought Slater the happy times with Hope leading up to it. If not for that one twist of fate, it was possible they could have gone all week, passing each other at parallels, never knowing. In the face of a love like Wyatt and Delaney's, a love that did seem destined, Slater felt his heart lighten a bit when he thought back over the week. No matter what happened, he would always have the memories he and Hope had created in this short extra bubble of time—and those were gifts he might never have gotten, otherwise.

"One of the most beautiful feelings in the world is when you discover the person who completes you—and not only in the flowers-and-poetry sense. No, the kind of love that's rare is when you find a person who is soft where you are rough, strong where you are weak, and steadfast when you feel like giving up. It is in our moments of despair and need where we discover if the love that we receive—and the love we have to give—is the real thing."

Slater's heart, which had only begun to slow from the rush to arrive on time, began to speed back up. Had he been unfair to Hope? Had he foolishly driven her away, when they might have worked things out if only he'd stopped to listen? If they had found where they could fit, instead of withdrawing at the first point of pain?

"And the road to that person isn't always the smoothest, the straightest, the easiest to traverse—"

Wyatt held out his hands, and Delaney took both of his in hers. Slater thought of all they'd been through just to get to this moment. And he'd dismissed Hope, after all these years, over the first stumble...

"But, in the end, it's worth it. You gain from the other person as much as you give. Marriage becomes more than a set of promises—it becomes a bond, pure and wonderful, blending two souls together until they are one light, shining for the good of both. For Wyatt and Delaney, that journey began in this very location, long before today. And I feel blessed to be here now to make official what many of you have seen for most of a lifetime—their commitment to the eternal love of one another."

Slater swallowed back tears. He looked around. There wasn't a dry eye at the ceremony; and it had barely begun.

The pastor smiled serenely at the crowd, and then turned his focus to Wyatt and Delaney. "So, without further ado, the vows."

Slater tensed, but relaxed when Delaney dropped Wyatt's hands to untuck a scrap of paper from a hidden pocket in her dress. He thought of the yellow paper with Hope's lyrics on it, wished he had it in his pocket now.

Delaney's voice shook as she began to read. "Wyatt, I am lucky to be yours and lucky to call you mine. Ever since we were kids, you have entertained me, challenged me, frustrated me"—Slater joined the crowd in laughter—"and supported me like no one else. You've trusted me in crazy situations where no one in their right mind would have gone along!" It was Delaney's turn to laugh, but she did so while wiping away tears, tucking the scrap of paper away again. "Today, I am so happy to celebrate us. Your love makes me better. And with you by my side, there is nothing I can't do. I love you, and I will cherish you for the rest of my days."

There was a brief, heavy pause as Wyatt gazed at his bride, his eyes brimming with love.

"But never again on TV. I promise that, too," Del added.

"Booo!" Alex called from the front row.

The crowd laughed, again.

"Wyatt?" the pastor prompted.

"I can't top that," Wyatt said, shaking his head. Slater felt himself tense again.

Say something, man!

Wyatt's head dipped, and he grabbed Delaney's hands again. When he raised his face, he was grinning, his eyes shining. "I'm not going to waste my time with vows, Del."

She smiled at him, but a few small lines creased her forehead as she waited to see where he was going with this. Slater thought that the whole guest list seemed to be leaning forward, expectant.

"I guess when you realize you want to spend the rest of your life with somebody, you want to start as soon as you can," Wyatt said.

Delaney laughed at Wyatt's movie reference and pulled Wyatt into her. They kissed as the guests all stood to their feet, clapping and cheering.

The pastor, grinning and shaking his head at Wyatt,

waited until the couple parted. "Okay, then. Let's wrap this up. The rings?"

Alex stood from her seat and walked Duke, resplendent in his own wedding finery, up to the altar. On his collar, tied with a satin ribbon, were the wedding rings. Wyatt and Delaney bent, untied the rings together, and gave Duke several seconds of behind-the-ears scratches for his service. The bride and groom stood, facing each other once more. Alex hurried back to her seat.

"Wyatt Andrews, do you take Delaney Phillips to be your wife? Do you promise to love, honor, cherish, and protect her, forsaking all others, and holding only unto her forevermore?"

Wyatt and Delaney only had eyes for one another.

"I do." Wyatt slipped the ring on Delaney's finger.

"And Delaney, do you take Wyatt to be your husband? Do you promise to love, honor, cherish, and protect him, forsaking all others, and holding only unto him forevermore?"

"You got it," she replied, managing what could only be described as a laugh-sob as she placed a thicker band on Wyatt's hand.

The pastor beamed. "Then, by the power vested in me, I now declare you man and wife. You may kiss the bride—again!"

CHAPTER 20

THE BALLROOM WAS DAZZLING, TRANSFORMED. The empty, cavernous space that she had peeked into a few days ago was now this swanky, glittering wonderland. And, stepping into it as the mid-afternoon sun filtered down through the ceiling skylights, she really did feel transported. Too bad the end of the week felt more like a mad tea party than Cinderella's ball.

Tall, cocktail-height tables lined the perimeter of the room, and on each was a bowl of water that housed floating candles. The center of the room was set with chairs draped in individual chair covers, silken and soft, dropping to the ground around each chair and flowing into the chair next to it to make each row look like one long confectionary seating option.

A stage, semi-circular, stood at the front of the room, and on it was a large, elegant podium that was made of clear Plexiglas—much like the rows of small awards that sat lined up on a table at the back of the stage. Hope knew what each of those awards was for—she'd ooh'd and ahh'd over them with Annie when they'd arrived—

but no "excellence in industry" or "best client relations" was going to cheer her up—giving or receiving.

Even in the air-conditioned interior of the ballroom—cold enough that she was chilled in her strapless dress—her champagne glass was sweating. Or maybe it was that her palms were sweating, nervous energy making her feel like it was many degrees hotter than was probably the reality. Her father wanted to announce her as his soon-forthcoming successor. Would he? She'd avoided him since their fight, and even Annie had said that she hadn't seen him all day, so Hope had no idea what would happen when he was up at the podium.

And though Hope's anger had caused her to defend to Slater the notion of her having to step into the top position at Beacon Financial, her gut twisted at the thought of actually accepting the job. Was it what she wanted, or was it, just as Slater had said, something she felt responsible to take, a place that she would accept—but not one that allowed her to follow her own dreams? She'd had her own misgivings about Beacon, and she'd never been a hundred percent sure that she wanted to helm it. But the business had been her only connection to her father for years, and she'd never wanted to clip that thread. Now, she was hopelessly tangled in it.

The air was thick with the soft, mellow jazz music that was being piped through the overhead speakers, loud enough to be heard but not so loud as to interrupt the murmurs of conversation between the attendees of the ceremony. The room was filling up, and soon everyone would be ushered to their seats. She guessed she still had about a half an hour before things really got underway. She knew, however, that, across the lake, Wyatt and Delaney's wedding would also soon start. Hope pinched the bridge of her nose with the thumb and forefinger on her free hand. The scent of the candles at the table where she stood was so sweet that it was making her nauseous.

"You look absolutely lovely."

Hope turned, her heart leaping in her chest. But the deeper timbre that had echoed in her ear must have been a figment of her imagination—because Jack Allen, not Slater, stood behind her. He was dressed to kill in a navy suit that made his close-cropped, salt-and-pepper hair even more debonair looking, and he held a champagne flute in one hand.

"I would have come with two glasses of champagne, but I wasn't sure if you might dump one over my head," he said dryly, one corner of his mouth quirking up in a half-smile.

"You? Why would I?" Hope clutched her own champagne glass close. "I have nothing to be upset with you about."

"Nor I with you," he admitted. "May I—can we talk?" He waved a hand a few tables back, and Hope nodded, grabbing her small clutch, her wine glass, and following him so that they could each take a seat at one of the farthest tables toward the back, out of the earshot of others.

Jack fiddled with stem of his glass, avoiding looking at her as he began to speak. She was a little taken aback that he seemed flustered, when he was usually so smooth and confident. "Hope, I admit that I can be a flirt sometimes—"

At her burst of laughter, he looked up, and the smile he gave her was a full one.

"But I shouldn't have pressed you to meet me outside of the bounds of the seminar events. I mean, lunch, maybe, because I do have legitimate questions about

Beacon's operations, but to ask for your personal time was wrong. And I admit to overreacting when you didn't show. My feelings were hurt, and I should have handled it better. I certainly shouldn't have called your *father*, for goodness sake." He looked chagrined.

Hope took a sip of her champagne. "I should have shown up, though, Jack. It was unprofessional of me not to. I honestly let time get away from me."

"And you should be able to. Anyone would want to in a place like this, with the right company." He winked, and she knew that he wasn't referring to himself.

"Yes, well, that company and I have a history..." She rolled her eyes, hoping he wouldn't press her for details. She was too embarrassed to admit to her outburst.

"History sometimes repeats itself," Jack added, his eyes sparkling. "And take it from a serial flirt who's spent way too much time making fleeting connections but never finding anything real—a history can be a foundation."

It was Hope's turn to look away. She swallowed thickly. "I think I put a few hefty cracks in that foundation recently."

Jack clicked his tongue sympathetically. "I'm sorry to hear that." He raised his champagne glass. "We're a pair of messes, aren't we?"

"But we clean up well," Hope replied, raising her own flute. She looked down at the mint-green dress that she wore, and down past the flowing hem to her painted toes, framed in delicate gold heeled sandals. Both of the heels were clean, no trace of lake muck, but she would give anything for a creaky wooden rowboat and a pair of strong, forgiving arms around her right about now. She looked up, managing a watery smile. They each sipped their champagne.

Someone toward the center of the room shouted Jack's name, and Hope turned to see a couple waving at them. Jack took the last sip of his drink and slid the empty glass to the edge of the table. "I'll just take my leave, now," he said lightly. "But we're good now?" He held out a hand toward Hope.

She took his hand. "We're good."

She expected him to turn her palm and kiss her knuckles, but he shook her hand instead, firmly, intently. "I'll give Beacon Financial a call once I'm back home and caught up."

Hope's eyes widened. "Jack?"

He smiled. "You've more than proven yourself. I can't wait to do business with you."

And, with that, Jack was gone, trotting toward the couple who'd waved him over. Hope felt her heart grow a little lighter, despite the heaviness that still lingered over the situation with her father, with Slater, and with—*ouch*—the wedding. She needed to tell someone, anyone, that at least the situation with Jack Allen was resolved.

Hope rummaged in her small evening bag and came out with her phone. She texted Annie to hurry back, even though the poor woman had left only minutes before the first guests had arrived, rushing to go get ready.

But Annie, as usual, was way ahead of Hope. No sooner had Hope hit send on the text, but Annie was swinging through the doors of the ballroom—and Hope's father was with her.

Hope froze. Annie spotted Hope immediately, and then her father did, and there was a brief moment when Hope thought he was going to flee, dragging her assistant along with him like a string of wedding cans on the bumper of a limo. But Annie planted her feet, whispered

Wedding in the Pines

something to him, and the pair of them walked toward Hope.

To say there was tension when they reached her was putting it lightly. Hope didn't stand.

"Hey," Hope said, hearing the strain in her own voice. "I didn't get your text that you were on your way down," she said to Annie.

Annie arched an eyebrow at Hope. "I left my phone in the room. Where am I going to put a phone in this dress?" Annie spread her arms wide, indicating the form-fitting, summer-yellow dress she wore. Hope looked, but there wasn't a pocket in sight.

He nodded tightly to Hope. "You look very nice," he said.

"Thank you," she replied woodenly. "You, too. But you're late." And he did look nice. Her father's suit was navy, like Jack's was, but it had a subtle pinstripe that ran the length of the jacket and trousers, making him look a bit taller, a bit more sophisticated than his usual solid suits. And although he was dressed well, he looked tired, dark circles stark under his eyes. Nervous, too, something that Hope could tell from the way his eyes darted everywhere, focusing on anything else but her.

"I'm going to grab a drink," Annie said. "You two play nice, okay?"

And before Hope could object, Annie was off. Hope drew a deep, steadying breath. Her father looked around one more time, and Hope only realized after he began speaking that he had been surveying the area for the same reason that Jack had ushered her back here moments ago—he wanted to be sure no one else could hear them.

Oh, no. What is he about to say? Hope braced for a

repeat of the encounter under the portico. She brushed her hand over the tablecloth that hung on her side of the table, scrunching the material between her fingers and then letting it sift out.

His features might as well have been set in stone. His mouth was pulled down in a frown, his brow was furrowed, and his eyes were pinched in what Hope could only describe as a glare. His jaw worked as though he were gritting his teeth.

"Dad..."

"I'm so sorry, honey." The four words came out brokenly, and her father's face crumpled with emotion. In the same second, he reached out to grasp her hand. He pulled, and she stood and went into his arms as he folded her into a hug.

Hope's throat closed up so fast that she had to breathe sharply through her nose to get air. Tears welled up at the unexpected apology. She could do nothing but wrap her arms around him in return.

"I was wrong," he said, his shoulders rising as he inhaled shakily. "I was wrong to give you an ultimatum. I can't live your life. It's not up to me to decide what makes you happy."

Hope pulled back, rubbing both of her hands up and down her father's arms to comfort him as she ducked to try and catch his eyes. "Dad, it's okay. Hey, come on." Before anyone could catch sight of them, Hope pulled her father through the ballroom doors and out into the hallway, where the soft jazz music dimmed to nearly inaudible, and they could talk in greater privacy. While he paced the hallway, back and forth, taking deep breaths, Hope backed up to lean against the wall most opposite him.

"I'm not sure what we're supposed to do here, Dad," she admitted, wiping at her eyes.

He shook his head, looking as confused as she felt. "I don't know, either. But I know that, after your mom…" He trailed off, eyes welling up again. When he'd gathered himself, he said, "No, before that. I thought I could keep you from making a mistake with music, with Slater. I thought that I knew better. But I didn't."

"It's in the past," she said, not believing it herself.

"But it's *not!*" he exclaimed. "Do you know what happened with Ralph Murphy, Hope? Why he's not here?"

Of course, her father knew that Hope didn't, but she shook her head anyway. "Ralph couldn't make it. That's what you said."

"I drove him away. I've been so unhappy that I let it spill over into everything, onto everyone around me. Ralph and I had an argument before we left to come here. It was a simple disagreement over a matter of stocks, and I should have compromised with him, bent a little, worked things out. But I insisted that Ralph see things my way. And things just blew up. Ralph is one of my oldest friends and one of our biggest clients. And now, he's probably not going to be either of those things. He's said he's pulling all of his accounts with us. And I can't hand Beacon over to you with that big of a loss hanging over its head. I can't let you—force you—to inherit a problem that I created because of the same mistakes I've been making for decades."

Hope came forward to put a hand on her father's forearm. "Beacon Financial is a great company. It's a huge accomplishment, what you built."

"What *we* built," he corrected, putting his hand over hers. "But I want you to build something of your own.

Not something that's weighed down with my baggage. And if that means you're not with Beacon, then I'll accept that."

Behind her, Hope had a vague awareness that the doors to the ballroom had opened, and that soft footsteps were thudding behind her on the plush carpet of the hallway. "You won't announce that I'm taking over Beacon Financial?"

"I won't," he assured. "Unless that's what *you* want."

"It's not." The words came out almost before she could weigh the wisdom of saying them. She put a hand over her mouth, horrified. And then Hope realized. If she and her father were truly ever going to heal their relationship, she had to stop her knee-jerk assumptions that she bore the responsibility for everyone's happiness—but her own. She looked over at him, half expecting to find him frowning.

But he simply smiled. "What do you want?"

The image of a ruggedly handsome face, cast in firelight, and broad, strong hands cradling a guitar flashed into her mind. "I think I know."

Her father nodded. "Then go."

"What about the awards ceremony? And what will you tell all the clients about Beacon and your retirement?"

"Hope, for goodness sake, the best man is waiting for you!" Annie's exasperated voice cut through the buzz that had started in Hope's ears. Hope turned to find her friend standing outside the ballroom doors, looking exasperated. Annie waved down the hall emphatically. "Go to the wedding!"

"Annie," Hope said hoarsely, and then, more excitedly, as she turned back to face her father. "*Annie* would be an absolutely perfect choice to take over Beacon."

Her father looked taken aback for a moment, but then

a thoughtful expression took hold. "You know, Hope, you might be—"

"Go!" Annie said, this time right next to Hope. Hope felt Annie grab her hand, squeeze it tight. "Girl, I would run every department at Beacon, from housekeeping to the C-suite, to get you to leave this side of the lake right now."

"I just...let me call." With shaking hands, Hope woke her phone screen and dialed Slater. The call went straight to voicemail. Her heart clenched in her chest. "He's not picking up."

Hope's eyes darted between her father and Annie, and she felt tears spilling over that she had been struggling to hold back. "Okay. Yes. Okay. I have to get to the Cabins." She patted her dress as Annie had earlier, and then opened her small clutch purse. "I don't have keys. I left the car keys in the room." She hesitated, and then bent to start taking off her high-heeled sandals. "I'll walk. Actually, I'll run."

"No," her father said, stepping forward before she had a chance to undo the first shoe strap. "I have an idea." He reached for Hope's hand. She took his.

He focused on Annie. "Ms. Goodman, I trust that you can handle the awards ceremony here without us?"

Annie's eyes filled. "Yes, sir."

He nodded. "Good. We have a wedding to attend."

Hope's heart was thundering in her chest as her father turned and strode down the hall. She went along, confusion still clouding her thoughts. "Dad, where are we—"

He pulled her out into the lush lobby of the resort and strode toward the clerk. "Alexandra Brent-Collingsworth, please. I need to reach her, now." Hope had always considered her father to be a commanding figure, but he was downright intimating as he stood at the front desk of the resort. So much so that Amelia—the young clerk who Hope recognized from the first night and the ballroom mix-up—immediately picked up the phone that sat by her left hand and punched in a number. After two rings, the call connected.

"Alex, this is Amelia. There's a gentleman here at the front desk who needs to speak to you. He says it's urgent."

Hope's father shook his head. "Please tell her that I took her words by the lake to heart. And now I need the help of some good people to set things right."

Amelia relayed the message, and there was a brief pause before the soft voice on the other end said something Hope couldn't quite make out. Then, Amelia hung up, opened a drawer, and took out a set of keys that was attached to a small, flat, coin-shaped cut of pine. A number was stamped on the rustic keychain. "Alex says take vehicle one. Go out the front entrance, turn right under the portico, and follow the sidewalk all the way down to the company parking area. It'll be in the spot labelled with the same number."

He grabbed the keys that she dangled. He smiled. "Thank you. Ready, Hope?"

Hope, more confused than ever, simply nodded. As they turned to start toward the front door, Amelia called out. "Oh! Ms. Bergman?"

Hope looked back. "Yes?"

"The wedding has finished and they're setting up for the reception. The music starts soon. Alex said you'd know what that means."

Hope nodded. "I do."

Her father held the door for Hope as they dashed out into the dusky, dwindling sun.

CHAPTER 21

THE RECEPTION WAS IN FULL swing. In true Cabins in the Pines style, after Wyatt and Delaney had been officially presented as Mr. and Mrs. Andrews, everyone had pitched in to transform the ceremony set up into the reception. Literally every wedding guest had grabbed a bench end, flower arrangement, pine bough, or tuft of tulle and joined in on what Slater thought of as a near-fairy-godmother-level scene change. Within twenty minutes, the benches were set off in a large U-shape around the dance floor, outlining the existing paver patio, as well as the wooden deck tiles that had been laid out to extend it.

Slater now sat on one of those benches, admiring the way the lights were starting to add a soft, romantic ambiance to the party. A huge, arching white pop-up canopy stretched over the dance floor, open on all sides, and out the far end of it, Slater could see the perfectly-framed view of the sun setting over the lake. He watched Wyatt and Delaney swaying through their first-song dance, and he leaned on his guitar case, which sat against his knee.

It was too bad that the instrumental band from the

resort hadn't been able to stay—but Rachel had come to rescue for the time being.

Maisie, Charles, Ursula, and Norman, along with Delaney's folks, stood at the perimeter of the dance floor, watching Wyatt and Delaney, who knew nothing about their surroundings—people or place—as they stared into each other's eyes. Alex was pacing behind the others, far enough away that Slater couldn't make out what she was saying as she spoke into her phone. Alex frowned, and then listened, and then broke into a gleeful smile before hanging up.

Must be about the cake, Slater thought.

The bench next to Slater shook slightly as he was joined.

"So, your date didn't show either, huh?" Rachel leaned her chin in her hand, propping her elbow on her knee. She looked over at Slater, and he hooked an arm around her shoulder, giving her a brotherly hug.

"Aww, kiddo, I'm sorry. He's a fool. You look lovely tonight. And any guy who would miss out on a fun night with a girl who can not only pull together a wedding play-list, ultra-last-minute, but also get it playing on a sound system that was borrowed *in pieces* from presentation audio equipment? Pfffft. Crazy."

Rachel managed a smile, though she did still look a bit glum. "The bummer being that I now have to leave my phone at Paul Bunyan's DJ booth." She waved toward an artistically stacked group of the benches that Slater had built, which had been repurposed into a waist-high surface where Rachel's phone now resided, propped next to an assortment of audio equipment. A motley group of speakers had been placed strategically around the dance floor.

The first-dance song ended, and the guests sur-rounding the perimeter of the dance floor clapped, and then moved under the tent, coupling off as the next song began.

Rachel bent, picked a few blade of grass, and then be-gan to peel them, throwing thin strings at her feet. "How about you? Why didn't Hope show?"

Slater ran a finger over the latch of his guitar case, shaking his head. "You know, we had a fight." He thought about sugarcoating the story for Rachel. She didn't need to know about what had happened between Slater and Hope. And it was embarrassing. He'd messed up, had been too reactionary when he should have just heard her out.

Rachel was waiting for him to go on.

"I let myself have way too many expectations about what was going to happen after this week was up, and I got angry when she hinted that she was making a choice that would kill any second chance we might have." He puffed out a breath. Man, had that felt good to get out.

Slater looked over to find Rachel, eyes wide, looking through him—past him?

"What?" he said. "Too honest?" Slater put both his hands up, palms up. "You're old enough to know that love doesn't always turn out the way we—"

"Want to dance?"

To the other side, opposite Rachel and over Slater's shoulder, there stood a tall, classically handsome man—well, Slater would have called him a *kid*—dressed in dark slacks, a crisp, white button-down shirt, and a mint-green tie that perfectly matched Slater's. That was odd. Only the members of the wedding party had known to wear that color.

"I'm so sorry I'm late," the young man said. "It couldn't be helped. But I came the second I was free."

The kid—sharp jaw, close-cropped hair, handsome in an apple-pie, athletic way—looked so familiar, and yet, Slater couldn't place him. And Rachel seemed too hypnotized to make a proper introduction. The kid held a hand out to Rachel, who practically levitated off of the bench beside Slater.

And, just like that, Slater was alone again. But he watched, amused, as Rachel floated in the arms of whoever her mystery-date-who-showed-up-late was.

The bench beside Slater shifted again a moment later, and Delaney arranged herself beside him, wedding dress and all.

"Check out who Rachel's date is," she said, trying to be subtle as she gestured toward Rachel and a tall, wheat-haired guy who seemed a couple years older. "Any minute now, he might start spewing melodramatic poetry."

Slater widened his eyes, turning to shake his head at Del. "Scott from *Lovestruck High*. I thought the surprise was a front-row seat at his Q&A?"

"The surprise is apparently that her Q was used to ask if he'd come to the wedding with her."

"And what he answered is pretty obvious," Slater chuckled. "Are we all going to be forced to add the wedding video to the rotation of every blooper reel, interview, and behind-the-scenes featurette that Scott has appeared in that was *ever* put on a DVD or released exclusively to fan-club members online?"

"Yes," Wyatt said as he walked up behind them, balancing three champagne glasses in his hands. "I guess fate has a funny way of finding this place."

"I guess it does," Slater agreed, though he could hear the dry edge to his voice. There would be no miraculous last-minute miracle for him. He'd dug the pit he was sitting in.

Delaney put a hand on Slater's shoulder. "Hey, don't worry about what happened. Sometimes, things don't work out for a reason. There could be something completely wonderful waiting for you in the future." Delaney reached back behind her and grabbed Wyatt's hand. He squeezed her fingers in his and smiled at her.

"You're right," Slater said. "But half of the problem was that..." Slater trailed off, swallowing. "My wedding present to you and Wyatt was going to be music tonight. Hope and I were going to sing. She even finished the lyrics for this old song of ours, and it was so perfect. You would have loved it."

Delaney took Slater's hand in her free one, speaking softly. "You have done *so* much. You have helped us tackle every problem that this wedding has come across. You have been tireless in making sure that we had an amazing day. We couldn't ask for a better friend, Slater."

Wyatt nodded. "You being part of this family is the best gift we could have had this week."

Slater nodded, touched at the deep show of affection.

"And you could always sing it, anyway," Wyatt said, nudging Slater's guitar case under the bench with his shiny wingtip shoe. "I'll take Del for another spin out there. Gotta get in all the dancing I can. Once her dad gets her out there, I won't be able to get her back all evening."

Delaney's musical laugh cut through the air, which was now dusky with night. Slater began to feel a smile tug at his lips. "I could," he said. "You can come sing the duet part, right, Wyatt? It isn't quite right without two voices. How are you at vocal runs?"

"No. Nooooo," Wyatt protested, holding up his hands, trying to keep hold of his flute at the same time. "I sound like a dented up eight-track when I sing."

Delaney stood. "Well, I would still dance to a dented up eight-track with you," she said, reaching for Wyatt. The bride and groom stood together, looking expectantly at Slater.

"All right," Slater said, acquiescing. "But it won't be quite smooth. I'll have to try and remember the second half of the lyrics. She kinda took 'em."

Slater popped the latches on his guitar case, picked up his guitar, and moved to the bench on the farthest side away from where he currently sat. The seat put his back to the pavilion, and it formed enough of an area in front of him, covered by the overhead tent, that it was stage-like, and the guests all instinctively faced him when the current song faded out. Slater looked over to see that Maisie was near Rachel's phone, tapping at the screen to stop the pre-made music.

The microphones from the resort musicians were still in a cluster at one corner of the dance floor, having not been gathered up and taken back yet, and Charles brought one over, trailing a long cord. Slater could only guess what it plugged into, but when he lowered it on the stand to its shortest height and tapped the metal screen, it popped with sound. It would do.

He placed his guitar over his lap, and strummed a few soft chords on the strings. The old acoustic wasn't fancy, but she was familiar, and Slater closed his eyes, knowing that he could play by feel. The crowd standing in front of him grew hushed.

He sang the first words softly, finding it impossible not to think of Hope as he did, of how they would never have the chance at the overflowing happiness that he had borne witness to today. It was possible, he knew— but not for them.

No matter where we start,
A million miles or breaths apart,
The stars might burn and all go dark,
But I would still find you...

Slater smiled as he heard a few sighs, but none of the sounds of dancing. That was okay. It wasn't really a dancing song. Even the slowest of dances wouldn't match this ballad. No, it was a song to sing to someone who needed to hear the words, a song to croon to someone in the dying light of a fire, leaned in close, so that the lyrics were for their ears only.

He rolled out the next lines, his voice wavering slightly toward the end.

If every old love leaves a mark
A broken trail to lead our hearts
Then let this new love be the spark,
That lights the way to what's true

And then, he lost the words. Exactly the way he'd lost *her*. If they had changed enough over the years, then there should have been a different ending. They should have both handled things differently this time around. Instead, it was clear that they'd both held on to old habits when it came to one another, and it had just made things fall apart all over. Slater couldn't blame Hope entirely. He'd foisted unrealistic expectations on her over a week's worth of days. He should have just treasured the time. He kept strumming for a few more notes, searching his brain for the rest of the song.

And then, the words came—but they never left *his* lips. The bench beside him shifted slightly, and another voice flowed through the microphone.

And I know this love can last
the storms that may
Come to block the light
until we barely see the rays

Slater kept playing out of instinct, and his eyes flew open to see Hope, sitting next to him, her eyes uncertain but her voice sure and strong as she wrapped her fingers around the microphone to bring it closer to herself.

But the love we share will
blaze through all the dark
And you and I will be the thing
that's weathered from the start

Slater couldn't swallow past the sudden lump in his throat. Somehow, he kept playing, his eyes locked on Hope, barely able to imagine what her being here might mean. He'd been wrong before, and he wanted to assume nothing in the moment. She looked right back at him, into him, and he wanted the song to never end.

Her voice trembled as she neared the last words.

Oh I never knew that love
could be the answer to a prayer

It was like the light came chasing you
and I was lucky to be there

Slater managed to join her in the last verse. Their voices carries through the warm, heavy night, and though he was aware that the entire wedding party was watching everything play out, like Wyatt and Delaney reciting their vows, there was only one center of the universe right now—and she was sitting next to him.

So no matter where we start,
A million miles or breaths apart,
The stars might burn and all go dark,
But I would still find you...

Slater put a little extra force into his last swipe of the pick, and the last note reverberated through the silence that hung for a few seconds after they finished. He still couldn't take his eyes off of her.

She dropped the microphone to her lap, where it half disappeared into the soft, mint-green satin of her dress. She was breathing fast, her wide eyes locked on his.

The gathered crowd burst into applause, cheers, and a few ear-splitting whistles. The noise broke the spell, and Hope dropped her chin, her cheeks coloring a deep pink as the guests continued their boisterous praise.

"What are you doing here," he whispered below the din of the cheers. "I thought..."

She shook her head, waving her hand to get him to stop speaking. "I couldn't let the best man go to the wedding without a date, could I? Besides, my dress only matches everyone else at this party."

He frowned, still not understanding. "But your father. And the ceremony. Your job at Beacon?"

She shook her head again. "That's not what's important right now. But, interestingly, my father drove me here." She pointed up and across the dance floor, past the crowd, to where he stood, hands in pockets, misty eyes trained on Slater and Hope. When Slater looked over, Dan gave a small wave.

"I'll be darned," Slater said, in utter disbelief. "You will definitely have to tell me this story."

"I will," Hope said, finally cracking a smile that made summer start in his heart all over again. It had been a long winter in there without her these past couple of days. "And did you know that vehicle number one at your fancy-schmancy executive resort is an old *golf cart*?"

It was Slater's turn to crack a smile. "I did."

No one approached them as Slater set his guitar and the microphone aside and stood. Instead, the wedding guests all drifted back out onto the dance floor as Rachel started up the wedding playlist again. A soft-rock crooner was asserting sonorously that love could never, ever feel so strong. The fireflies at the edges of the overhead canopy made lazy curlicues, swooping into puddles of light cast by the strung bulbs, and then winging it back out into the velvet dark, where Slater could see them more distinctly.

Slater took a steadying breath and tried to make eye contact with several of his friends, but it almost seemed as though everyone was avoiding looking at them. He finally managed to catch Ursula's eyes, and she frowned, shook her head, and jerked her chin in the direction of the dock, giving him only a moment of attention before turning back to her dancing partner, Norman. When

Norman's head drifted toward Slater and Hope, Ursula reached up and turned his face back to her.

Wyatt and Delaney studiously avoided looking at him. Maisie and Charles looked pretty lovey-dovey as they danced, so Slater wasn't sure if they were in on whatever this was or if they were just that into each other. Delaney's folks were leaning over the refreshment table. Rachel was once again in the arms of sonnet-swapping Scott. Delaney's Aunt Tildy was trying to coax Dan Bergman onto the dance floor.

Well, this *was* the matchmaking side of the lake.

Slater looked down at Hope, who was still sitting on the bench. He was afraid to guess at—or wish for—the reason she was here. But he hadn't taken the time to listen to her before, and so, regardless of her reasons, and regardless of the outcome of the conversation, he owed her the time to talk things out. All those years ago, they hadn't taken the time. They'd almost missed the chance when they'd let emotion overcome reason in their disagreement at the lakeshore.

Her circumstances had cut their time short, all those years ago. And he was wise enough now to know that he had let pride prevent him from listening at the time *and* let it get in the way reaching out to her after their split. They had reacted, back then, not *faced* the obstacles together

There was a glimmer of dream that still nestled in his heart—that there might be a way she would stay, a way that they could change the mistakes of the past into a beautiful new future. But it should start differently than it had ended last time.

"Did I tell you that you look beautiful in that dress?" Slater asked, working up his courage.

"You didn't," she replied.

"Do you want to take a walk with me?" he asked, holding out his hand.

She slid her palm against his. "I do."

CHAPTER 22

H OPE TRIED NOT TO LOOK at Slater as he led her away from the wedding reception. Her heart was beating at Olympic speed, and his hand felt warm and strong, firm in hers as they walked hand in hand away from the soft, golden harbor of light where all of his friends—his family—celebrated.

She had no idea what to say, how to explain. She burned with embarrassment at the thought of trying to justify why she had been so angry, feeling history repeat itself at their argument at this very spot days ago. And Hope certainly didn't have any idea of where they should go from here. What did he want? What did she want? Where did those two dreams intersect? So she stayed quiet, concentrated on slowing her breathing, organizing her scattering thoughts.

It had been exhilarating, singing with him again. And not only singing. This week, she'd felt freer, happier, when they'd been eating dinner, hanging out with his friends, making plans for when they would see each other the next day, than she had in many years. When Hope thought about the way she felt walking into her life away from here, walking into work every day, she wasn't unhappy—she was confident, ready to handle whatever was thrown at her, and felt satisfaction as Beacon had grown under her efforts. But at the end of the day, walking into her empty apartment with its bare walls and the piano that no one ever saw her play, she never felt whole.

Here, with Slater, she did.

They reached the end of the dock, and Slater sat, pulling her gently down with him. When she settled, he released her hand and began to take off his dress shoes, setting them behind him. His socks followed, and he was rolling up the legs of his tuxedo pants when she reached for the straps of her own sandals. A moment later, they were both dangling their feet into the dark water of the lake. Out from where her feet caused ripples in the water, the trees were reflected in the surface, dark lengths of shadow interrupting the glittering surface of the water.

Hope couldn't help but shiver a little when she sunk her feet in, even though the water was pleasantly warm. He noticed and tipped his head at her curiously.

"A little scary," she said, looking down into the water.

"It is," he agreed, and she felt that the weight he gave the words covered so much more than the slight trepidation that came with putting your toes down into the unknown. She slid her hand along the smooth plank of the dock between them until her fingers found his again. He curled her hand into his completely, staring quietly out across the water as though he were waiting for her to speak.

"I guess I should start out by saying I'm sorry."

He laughed softly, rubbing over the back of her hand with his thumb. "What in the world do you have to be sorry for?"

She tugged at his hand until he looked at her. "Slater, I walked out on you. I left you by *note*."

"True. And I did say that it was a pretty cold move." He pursed his lips. "But I never took the time to understand why you would," he admitted. "I shut you out at the first sign that things would get hard. I was too preoccupied with my own pain to stop and see how painful the choices you had to make were. If we had just talked back then, we might have worked it out."

Hope nodded seriously. "Honestly, it was easier to do what my father wanted. And he thought that what he was asking me to do was right. And my mom..." Her eyes began to burn, and she put a hand to the bridge of her nose.

Slater put a hand on her cheek. "Hey, he was right about that. About your mom. You did need to go home, to take care of your family. Ever since I came here, the importance of cherishing the time you have with the people you love has become clearer all the time. And when you showed back up, well, it became *crystal*. When I think about how I might have convinced you to stay with me back then, how you might have missed that last window of time with your mother, man, it makes me shudder. I would never have asked that of you—but it could have happened."

She put her hand over his, holding his palm against her skin. "But changing majors, breaking up with you? I didn't have to do any of that."

"Things have a way of getting out of hand when we're running on emotion. And we can't control the outcome when we lash out mindlessly. Sometimes, the things we do in hurt, in anger, or out of fear—they change our lives forever."

Hope watched him speak. His handsome face was softly illuminated by the moonlight that reflected off of the lake water, and it was clear from the way he paused to press his lips tightly together in the middle of speaking that the words, as well as his struggle to keep the tremor out of his voice, that they were hard for him to say. Hope realized that Slater was afraid. And not in a dip-your-toes-into-the-dark-water way. She had broken his heart before, and he was opening himself up again, admitting his own part in their troubles. Not that she blamed him for her own past reactions; those had been all on her. And he had no way of knowing that she wouldn't do it again now. It was a lot of feeling to deal with in a short time; intense, but not, as it had been when she was younger, confusing. She loved him. It was simple. The complicated part was what to do about it.

"What you don't know, Slater, is that if I leave again the way I did before, a part of me will still be here. And I already live without that part of me every single day."

He stared at her, and she pulled her hand from his to start worrying the fabric of her dress. Starting to smile, he chased after, recapturing her hand and enveloping it in both of his. "You have nothing to be nervous about. You can say anything to me."

She smiled, nodded, and dropped her eyes to avoid the intensity of his gaze.

"I was telling the truth, Hope, that day in my office. I never stopped caring about you. I—so, so stupidly—I wanted to get away from the hurt you'd caused me. And, if that meant cutting you out and changing schools, I didn't care. Just like it was easier for you to give in instead of fighting for what you wanted, it was easier for me to run away and not deal."

Hope wanted to pull him in and kiss him, but the moment seemed so raw and open that she didn't want to risk mistaking the intent of his speech. She couldn't read him. Was this goodbye again? Was he giving her—them—the closure he thought they needed so that she could leave when the new week started, able to look back on her time here in fondness, reminiscing without bitterness as she went on to live without him?

She scooted closer to him so that they sat hip-to-hip. She wound her arms through his and tipped her head back, looking up at him. Those eyes—the same ones she'd always gotten lost in—were swimming with a mixture of sadness and hope. They were both so vulnerable here that she dared not make another move. She needed to make very clear where she stood on the point of their heart to heart. Then, everything would be up to him.

"Let me put it out there, then. No qualifications. I need you, Slater. I've needed you for many years, and I've only been pretending that I didn't. It was easier than admitting that I took the path of least resistance back then. But you're worth it. You're worth the rough patches, worth the work to figure things out." Hope could hear her own voice faltering. "And I won't go, not if you still want me."

Slater's face passed from sadness to joy, and Hope could practically see his brain working, trying to figure out the next right move.

"I mean that I love you, Slater. I'm sorry I hurt you, that I didn't fight for you, for us. And if you give me another chance, I'll—"

His fingertips pressed against her lips. Her eyes widened at him.

"Hope." He took a breath that seemed as though he'd

been starved of oxygen for a long time. "Please don't say it if you won't stay."

She grabbed his wrist and gently drew his hand away. "You will have to toss me in the lake to keep me away from you."

He leaned over and put his forehead on hers, closing his eyes. "I love you, too. I always have, and I will never stop."

Hope was a little disappointed, in the moment, that the wedding reception didn't include a concert of nicely-timed fireworks. Because she wanted big, sky-high bursts of light showering over the lakeside to mirror the happiness that was bursting in sparkling arcs inside her.

One moment, she was rejoicing in Slater's words, and the next, she was gasping with the thrill of him suddenly kissing her. The warmth of him as his hand came up to cup her upper arm made her feel as though the world had narrowed to two points—where his fingers touched her skin and where his lips touched hers. His other hand wrapped around her waist, pulling her in impossibly closer. And despite the joy of his long-yearned-for embrace, Hope found herself crying.

Slater pulled away, both of his hands rising to cup her cheeks. "What is it?"

She shook her head. "We waited so long," she said. "We wasted so much time."

He pulled her into him, wrapping his arms around her. "That's another thing I've learned," he said softly. "There's always a way to start over. I mean, I've seen it happen here, but I never fully believed until now. I was always afraid that our past would never let us be together again."

She looked at him, those wide, summer-blue eyes full of love. "If I can help it, Slater, we'll never be apart again."

It was Hope who leaned in now to capture Slater in a second kiss.

Hope and Slater returned to the reception hand-in-hand, and Slater hesitated slightly when Hope pulled him toward her father, who now sat on one of the log benches, talking with Maisie. Though Dan Bergman looked relaxed and happy, even laughing at something Masie was saying, Slater was hesitant to stir up any angst, when he and Hope had just reached such a joyous place with each other.

"Hope, I don't know if now..." Slater pulled against her lead.

"It's the perfect time. It's overdue, actually." She squeezed his hand, looking over at him with eyes that were calm and sure. "Trust me."

Slater nodded. "Lead the way." He tightened his hold on her as they walked over to where Dan Bergman sat. To Slater's surprise, as they neared, Dan jumped from his seat and met them at the edge of the dance floor. He was wringing his hands, his face pinched with worry. Slater could see that the reception had shifted from dancing to more of a social mingling, with everyone grouped in small clusters, talking.

Slater and Hope stopped in front of Dan. Hope let go of Slater, and Slater took a step forward. Dan started in on what he'd obviously been holding since they'd left. "I owe you an apology, young man." Dan held out a hand, which Slater readily accepted.

"I made a lot of mistakes in the past with good intentions but short sight. And it hurt my daughter, and it hurt you, and I can't ever take that back." Dan looked at his daughter, and Hope came to stand beside her father as Dan's voice trembled.

"But if there's anything I can do, anything in my power that can help either of you regain some of the lost time—I will do it. Because I've been *so* blind, but trust me when I say that I know the pain of having had a deep, abiding love that is too suddenly gone." He looked resolute, though pained.

Slater looked directly at the man who'd been instrumental in separating him and Hope. But he didn't see an enemy, nor a person who'd wrong both of them. What he saw was a man who loved the same woman that Slater did—and Slater himself had been guilty of some pretty bad decisions where she was concerned, too. And now, that same love, the love of a father, allowed Dan Bergman to lay his soul bare and offer to make amends.

"Sir," Slater said. "If fate is giving Hope and I another chance—if there can be forgiveness and an opportunity to start over between your daughter and me, then I don't believe it should be any different with you." Slater held out his hand for another shake.

Dan grasped it, and then pulled Slater into a hug.

It lasted until, as with many moments surrounded by his friends, a voice broke in. But Slater thought it was pretty warranted—it was *her* wedding, after all.

"So, how about we all celebrate new beginnings? With cake." Slater, Dan, and Hope looked toward Delaney, who stood a few steps back. The rest of the crew—Wyatt, Maisie, Charles, Norman, Ursula, and Rachel—were standing behind her. Slater almost guffawed when he caught sight of Rachel's wedding date, Scott, also standing with the group. He was cozied up next to Rachel, and he looked utterly enthralled by the scene that had just played out in front of them.

Over Delaney's shoulder, Slater saw Maisie's face pale. He must have reacted, because Delaney turned to look at her friend.

"About the cake..." Maisie said.

"What about the cake?" Only Wyatt could make a four-word question sound like a full-blown panic attack.

"There was a problem at the bakery. Plumbing. They had to shut the whole place down for a few days, and they weren't going to be able to make the cake," Maisie explained carefully. Slater had never heard someone speak as though they were navigating a landmine with speech. He watched Wyatt as his friend wobbled a bit on his feet.

"Alex said she took care of it," Masie finished.

"And she did," Dan Bergman said. All eyes shifted to Hope's father, and every face held the same expression—utter confusion. "Actually, I gave Alex the keys to the golf cart when Hope and Slater went to the docks. She should be back any minute now."

As if on cue, the sound of a diminutive horn beeped. Alex steered the golf cart off the trail and onto the lakeshore, winding it carefully past the dance floor and pavilion to swing it in front of the gathered group, easing to a stop. There was a huge box on the back seat of the cart, tied down with so much twine that Slater doubted that they would ever get into it to find out what was inside.

Alex hopped out of the golf cart, waving at the gathered group. "Boys, I need one of those tables from under the pavilion brought to the side of the dance floor. Everyone else, check the plates and napkins."

Slater got a move on. In another impressive show of Pines solidarity, everyone went to work. A table, covered in some of the wedding tulle and stacked with plates, napkins, and silverware, materialized. Under Alex's direction, the twined-up box was freed from the gold cart and carefully lifted onto the table. Everyone circled around as Aunt Tildy—who had produced a small Swiss Army knife from her handbag—cut the remaining strings.

The cardboard fell away to reveal a towering, four-layered cake, each tier slightly bigger as it cascaded to the base. The confection was frosted in a rich, deep chocolate and sprinkled with...

"Are those marshmallows?" Delaney said brightly.

And they were. Along with cascades of miniature marshmallows, the surface of the cake was punctuated with tiny graham crackers and chocolate chips. But, as impressive as the cake was, it was the topper that drew everyone's attention. A tiny, realistic fondant campfire topped the cake, looking for all the world as though it were realistically glowing. And sticking out of the cake beside the campfire, angling over, was a shiny, sugared pretzel stick with a full-sized marshmallow skewered on the end. Stuck into that marshmallow was a minuscule replica of an engagement ring.

Everyone saw it—and realized—at once. And everyone roared with laughter. Except for Wyatt, who blushed and grumbled, "I am never going to live that down."

Slater had to hold his sides.

"But how?" Hope asked Alex, when the laughter had faded.

Alex paused, but Dan nodded, and she said, "Mr. Bergman baked it."

Slater had never known so many jaws to drop at once, his included.

Hope stuttered. "Dad? How? When?"

Dan looked sheepish, but he waved toward Alex. "A friend helped me see, after our argument, Hope, that we should take our happiness when we have the chance *and* that we should do our best to create joy in others. I know that—*knew* it—but I'd forgotten. Alex was kind enough to lend me the kitchen at the diner last night. I used what was available there."

"It must have taken you all night," Delaney said, awed.

"That's why you were late to the awards today," Hope added, her voice thick with emotion.

Dan looked at his feet, laughing. "Can't quite bounce back after an all-nighter like I used to." Hope's father was still looking down, and so he didn't see it coming when the entire Pines crew—Slater, Hope, Maisie, Charles, Ursula, Alex, Norman, Wyatt, Delaney, and Rachel—moved in to surround him in a group hug.

Scott stood respectfully to the side, but when everyone released Dan Bergman, who was laughing and wiping at his eyes, Slater could see that Scott looked a little misty, too.

As the wedding party and all the guests converged on the cake, Slater caught Hope's hand and drew her back from the crowd. She stilled in front of him, her back to his chest. They watched together as Delaney and Wyatt fed each other the first cake slices, and then cut and served the rest of the party. Hope turned her head and looked up at Slater, her eyes luminous with unshed tears. But she was smiling, and it was a smile he'd missed for many long years. Slater snaked an arm around her waist, holding her against him, and his other hand found hers. He pressed his cheek against her hair.

With the two of them wrapped up in each other in perfect harmony on this perfect night, surrounded by so much love, Slater knew with a final certainty that nothing else mattered but keeping Hope a part of his world from now until forever.

EPILOGUE

I T WAS A PERFECT SATURDAY. Slater and Hope sat at the lakeside, a crisp fall wind blowing over the surface to bring damp, autumn-scented air to the shore. The deciduous trees that were woven between the pines had burst into a brilliant rainbow of spiced colors, creating a breathtaking living canvas that changed with each day that progressed toward winter. Hope looked across the lake at the resort side, noticing that swaths of the opposite shoreline normally hidden by the summer foliage were now starting to reveal themselves.

Slater strummed his guitar, and Hope listened, tapping a pencil against an open, leather-bound notebook. The hushed whisper of the breeze through the trees seemed to stir something in Hope, and she leaned down to scribble a few single words, each on their own lines, onto the paper.

"I'm not sure about that near-rhyme," Hope huffed, thinking hard.

Her train of thought was interrupted by Duke, who trotted over from his place under the pavilion, where he had been begging with the most pitiful whine that Hope had ever heard for some of the burgers and hot dogs that Wyatt and Delaney were grilling. The pup wiggled his way into Hope's lap, and she let him settle there, stroking his soft fur absently. He was slightly damp from his trek through the carpet of fallen leaves that covered the ground between the pavilion and where Hope sat.

"How about this, with the same words?" Slater tried a different arrangement.

Hope leaned back and placed both of her palms in the grass, watching him as he strummed. His hair had gotten longer, and now it just reached the collar of his green plaid shirt. It fit him, and she thought to ask him not to cut it too much on his next visit to Joe's. When Slater realized that Hope was staring, he looked up, and—it never failed—she was immediately lost in the depths of his eyes.

"What?" he said.

With the changing of the seasons and the landscape around the property, Hope was even more aware of how much other things in her life had changed lately. She loved the way the water had gotten cold, meaning that dipping her toes at the edge of it brought a chill, how the air in the mornings would be heavier with dew, and how the mist continued skimming across Lake Fairwood now until well into the morning. And she loved that she was here, for good, to see it all happen. So much different than the view she'd had outside her office window at Beacon Financial—of nature and on life.

And the view from where she was sitting was pretty good, too. Slater's smile widened, but he was still waiting for her answer.

"Nothing," she said. "I'm just happy."

"Don't tell him that," Wyatt said, plopping down next

to Hope on the blanket that Hope had spread out, two plates in hand. "I'm here as a witness to testify that this man hates immeasurable happiness and undying love."

Slater picked up a handful of leaves and tossed them at Wyatt. They fluttered ineffectually down onto the blanket before reaching their intended target. Wyatt held out two plates laden with food.

"You're working too hard, lovebirds. Delaney says eat." Wyatt handed the plates to Hope, who accepted hers with a smile, and Slater, who set aside his guitar to take the other.

"Thanks," Slater said. "Where is everyone? I thought we all said 12:30 for lunch."

Wyatt shrugged. "Well, Charles had to drive into town, and I think Masie went with him. Ursula's yoga class should just be finishing up over at the resort, but I know she said that Alex was going to ride over with her once the video call with Jack was over."

Hope wiggled her eyebrows. "Jack Allen. That seems to be getting serious."

Slater paused between bites of potato salad. "She says it's strictly business."

"That's usually the starting line around here," Wyatt observed dryly.

Delaney was next to appear, and she took a spot on the blanket at the other side of Hope, carrying plates for Wyatt and herself. Wyatt snagged the plate closest and leaned over to give his wife a quick, sweet kiss. Hope looked up into the gray-blue sky, giggling as they met in front of her.

When Delaney sat back up, she untucked her phone from her pocket and waved it at Wyatt. "Rach texted and said to save her some leftovers for after school."

"Food? Yes. Dessert? Depends on what Maisie brings." Wyatt's deadpan face made his wife laugh.

"And what about Norman?" Slater asked, pointing his fork at the director, who was sleeping peacefully in a hammock strung between two nearby trees. Even from where they sat, they could hear him snoring softly.

"We'll save him lunch, too," Wyatt said. "My stance on dessert is still unchanged."

Grinning and shaking her head, Delaney unfolded a red-and-white checked napkin onto her lap and set her plate down. Delaney looked over at Hope.

"When does your moving truck get here?" Delaney asked.

"In about two hours. I'll be glad to have my stuff. The new place is so empty, it's kind of a downer." Hope took a bite of her burger, closing her eyes in delight. She opened them when Duke popped up from her lap, having suddenly gained interest at the smell of food. She shooed him gently off to one side, and he whined, did a few circles in the fallen leaves, and then dashed off to the tree line.

"Where's *he* going?" Slater mused. Momentarily, Duke came back, barreling out of the same spot he'd disappeared at the trailhead. And he wasn't alone. Ursula, Alex, Charles, and Maisie followed him, chatting and laughing.

The group was soon settled with Hope, Slater, Wyatt, and Delaney, and the time passed too quickly. Before she knew it, the alarm on Hope's smartwatch was going off, and it was time to go meet the moving truck. Hope smiled, thinking of how the same alarm had only been used recently to remind her of happy things—her flight here after she'd packed up her old apartment, the time Slater would pick her up to meet Wyatt and Delaney at the movies, and the arrival of the moving truck, signaling that she would be here in Fairwood for the foreseeable future.

And, come Monday, it would wake her up so that she could start at her part-time financial consulting position—at the Cabins in the Pines Executive Resort. Her new office was right next to Alex's. The part-time bit thrilled her, especially since her other part-time passion was happening alongside the new full-time love of her life. She was writing music again, and she and Slater had many, many future afternoons just like this planned out.

Slater mock-pouted. "Do we really have to go?"

"We do. Not only do we have to unpack the moving truck, but you have to get back to your place in time for an early turn-in. My dad gets here at practically dawn, and you know he wants you to drive him around town to look for his retirement pad."

"Dan at dawn. I can handle it." Slater stood, dusted off his hands, and put his guitar in its case.

After he and Hope had both gathered up their trash and tossed it, they returned to the group to hash out plans for Hope to come back tomorrow so that she could move stuff into her new workspace. And then, they were ready to go. Slater held out one hand to Hope and hefted his guitar case in the other. She took his hand.

They bid their goodbyes, with Ursula the first to mist up and set off a chain of bittersweet tears in Maisie, Delaney, and Rachel. Hope kissed cheeks and gave hugs, a little sad herself to be leaving. But this special place—and these special people—would be here when Hope returned. With her hand wrapped in the warmth of Slater's, her songbook in her other hand, Hope put Lake Fairwood at her back and started up the embankment to the trail. With each step, she thought about how, with just the slightest difference in decision, she might never have ended up right here, right now. She wiped at her suddenly welling eyes.

As they neared the trail, Slater looked over at her. "You okay?" he said, squinting curiously. "You went somewhere there for a minute."

"I'm fine," she said, tightening her hold on him. "And don't you worry, Slater Evans..." She stopped, tugged on his hand, and brought him close. "I have no plans to go anywhere anytime soon."

His smile, which made his handsome face as warm and inviting as the sweep of fall along the shoreline, disappeared in the next moment—stolen away as Hope's lips met his.

THE END

CHICKEN A LA ROSE

A Hallmark Original Recipe

In *Wedding in the Pines*, Hope surprises Slater by making him a homemade dinner...including Chicken a la Rose, her late mother's recipe. Over dinner, they both do their best to ignore the feelings they still have for one another. Make our Chicken a la Rose recipe any time you want a dinner that's as easy as it is elegant.

Prep Time: 10 minutes
Cook Time: 15 minutes
Serves: 6

Ingredients

- 6 chicken breasts, boneless, skinless
- 2 tablespoons butter, divided

- 2 tablespoons olive oil, divided
- 4 cloves garlic, minced
- 1/4 cup almonds, sliced
- 2 tablespoons lemon juice
- 2 roses, petals, chemical free
- 4 tablespoons honey
- Salt and pepper to taste

Preparation

1. Sauté salt and peppered chicken breasts in a large skillet with 1 tablespoon butter and 1 tablespoon olive oil over medium heat, about 5 minutes per side.

2. Remove to a serving platter and keep warm.

3. In the same skillet, sauté garlic in remaining butter and olive oil for about a minute.

4. Add almonds continue another 2 minutes.

5. Turn off heat or remove from stove top and stir in lemon juice to deglaze the pan and scrape up any brown bits.

6. Crush the rose petals to release aroma and natural oils, then gently stir in pan with honey and season with salt and pepper.

Thanks so much for reading
Wedding in the Pines. We hope you enjoyed it!

You might like these other books
from Hallmark Publishing:

Love on Location
The Perfect Catch
Rescuing Harmony Ranch
A Simple Wedding

For information about our new releases and
exclusive offers, sign up for our free newsletter at
hallmarkchannel.com/hallmark-publishing-newsletter

You can also connect with us here:

Facebook.com/HallmarkPublishing

Twitter.com/HallmarkPublish

ABOUT THE AUTHOR

With strong, relatable heroines and heroes too lovable not to fall for, Cassidy Carter crafts sweet, fun, family-centered romances that will win readers' hearts. When she's not writing, Cassidy can be found digging in the garden or lost in a good book. Originally from the South, she now resides in the desert Southwest with her husband, two daughters, and a cattle dog that has never seen a lick of ranch work.